Georgia walked into the bathroom and stepped up to the mirror. She studied her face closely, transfixed by the skin around her eyes. What was it about age? Was she, at thirty-five, ancient? Or was she still, just barely young? It depended on how you looked at it. If she saw an article in the paper about a thirty-five-year-old woman falling to her death in a failed parachute leap, she'd think – My God, she was so *young*. If, however, she saw an article in the paper about a thirty-five-year-old actress out on the town with her twenty-two-year-old toyboy, she'd think, My God, she's so *ancient*.

'Mirror, mirror on the wall, who's the likeliest candidate for a facelift of them all?' she addressed her reflection.

# GIRL TALK

## CINDY BLAKE

Futura

A Futura Book

ISBN 0 7088 4356 3

Photoset in North Wales by
Derek Doyle & Associates, Mold, Clwyd
Printed in Great Britain by
BPCC Hazell Books
Aylesbury, Bucks, England
Member of BPCC Ltd.

Futura Publications
A Division of
Macdonald & Co (Publishers) Ltd
Orbit House
1 New Fetter Lane
London EC4A 1AR
A member of Maxwell Macmillan Pergamon Publishing Corporation

*To*
*Y.A. Tittle and Betty White*
*with love*

# Chapter One

'George? It's Sam.'

'Sam? Where are you?'

'I'm in New York. Is this an OK time to call?'

'A great time. Andrew is out interviewing someone about the 1960s and I'm reading the latest Judith Krantz. The handsome blind brother has just saved the beautiful movie star's life. I was hoping they would both be shot. Perfect timing.'

'Listen, George, I'm coming to London in ten days. I have an assignment from *The Travellers' Guide*: What do the British *really* think of Americans? In 3,000 words. Would it be all right if I stayed with you?'

'Terrific. As long as I get to be an authority you consult. You know how good I am on that subject. Seven years in London and I know all about the Anglo-American love-hate relationship. The Brits love to hate us. What about David. Is he coming?'

'David and I are divorced.'

'Jesus, Sam, you scumbag. You need to deliver bombshells like that in the first sentence, especially if it's a transatlantic phone call. Are you OK?'

'Sure.'

'Sure. Look, get your ass in gear and come over as soon as you can. I want all the details. You're not old enough to be divorced.'

'You said last year I wasn't old enough to be married.'

'Samantha, listen. *No one* is old enough to marry David. No one is young enough, either. You fucked up.'

'Thanks.'

'No problem. Look, just get on a jumbo. Tell me what flight it is and I'll meet you. Don't worry about the air controllers here being overworked, over-wrought and over the hill. Or the ground staff there being coked to the eyeballs. I'm sure they'll be fine on the night.'

'You're so reassuring.'

'Well, remember, I promised you that if you died in a plane crash I'd have a sex-change operation, so at least you'd be laughing on the way down, thinking about me under the knife.'

'Georgia, you never promised me that.'

'You shouldn't have told me I didn't. Dumb. Dumb. Dumb.'

But Samantha was, thought Georgia when she hung up the telephone, just that. Dumb. She was a good, dependable feature writer, she had a sense of humour and was easy to be with. But something was missing. A sense of power? Dumb in such a good-looking girl who had her own money and her own brains. Maybe all American preppy women with East Coast backgrounds and bank accounts were doomed to be dumb. She had to be dumb to fall for David. And dumb to get ditched, which, Georgia reckoned, must be the case; Samantha didn't have the balls to walk out on anyone. Dumb, dumb, dumb.

Georgia tossed the novel off her bed, picked up a pair of jeans from the floor and lay back down on the duvet. Successfully manoeuvring the tight jeans over her hips, she took a deep breath and yanked the zipper up its tortuous path. Then she took an even deeper breath and snapped the button in place. As soon as she stood up the zipper raced back down its track. She swore, found an extra-large sweatshirt on Andrew's chair, pulled it over her head and undid the button of her jeans with true relief. 'What they can't see can't disgust them' she said, then walked into the bathroom and stepped up to the mirror. She studied her face closely, transfixed by the skin around her eyes. What was it about age? Was she, at thirty-five, ancient? Or was she still, just barely, young? It depended on how you looked at it. If she saw an article in the paper about a thirty-five-year-old woman falling to her death in a failed parachute leap, she'd think – My God, she was so *young*. If, however, she saw an article in the paper about a thirty-five-year-old actress out on the town with her twenty-two-year-old toyboy, she'd think, My God, she's so *ancient*.

'Mirror, mirror on the wall, who's the likeliest candidate for a facelift of them all?' she addressed her reflection.

'Don't answer that,' she commanded, then carefully stretched the skin back towards her temples with her fingers. That's more like it, she thought. Maybe all women over thirty should walk around with their hands at their temples. Everyone will think we're being incredibly earnest and contemplative all the time. It's worth a try, anyway.

'George – is something wrong? Why are you looking so pained?'

'Don't I look younger?'

'No.'

'No?'

'No. You look like you've got a migraine, actually.'

'Oh, damn.' Georgia took her hands from her head and banged them on the table. 'And I thought I had the answer there. Instant facelift. No expense, no operation, no sweat.'

'No good.' Eugenie Woodrow laughed and picked

up her chopsticks. 'Which reminds me. Why do you keep dragging me to these nasty Chinese restaurants when your huband is working late? If we have to go Chinese, couldn't we go up-market Chinese? I think I see a caterpillar climbing out of my spring roll.'

'This is research, Eugenie. I'm trying to find a stunning new Chinese chef I can sign up. Do you know how successful cookbooks are? And do you know not one of my authors writes cookbooks? I need to discover a chef.'

'But why a Chinese chef?'

'Because I've thought of a perfect bestselling title. *Take A Wok On The Wild Side*. Which reminds me – have you thought of a title for your next masterpiece?'

Eugenie swept back her dark hair and took a sip of wine.

'No. Do we have to talk business tonight?'

'Not if you're not up to it. What about your love-life? Is that a safe subject?'

'My love-life', Eugenie took another sip of wine, 'is a very safe subject. Because it's non-existent. I am now thirty years old, unmarried, and fast coming to the conclusion that men are selfish and dumb to boot.'

'I know. Don't you love them? They're so self-obsessed and tacky and useless they're kind of cute.'

'Cute?' Lighting a cigarette, Eugenie glared across the table at Georgia. 'Cute?'

'Sure. Despite feminism, most men will never take women seriously. Most men can't even take more than two minutes of foreplay seriously. So I don't see the point of taking them seriously.'

'Am I supposed to take you seriously?' Eugenie laughed.

'As your literary agent, yes, of course. As your friend, absolutely. But we're not talking about me. We're talking about men. You're pissed off with men

10

because you fell in love with Duncan and he refused to leave his wife, and you've taken that seriously. But tell me something – when Duncan used to get undressed in front of you didn't he look foolish in his underwear?'

'Yes, he did, actually.' Eugenie smiled, remembering. 'He always wore boxer shorts with silly patterns on them.'

'Exactly. And it's even funnier when they wear Y-fronts. Have you seen those jean commercials where some sexy man strips? It's fine until he's standing there in his briefs – then he looks ridiculous. Just like when you go to the beach and see all those aspiring studs with bulging little bikinis. You have to laugh.' Georgia looked down at her plate. 'I think your caterpillar has a boyfriend over here. Anyway, think of Duncan in his boxers and you won't be so heartsick. Sure, men are hopeless, but that's what makes it fun for us. We can sit here and bitch about them. We can talk about all the things men are frightened to death women talk about when we get together.'

'Such as how they look in their underwear.'

'Right. Or how they perform in bed. Just think – the whole story of creation might have been different if God had been inspired to yank a few extra ribs off Adam and make some more women. Then Eve could have had female buddies to shoot the breeze with. As it was, she was left alone with a guy who roamed around the garden communing with nature all day. Boring. No wonder she was reduced to talking to a snake.'

Eugenie put out her cigarette and immediately lit another. 'Maybe God *is* a man, George. Male solidarity. He'd hardly want a bunch of women laughing about the size of Adam's fig-leaf. But is that what women really want? A group of girlfriends they can be vicious with?'

11

'Eugenie, you numbskull. Women really want stunning, perfect children, stunning, perfect careers, and stunning, perfect men who will make stunning, perfect love to them at least twice a day. We want it all.'

'And failing that?' asked Eugenie.

'Failing that, we'll take almost anything. And do almost anything to get whatever measly love and attention is on offer.' Georgia put her hands back to her temples. 'Are you absolutely, positively *sure* I don't look younger doing this?'

I was dumb to call Georgia. Samantha thought as she sat on the British Airways 747 bound for London. She's fun and she's funny, but she's not the kind of peson to be with when your heart has been surprise-attacked. She is anything but nurturing. She'll jump on everything I say. And she'll want to know exactly what went wrong with David. How can I tell her when I don't know?

The man sitting beside Samantha in Club Class closed his briefcase, placed it on the floor with a decisive gesture, and turned to her. 'I always think I'm going to work on these overnight trips, but I never do. Airplane trips should be fun, don't you agree?'

He was dressed entirely in white. White sandals, white socks, white trousers, white T-shirt, and white linen jacket. His hair was dark and curly, but with fashionable blonde streaks running through it. He looked like a male model, Samantha thought, and he looked foreign. Samantha picked up her book, *A History of Western Philosophy*.

'I like to read,' she said. She didn't want to be rude, but she didn't want to talk, either. She wanted to think. David had walked out of her life five months ago and was now in the Caribbean somewhere with his girlfriend. She didn't know what she had done wrong, but she must have done something. It was, she knew, all her fault.

When things went wrong, it was always her fault. She would even blame herself if she and David were driving somewhere and there was a traffic jam. She knew she hadn't created the jam, but as she would watch David get increasingly annoyed at the wheel, she'd feel responsible. She felt responsible every time he lost his keys, or got a parking ticket, or had a stomach ache.

He had left her for another woman, and she never asked him to explain why. She knew it was somehow her fault, so there seemed no point in arguing, or trying to stop him. But what exactly had she done wrong in their two years of marriage? She felt like an inept detective investigating a crime, but she wasn't sure who had robbed whom of what. She was, in short, clueless.

'I like to read too. Look here ...' The man in white pulled his briefcase back onto his lap, unfastened it and hauled out a copy of *Cosmopolitan*. 'See – see this article on Yugoslavia. It says that the most handsome men in the world are Yugoslavs. So where do you think I'm from?'

'I don't know. I'm not good at guessing games.' Samantha replied. His teeth were distracting her. She'd never seen any so obviously capped. And whoever had capped them seemed to have forgotten that teeth have gaps between them. His were two solid, shiny white plates, upper and lower.

'Yugoslavia of course.'

Samantha immediately wondered about dentistry behind the Iron Curtain. Did he have to pay?

'I must say, I must tell you that you have beautiful breasts. Would you mind unbuttoning the top button of that blouse?' He leant towards her. She backed away, so that her head was up against the window. 'I

13

have had many, many adventures,' he continued, looking at her blouse and not her by now slightly frightened face. 'I know I don't look thirty-two years old, but I am. My first sexual experience was when I was nine years old. I was in bed with my sister, and it happened. Beautiful, wonderful adventures have kept happening since. I love women. I love your breasts. I love airplanes. I love sex on airplanes.'

Samantha looked at him. She couldn't believe it. The man suddenly leant away and lit up a cigar. He was beginning to look more like a failed TV evangelist than a male model. Cigars weren't allowed on airplanes, she knew. But then was this kind of talk allowed anywhere but on Dr Ruth's chat show?

'I'm sorry, but I'm only interested in reading my book,' she said, feeling that, while he was smoking his cigar, she could safely move back to her original position.

His face took on a look of petulance, an official crossed. He might not be a Communist, but he was obviously a believer in parties.

'You don't know what you're missing,' he said, and leant across her yet again, closed her book and put his hand on the top of her black blouse, at the same time exhaling his cigar smoke.

The plane hit a bump, the smoke hit her straight in her face and a collision occurred in her stomach. Reaching across his hand for the sickbag, she pulled it up to her mouth, doubled over and threw up.

'God, I'm sorry,' she mumbled as she stumbled across his legs to the aisle and the lavatory.

'I've never had such an effect on a woman,' he said when she returned. His face, which she had remembered as deeply tanned, looked pale.

'I'm sorry. It's not you, it's the cigar.'

'Yes, well, I've put it out. I think perhaps we are not destined for a beautiful experience.'

'Maybe not.'

Samantha felt awful. What a way to put the man off. Why was she so inept? Other women, she felt sure, could have handled the situation a lot better. At least they wouldn't have thrown up immediately after being propositioned. She pushed the button and eased her chair back. It was time to stop thinking about her own inadequacies. It was time to fall asleep.

The stewardess woke her up when they were forty-five minutes away from Heathrow. She asked for coffee, and then noticed that the stewardess and the Yugoslav had obviously hit it off during the night. They were joking flirtatiously with each other.

'Well, how is the woman with beautiful breasts who likes reading philosophy feeling now?' he asked, with what Samantha thought was some concern.

'Fine, thanks. I'm really sorry about that.'

'Oh, not to worry. At least you managed to hit the bag and not my clothes.'

Samantha smiled. He was a nice man. He didn't blame her for throwing up. She had never been the object of such a come-on before, and although she thought he was ridiculous, she was vaguely pleased. She was used to sitting beside doting grandmothers who showed pictures of little Johnnie and Barbie the entire trip. The Yugoslav was a new experience, something she could tell Georgia about.

'I'm in Public Relations and I have a big meeting in London this morning, as soon as we arrive. People think I look like a gigolo, but no, I'm not so lucky, you know. I work hard. And I care about clothes. I love clothes. These white clothes are for a reason. I love the purity. I love the white theme. It's part of my style, my ability to get my pitch across. The English don't know how to dress. I dress Italian. I love the Italians. The people at this meeting, they'll love my white. It's easy, so simple. Pure white.'

The stewardess returned and handed the coffee over to Samantha. As she reached across and took it, her finger got twisted in the handle. The amiable Yugoslovian lecher with a theme was suddenly and irrevocably transformed into a man in a white suit who had just had a steaming cup of coffee dumped all over him. And he didn't love it at all.

'Hold on a minute. I can't hear you properly. There's a 747 going over.'

John Rankin, standing on his balcony in Chiswick, watched as the plane, its landing gear lowered, moved closer to Heathrow and the din subsided. 'I'm sorry, what were you saying?'

'I was saying that I hoped I hadn't woken you up. Am I interrupting you?'

'Not exactly,' John Rankin replied, reaching for his cup of coffee.

'Well, I just wanted to say thank you for the other night, and to apologize for getting so drunk. I don't usually drink that much, really. And, um, I can remember passing out, but I don't really remember anything after that.'

'It would be hard to remember anything during a state of unconsciousness, wouldn't it?' John Rankin had almost forgotten how much and how stupidly she talked. He did remember that, looking at her inert body on the bed beneath him, he had been pleased she couldn't rattle on anymore.

'Anyway, I was just calling to ask, well, I mean to find out – I mean, we did have fun the other night, didn't we? I mean, you know, did we have a good time?'

'Yes, we had a good time.'

'Oh, really? That's great. Maybe we can do it again sometime. I don't mean me getting drunk. I mean, you know, whatever we did that was a good time.'

'Sure, Shirley.' That was her name. He gave himself a pat on the back. 'I'll call you.' John Rankin watched another 747 begin its descent, and imagined he had a heat-seeking missile stationed on his balcony. How many planes could he shoot down before they changed the flightpath?

'John?'

'Yes?'

'I was saying that I'm around for a while. I mean, I'm going out tonight, but I'll be here tomorrow.'

'Good. Have fun tonight.'

'Thanks. Did I say that I'd be here tomorrow? Um, you have my number, don't you?'

'Yes to both questions, Shirley. Goodbye.'

'Byeeee.'

He put the phone down, and pulled the belt tight around his white towelling dressing gown. It was beginning to rain. He closed the balcony doors behind him and walked back into his kitchen.

The girl in his bedroom was worth waking up, no doubt about it. But he'd have another coffee first.


'Listen, Sam,' said Georgia as she guided her to the carpark of Terminal 4, 'I love tales of human misery, but I won't press you about David if you don't want to talk. The last thing you need is a cross-examination. You probably should have stayed in a hotel. At least you'd have room service and anonymity. Not to mention mini bars. Here's the car. Dump your things on the back seat there. As you can see, it's raining and miserable as usual. Welcome to England in June. I now understand why the British are obsessed by th weather: it's always lousy. You can try to forget ab it for a while, but it's relentless. The sun may never set on the British Empire, but it sure a doesn't bother to rise here in England.'

17

Georgia may have a right to complain about the weather. Samantha thought, but she was one of those women who didn't need a tan. Tall, pale, with scattered freckles and long, carefree red hair which looked as if it had a life of its own, Georgia had already gotten her fair share of help from Mother Nature.

Samantha always agonized about whether to use sunbeds and always, in the end, decided against them. She would have liked a tan, but she never seemed to have time to sunbathe on a beach and didn't want to subject herself to a sunbed. She was terrified of the top becoming unhinged and crushing her, and could imagine her body lying on a slab in the morgue, resembling a squashed lobster. As a result she was pale most of the time. But not, she knew, attractively pale like Georgia.

Samantha sat back in her seat and looked around her as they made their way onto the crowded motorway. She didn't mind the drizzle. She wished Georgia would turn on the radio – an English voice, a comforting English BBC broadcaster's voice – that was what she wanted. It might take her mind off her guilt about the Yugoslav in the stained white suit. She couldn't tell Georgia about him now, it would be yet another embarrrassment, another tale of human misery. Her own.

Georgia's car, an old MG with a sun-roof, was beginning to leak as the rain continued and they drove on towards the centre of London. The traffic on the motorway, as it narrowed to two lanes, became like a shoelace tightly knotted, almost impossible to untangle: but Georgia, switching lanes continually, made ome progress. It was not unlike the Long Island pressway at rush-hour, thought Samantha, but as came closer to the centre of London she noticed a ence. There was no dramatic skyline, only s, shops, a few tallish apartment blocks and offices, gradually becoming denser.

Driving into any large American city from the airport, particularly New York, there was a definite switch in architecture from suburb to city – an announcement, in effect, of arrival: 'You've made it to the big time.' That may have been the reason, Samantha thought, as Georgia drove on, why there were exuberant songs about cities in America: 'New York, New York', 'Chicago, Chicago'. The only song about London she knew of was, 'It's a Foggy day in London Town', a low-key, slightly plaintive tune.

Part of the American dream was the belief in the promise of the big city, the idea that a city would change your life. And that, Samantha realized as they were stopped at a traffic light, was exactly what she wanted as well. She was hoping that two weeks in London would change her life.

'Oh my God. Oh no.' Samantha crouched down in her seat.

'What is it, Sam? What's the matter? Jesus, what are you doing down there?'

'That taxi.'

'What taxi? What are you talking about? There are lots of taxis. Which one?'

'The one beside us.'

'What about it? It's big. It's black. The driver, as far as I can see, isn't pointing a gun at us. Are you on the run from the law or what? This is exciting.'

'There's a man in a white suit in the back.'

'There *was* a man in a white suit in the back.'

'Oh no. Has he gotten out? Is he coming toward us?'

'No. The taxi has just made a left turn. The man in the white suit is off in a different direction. So who *is* this mysterious fellow? And what has he got on you? Old love letters? Pictures of you in compromising positions with Liberace? What?'

'He doesn't have anything on me. He's got a cup of

coffee all over him. His white suit. I spilt it on the plane. He was furious.'

'Well, fuck him if he can't take a joke. People will think he takes his coffee white.'

Samantha didn't laugh. Georgia wondered whether she'd lost her sense of humour. Last year Sam had laughed at all her jokes. She drove on while Samantha collected herself and sat up.

'So what *did* go wrong with David? I'm incapable of playing coy anymore. This is a need to know situation.'

'He left me. He went off to the Caribbean with one of the models he was photographing and got a quickie divorce.' Samantha ripped open the carton of duty-free cigarettes at her feet, yanked one from the pack and lit it.

'Oh. I see. Gosh, I thought it was serious. Like maybe you'd spilled a cup of coffee all over his Hasselblad or something.'

Georgia, Samantha thought. Georgia's jokes. They seemed funny last year when there were about other people's problems.

None of Samantha's friends in New York had joked with her about David's departure. They either said that all men were shits or they left it alone. Men weren't as important as jobs in New York. Samantha had a good career as a freelance journalist, therefore she was fine. Marriages came and went, but reasonable jobs and decent apartments, they were rare and precious gifts. Samantha could imagine some of her female friends giving her hours of comfort if her analyst had ditched her, but she had never had an analyst. And now she didn't have a husband.

'Well, sweetheart, I could spend a long time trashing David, and his bimbo model, but I won't. At least not now. What you obviously need is a good fuck. I know a couple of men who are hot stuff in bed, according to my grapevine.'

'Georgia, please, that's the last thing I need. You playing pimp. I'm fine. And the less we talk about David, the better.'

'Your marriage has broken up but you're fine and you don't want to talk about it.' Georgia turned from the wheel and looked quickly at Samantha. 'Am I beginning to see a stiff upper lip setting in? No wonder you came to England. You sound like a typical Englishman, and a typical Englishman sounds mute.'

Samantha was beginning to worry. Georgia, whenever she spoke, talked with her hands as well, and was in danger of losing control of the car. Samantha didn't want to appear frightened, but she wished Georgia would concentrate on the road ahead.

'I'm tired and jet-lagged. I'm sorry.'

'Don't, please, apologize. We're almost home, and you can go straight up to bed. I promise you a couple of hours of peace and quiet.'

Georgia drove on, taking a right turn just before Harrods, winding her way through Belgravia and into Pimlico. Parking on a yellow line outside her house, she swore at the prospect of a clamp on her car, then took Samantha's two bags out of the back, opened the door and struggled with a small key to turn off the alarm which was, within seconds, sounding at full force.

'I can never get this thing right. Hold onto the side of the bell there to muffle the noise a little. There – whew. This is connected to the police station, but they must be used to me by now. If a burglar ever comes, they'll just assume it's me being hopeless again. Come on up to your room.'

Hiking upstairs, Samantha saw that the house hadn't changed from the previous year. It was in its habitual state of disarray. She was led, her head still clanging from the alarm bell, into a spare room she had not been in before, a feminine room with a small single bed and wallpaper with strawberries floating through it. Samantha thought of Wimbledon, of strawberries and cream and grass tennis courts, and the throbbing of the alarm began to fade.

'Just relax, take a nap. I've got work to do, but come downstairs when you wake up and we'll have some coffee.'

Georgia sat down on the bed as she said this, making no move to leave. All Samantha wanted to do was collapse, but she stood awkwardly beside her bags, waiting for whatever Georgia was obviously determined to say.

'You know, Sam, we don't know each other that well, and all this sisterhood stuff bores me, but I sometimes think that women *do* have something in common, at least all women over the age of twenty-one. I think we're all like aging singers afraid of losing our voices – except in our case, we're afraid of losing our looks, or our boyfriends or husbands, or our children when they grow up, or our ability even to have children as we grow older, or, of course, our careers.

'And it sounds to me like you've lost David. But you're only twenty-five, and maybe that's the best time to lose something – early. You can recoup. It's not as if you were Ferdinand Marcos and had lost something big.'

Samantha stood silently – what was she supposed to say? To her mind a husband was, after all, a big thing to lose.

'Anyway, maybe if we handle life the right way, we can all be like Frank Sinatra, an aging singer who has lost his voice but is still a superstar. Maybe it's all in the phrasing. Or the toupee.'

Georgia stood up and gave Samantha a hug, then went out and closed the door. Taking off her clothes, and climbing under the duvet, Samantha wondered what she should make of that speech. By Georgia's standards, Samantha knew, it was serious. But what did it mean? 'I don't feel like an aging singer, I feel like someone with an economy ticket sitting in Concorde,' she thought, 'I don't belong with Georgia – she's too fast for me. She waves her arms around and talks like a rapid-fire machine gun and I don't understand what she's saying. We don't speak the same language. What does she mean by "it's all in the phrasing"? And what does Frank Sinatra have to do with women losing husbands?'

As she hovered on the edge of sleep, Samantha's thoughts whirled around Frank Sinatra, back to 'New York, New York', the song she had thought of in Georgia's car, and her wish that her trip to London might somehow erase the failure she had been feeling since David's departure. 'Georgia,' she said as she turned onto her stomach and put her nose into the stained, caseless pillow, 'Georgia is the name of a song as well. Why did I immediately think of Georgia when I saw David in bed with that woman? Why did I wangle this assignment to London the day I got my divorce papers? What am I doing here with her? Georgia. Georgia on my mind.'

# Chapter Two

Georgia Green picked up a manuscript from a pile on her desk and tried to concentrate. There was work to be done, and she was supposed to do it while Samantha slept off her trip upstairs. But she had no desire to read any books or call any authors or persuade any publishers. What she wanted was to curl up in her own bed and cry.

Here she was, a literary agent in a foreign city, childless at thirty-five, with a husband who was becoming more remote by the day. This morning, before she had gone to Heathrow, she'd tried with Andrew, she'd tried hard, but she'd gotten a lacklustre response. He had rolled on top of her briefly, grunted away, and rolled off. It reminded her of the scene in *Ryan's Daughter* – Robert Mitchum and Sarah Miles on their wedding night, an exercise in sexual boredom. What was she doing wrong? Did he expect her to come up with different moves? Astonish him? After five years of marriage, how could she pretend to be Kim Basinger in *9½ Weeks*? Sexual interaction between two people was limited after a while, wasn't it? She would have to think of something, and soon. Her IUD had been removed almost a year ago, and her gynaecologist had encouraged her, if she wished to get pregnant, to 'cover' the fertile days in her cycle. Lately those crucial days had been left blank, and she wasn't about to plead with Andrew. She had some pride.

She had a lot of pride. Georgia threw the manuscript back down on the desk and began to pace her study to keep herself from crying. Andrew hated weakness in women. He had made it clear early on that demanding, neurotic, tear-prone women were not his cup of tea. For a while, at the beginning of their relationship, she had been able to talk about her fears and insecurities. Until she began to notice that his eyes glazed over and his attention wandered whenever she became 'emotional'; then she learned quickly that if she played it tough, if she were cocky and feisty and funny, he would snap back and look at her with respect. Well, she didn't want to be a weak woman; she wanted to be a woman he was proud of. The superstar who's not fazed by any adversity. Frank Sinatra. Frank Sinatra? Was he really such a great role model? Samantha must have thought she was crazy.

Would Andrew be like David and do a bunk? That thought made her stop, sink down into her desk chair, and begin to examine the split ends of her hair, a nervous teenage habit she had never quite dropped. Andrew and David were friends – that's how she had met Samantha the previous year. David had brought his new wife to England, and the two couples had spent a few days together. Georgia had been curious about Samantha, not least because she had never liked David. He was overbearing and full of himself. Thrilled to be the rising photographer rivalling Annie Leibowitz in trendy magazines like *Interview*. Pleased as punch that he had spent a year at Oxford, where he had cultivated a group of English friends, which included Andrew.

Georgia sensed that David felt above Andrew now, disappointed that his clever English friend hadn't made more of a splash so that he could drop his name more often. When he talked about Andrew's books, the dictionaries of slang, jargon, quotes on different subjects, he was extremely civil. David was, thought Georgia, like many rising, conspicuously polite hot-shots, honing, amiability at the same time as hoarding superiority.

Samantha had been sweet, shy, almost awkward, and Georgia wondered what had made David choose her. Perhaps he had been attracted to her Hitchcock heroine looks – the blonde with the refined features and innocent, open face, or perhaps he had been impressed by her upper-class background. Whatever the case, Georgia had not been surprised by Samantha's news of the break-up.

Would Andrew do the same to her, would he bugger off? There wasn't another woman, she would be able to tell if there were. But Andrew was capable of leaving without having someone waiting in the wings. Maybe she should confront him, ask him why his feelings had changed, why he wasn't sharing himself with her anymore.

No way. Georgia found another split end and tossed her hair away in disgust. If she confronted him, she knew she would cry and blurt out ultimately stupid moans like, 'You don't give me little presents anymore – remember how you used to give me presents?' Or 'You don't write me little love notes anymore – remember how you used to write me little love notes?' Then she'd watch as that chilling dismissive glaze took over his eyes. It would be a scene from a situation comedy that wasn't funny.

She was tougher than Samantha, and she intended to stay tough. She wouldn't fold under pressure, she wouldn't break down and be a wimpy wife, asking him what was wrong, pleading with him for more love. She would rise above any problems, make light of them. After all, she had advised Eugenie to stop taking men seriously – she should follow her own counsel. If she was good at joking through life, she should stick to what she was good at. And think of something wonderful to do in bed.

The fax machine had started to buzz and Georgia was grateful for the interruption. She didn't like too much time to think. In the end, it was unsettling. When she leant over and read the copy coming through, she laughed.

'Georgia, you little devil. I have just read *Let Yourself Go*. What a lucky agent/creature you are to have Eugenie Woodrow as an author. Of course I have to think about taking an option for a mini-series. Am I a fool? Only with the ladies.

Sure, I balked a little at the idea of three glorious-looking, super-wealthy women being simultaneously kidnapped by a ravishing, down-on-his-luck, leftover sixties hippy with ideals. I mean, I was a hippy at college, wasn't I, sweetheart, and I don't remember *ever* having ideals. All I remember is pretending I had ideals so I could take incompletes in all my courses. Maybe you were purer than I was. I doubt it. Remember, I knew most of your boyfriends.

Anyway, I adore the way the three beauties all do a Patty Hearst and fall in love with Storm. Great name for a hero, by the way. Believe it or not, I've just been to a dinner party and every delicious little female titbit there admitted to having a secret sneaking crush on Claus von Bulow. I don't think we could get Claus to play Storm do you? Too old. But I see Michael Douglas. Or William Hurt. Or John Hurt. Or anyone who *looks* hurt. And sexy.

As you know, my last movie was such a spectacular flop that I have, in LA lingo, failed up. So anything goes. I'll be back in touch when I know more. Don't count the money yet, but you can think about it and salivate.

Power to the People, and that means us, honeychild.

Rick.

PS If Miss Woodrow thinks that she made up that sex scene with the Chinese basket chair every woman is now talking about, please inform her that little Ricky was doing it before his balls dropped. And it's better in real life than on the printed page.'

Samantha woke up, displaced. Where was she? The strawberry wallpaper came into focus and she remembered. Georgia's house. England. London. Pimlico. She had been dreaming of David, damn it. David and she in bed together. It was a recurrent dream and she hated it. David and she going through the motions, starting off with him on top, then flipping over so that she was on top, then turning sideways, her arms around his neck, his hands on her bottom, David pumping away until he had finished. She had the strange sensation of being a gas tank in a car, filled up by the nozzle until the trigger clicked, signalling the end. The transaction was complete. And then David sat up in bed. 'Samantha,' he said 'Sometimes I'm amazed by the things you don't know.'

The dream finished there. So had real life. Because that had actually happened one evening. He had delivered that line, gotten up and gone into the living room to watch CNN. And she had stayed in bed, terrified. *What* didn't she know exactly? They had been married for a year. If there were things she didn't know, why didn't he tell her? Of course it was all her fault for not knowing these things, whatever they were. She'd only been to bed with one man before David, a business school student, and he couldn't be classified as a raver. Just a nice, sensible man with a nice smile who had lived with her for a nice two years until he moved to the Mid West and they exchanged nice goodbyes.

David was another proposition altogether. He'd had lots of women, lots of success in every aspect of his life and she hadn't been sure why he had chosen her. But he had. Their first night out together, he had said, 'You're the one for me,' and she had been stunned. But David was like a steamroller, you either got out of his way or you were flattened, and all that she wanted was to be flattened by this attractive, self-confident photographer. She had thought that his assurance might be contagious, that together, he the photographer and she the journalist would flatten the world. It hadn't happened quite that way.

Samantha sat up in bed, chewing on her thumbnail. Not knowing 'things' was all her fault. Or was it? He could have taught her, he didn't have to go watch TV. But then *she* could have asked him to teach her, instead of pretending, as she did, that he hadn't said it. It *was* all her fault. All her fault for being such a wimp. She looked down at her gnawed thumbnail in disgust, grabbed a cigarette and lit it. It was time to go downstairs and face Georgia. Could she take lessons on not being a wimp from Georgia? Was that what she was here for, really?

Georgia had impressed her last year by her flamboyance. She had talked like a maniac, told anecdotes and jokes without any sense of self-consciousness or fear of boring people. Samantha had been brought up never to impinge. Never, her parents had taught her, talk about money, sex, or yourself. Ask questions, be polite, be a good WASP, always slightly distant from the fray. Above it. And look what happened to polite WASPS – they were regarded by everyone else as weaklings. Polite behaviour and self-effacement weren't the key to advancement in the eighties.

During her boarding-school and college days, she'd never met any woman as crass as Georgia. Well, to be honest, she had, but she had avoided them. Now she was travelling straight into the maelstrom. Was she hoping that Georgia's devil-may-care attitude toward life was contagious, as she had hoped David's self-confidence would be?

'Fuck 'em if they can't take a joke,' she said out loud, trying to mimic Georgia. It sounded lame, like George Bush trying to tell a dirty joke.

Rick Holland poured himself a cup of coffee, re-read the fax he had just sent to Georgia and chuckled to himself. 'She'll appreciate that,' he thought. 'I wish she'd been here tonight.' The beautiful blonde bimbo sitting beside him at dinner had been so young and so inarticulate she shouldn't have been allowed to eat at the table with grownups. He had asked the waiter if there were any high chairs available and the whole party had cracked up. She certainly shouldn't have been allowed to share his bed. But of course she had. Jesus, what an experience. Georgia and he had often amused themselves in their college days by speculating on which women in their classes were 'moaners' and which were 'screamers'. This little piece of quivering flesh was a screamer, all right, a true screamer. He'd thought at one point during the activities that she'd perforated his ear drum. Luckily in La-La land you could send them home early – everyone in Hollywood was hooked on beauty sleep.

Why couldn't he find an intelligent woman who was dumb enough to fall for him, he wondered. Romance hadn't materialized for him, or rather, it had – often – but the material hadn't stretched far. He loved women and they loved him. For brief periods of time. Once he had entertained Georgia by drawing a graph charting the progress of a typical love affair. The line shot heavenwards, up the scale, for the first few weeks. Then it evened out for a month or so. And then he drew a line straight down, dropping as precipitously as a stock-market crash. 'What's happened there, Rick?' Georgia had asked. 'Why the plunge?' 'Let's see,' he had answered, 'It could be that her old boyfriend calls up from Alaska inviting her on a fishing trip in the wilds. Or I suggest she go on a tiny diet and she suggests I get a brain transplant. Or, to put it bluntly, it's the logical consequence of a few months of sustained intimacy. And now, sweetcakes, our line goes so far down, we run out of paper. This is when the loving couple start getting into heavy duty war games. And we start a whole new graph – give me your arm and a knife, darling, and we'll draw it in blood.'

Picking up *Let Yourself Go* he turned it over and looked again at the picture of Eugenie Woodrow on the back. A raven-haired beauty, and, he hoped, a moaner. Georgia would probably know for sure; she had a knack of finding out every little detail of everyone's love-life, the little squirrel. He was glad he'd never been to bed with George – thinking about it, he laughed. Those AIDS pamphlets warned you that if you go to bed with a woman, you're sleeping with all her past lovers too. In Georgia's case, if you'd slept with her, you would have effectively fucked all her girlfriends as well – she would have told them every single move the next day. Still – he missed her friendship. Bimbos were all very well, but a steady diet of them was like eating Chinese food. A few hours after you'd finished, you felt hungry again.

Rick got up. tuned his radio in to the classic oldies station and listened to Jennifer Warnes and Joe Cocker singing 'Love Lifts Us Up Where We Belong'.

'Nice idea, you little doggies,' he said out loud. 'But how can I fly up there like an eagle when I'm surrounded by turkeys?'

# Chapter Three

'Twenty minutes,' said John Rankin, lounging back in his chair on the balcony of his flat in Chiswick, overlooking the Thames. 'All women have twenty minutes in their lives when everything comes together. Their spirit and their body simply take off, like a magnificent bird, and soar. The skin and hair shine, the face takes on a Madonna beauty, and the psyche is at peace. If you are a man fortunate enough to be present when this happens, you are ineffably lucky. Looking at you right now, I feel that I'm a lucky man.'

'Is that a line you're using to get me into bed? Because if it is, it's a pretty good one. Even if it is lunchtime, and lunch is not my time for playing.'

'It is a simply observation – it has nothing to do with sex, Linda. Although, of course, if you have your twenty minutes and *don't* go to bed, you're inevitably missing something special. Look –' John Rankin leant over to where Linda was sitting with her elbows on the table and stroked her forearm. 'Don't you feel different? Isn't your skin unusually sensitive? And your cheekbones' – he traced them with his two forefingers – 'these are intelligent cheekbones. They know what's happening. But it's your choice. You're about five minutes into your twenty right now. What do you want to do with the next fifteen?'

'Only fifteen?'

'Only fifteen.'

'What are we waiting for?'

Samantha put on the black skirt and blouse she had worn on the plane and went downstairs, feeling a little like a Marine recruit on the first day of training. Georgia would zero in on her now. She'd only slept an hour, her dream about David had upset her, and she wasn't sure she could face being alone with the Grand Inquisitor. Especially if the Grand Inquisitor was going to talk about Frank Sinatra. As she reached the bottom of the stairs, she stopped and listened to Georgia's voice, coming from the kitchen.

'You should see the black get-up she arrived in. She may well have gone Amish without telling me. Divorce can make people religious sometimes. I'm supposed to be jealous of twenty-five-year-olds, not feel sorry for them. Sam was quiet that week here last year, and shy. But she had a certain endearing style. Even Andrew, who, you know, never notices much, said he thought she was pretty. I wonder what he'll think now. She looks thin and wasted. At least I won't have to worry about him fancying her. Anyway, you'll be here soon, you can check her out for yourself. Maybe we can cheer her up.'

Samantha heard the phone being put down, then walked slowly into the kitchen. There was no point in avoiding Georgia, and even less in changing her clothes. Everything in her suitcase was either black or grey.

Entering the kitchen, she saw the familiar mess. Dirty dishes in the sink, a floor with sticky patches of Coca-Cola spilt over it, a hoard of fruit-flies gathered around a bunch of overripe bananas on the counter. David and she had never eaten at Georgia's house – Andrew had warned them off. 'We call it Chateau Botulism' he had said. 'It's best if we stick to restaurants.' Samantha sat down at the counter and waited for the worst.

'The thing about David ...'

'Do you mind if I have some coffee first, George? I'm still tired.'

'Sure. Of course. Right here waiting for you in the Mr Coffee machine. Even I don't mess that up.'

'Thanks. That is a really pretty room I'm in.'

'The spare room? Yuck. I haven't gotten around to redecorating it, so I'm stuck with Laura Ashley.'

'What's wrong with Laura Ashley?'

'She's dead.'

'Georgia, you're sick.'

'To get back to the real nitty-gritty, I mean, sure, David was a half-way decent photographer. But he didn't have much of a sense of humour, you have to agree.'

'You're talking about him in the past tense. He's not dead.'

'No. Do you think Laura Ashley may have redecorated heaven? David could take pictures of it when he *does* die.'

'Georgia, David takes pictures of people. Not rooms or food or anything else. People.' Samantha repeated, surprised that she was talking back to Georgia, even more surprised at her own wish to defend David.

'Did he take pictures of you in sexy poses? And since when did you start smoking?'

Inhaling, Samantha immediately decided that coming to stay with Georgia was the biggest mistake she had ever made.

'Ah, there's the doorbell. It's probably Eugenie – you didn't meet her last year, did you? She's my best friend, not to mention my best client. I was just talking to her in her car. I still get a kick out of calling someone in a car.'

Samantha's brain clicked on the name Eugenie.

34

Eugenie Woodrow, of course – the Englishwoman who wrote *Let Yourself Go*, the racy book about the three kidnapped heiresses. She had seen Eugenie on Phil Donahue talking about people falling in love with their captors, and it was clear to Samantha that Phil himself had been taken captive by the beautiful Ms Woodrow.

Another rousing female success story. Samantha stirred some milk into her coffee. Who else but Eugenie Woodrow would be Georgia's best friend? Samantha didn't know that people over the age of eleven had best friends, and the prospect of seeing Eugenie Woodrow in person made Samantha feel the same as she had when she saw her on television the year before. Slightly sick.

'Samantha, this is Eugenie, Eugenie Woodrow. Eugenie, Samantha Lewis. Sam's just gotten divorced and Eugenie has just fallen in love. You two should be a great combination.'

'I'm in love with my gynaecologist,' Eugenie announced as she went straight to the Mr Coffee machine, poured herself a cup, then lit a cigarette and sat down.

Samantha compared these two women as she sat opposite them at the kitchen table. Georgia was blatantly sexy, obviously attractive in an almost macho sense, while Eugenie was more discreet. Perfectly discreet. The nails were manicured. The blue eyes were quietly made up with brown eyeliner and eyeshadow, and her dark hair was pulled back, but not severely. She looked pampered, protected, and absolutely aware of her femininity. In fact, she looked as if she were calmly sitting on top of a powder keg. If she chose to, she could light a match and blow up anyone in her vicinity.

'And Georgia admitted to me on the telephone a few minutes ago that she's in love with her gynaecologist as well. I think it's a natural phenomenon, and much healthier than falling in love with your analyst. Or your dentist. Don't you think so, Samantha?'

Samantha nodded.

'Are you in love with yours?' Eugenie continued questioning Samantha, focusing on her. Samantha was acutely aware of her dowdy black outfit – why in God's name hadn't she packed a different set of clothes?

Eugenie was wearing jeans with a green and purple striped silk blouse, short purple suede boots and huge, heart-shaped green earrings.

'Well, I've always had a female gynaecologist,' Samantha admitted, blushing.

'You poor thing.' Eugenie turned to Georgia, who was already talking.

'Yeah, seriously, who wants a woman looking up your pussy? That's why I'm in love with mine. He spends all that time looking and prodding around in there and he doesn't throw up.' Eugenie started to laugh. Samantha was speechless.

'Well, it's true. That's what every woman wants, no? Some man who will spend a lot of time down below and act as if he's getting paid for it. Right?'

'Undoubtedly,' said Eugenie, looking at Samantha again, a look which seemed to offer an invitation to join in. But Samantha was still blushing, and looked down at her coffee as Georgia went on.

'My gynaecologist is the only man who can call me "honey" without pissing me off. I figure it's a compliment in those circumstances. Anyway, this one's a hell of a lot better than the last guy I went to. He suddenly looked up at me in the middle of a smear test and said, "I wonder why I do this job." That made me feel great, I can tell you.'

Squirming on her chair, Samantha looked for moral support from Eugenie. All she got was a friendly, open smile. Of course this kind of talk wouldn't bother her, Samantha realized. She writes steamy novels. What had all that fuss been about a Chinese basket chair – she couldn't remember, but she could recall Donahue arching his eyebrows and provoking a great laugh from the audience when he asked Eugenie whether she was seated comfortably. Why can't I be like Eugenie and take all this in stride? Samantha wondered. Why do I feel threatened by it?

'Maybe I should have a sex scene in a gynaecologist's office in this next book. What do you think, Georgia?' Leaning forward on her elbows, Eugenie's face tightened.

'That's what I need to talk to you about. Women loved that idea of three rich bitches falling in love with their kidnapper – it appealed to some primitive Mills and Boon instinct, I guess. But I can't work out what the theme of the next one should be. Perhaps I should have Storm, after serving his term for kidnapping, study medicine and become a gynaecologist. Women are at the mercy, more or less, of their gynaecologists.'

Eugenie had an extraordinarily deep voice which verged on hoarseness. Strangely, it added to rather than detracted from her aura of femininity.

Georgia squinted slightly as she pushed her red fringe back from her forehead with both hands.

'I think you've played Storm out, Eugenie. You need a new set of characters. But you told me you'd started already. How far have you gotten?' she asked in a tone which was not altogether casual.

'Not far. First chapter. In the first scene the heroine, who is basically frigid, walks in on her husband in bed with another woman, some long-legged busty model type. You know, the mega-rich, successful, married businessman gets caught with a Page Three bimbo. But maybe I should scrap it. It's a ridiculous, clichéd situation, and who wants a frigid heroine?'

'Nobody does,' said Samantha quickly, surprising the other two. 'Nobody wants a dumb, frigid, mediocre heroine, no matter how endearing she may be.' She got up and left the kitchen.

Georgia, for once was quiet. Eugenie looked at her and lit another cigarette. 'Did I say something wrong?'

The white linen tablecloth was gradually being covered in black ink. The couple at the table were both writing on it, beneath the question John Rankin had penned in the upper left-hand corner: What would you do with a million pounds? There was a dividing line bisecting the tablecloth – her answers were on the left, his on the right. Occasionally he would reach across and put a question mark beside one of her answers, or she would lean over to his side and put a cross through one of his.

'John, this is supposed to be serious,' she giggled. 'You can't possibly want to buy a pig farm.'

'Why not? You can't ridicule me when I see there that you would like to buy Gregory Peck for one night. Isn't he a little old for you?'

'I don't care how old he is. He could sit in a chair all night as far as I'm concerned. I'd be happy just to watch him.'

'Well, I'd be happy to watch pigs. But I'm deeply offended, Libby. You are almost at the end of the tablecloth there and you haven't said you wanted to buy *me* for a night. What's Gregory Peck got that I haven't?'

'Star status.'

John Rankin reached into his pocket and put on a pair of sunglasses. 'Do these help?'

'A little.'

'What if I went over to that man at the corner table there and borrowed his gold necklace? Would that be Hollywood enough?'

'You wouldn't dare.'

'You want to bet?' John Rankin got up and strolled

over to the man in the corner. Libby watched as, after a few minutes, the man took off his necklace and handed it over.

'I win,' John said as he sat back down beside her, undoing his shirt buttons and displaying the necklace.

'This is the most bizarre first date I've ever been on.'

'So I'll make a deal with you. You pay for dinner and I'm yours for the night. Only don't count on me just sitting in a chair.'

The waiter watched as the woman signed a cheque for the meal. Not bad. He hadn't seen him do that before. Then, as they left, he walked over and started to clear off the table, studying the ink-stained cloth. The manager would have to move from linen to less expensive tableclothes – he'd seen a lot of these, and they were a bitch to clean.

Samantha was jet-lagged on her first full day at Georgia's house in London. She got up at ten in the morning, fished a grey cotton dress with black horizontal stripes from her bag and went downstairs, hoping for the chance to have a cup of coffee on her own.

The previous day had been harrowing. After she had left Georgia and Eugenie in the kitchen she had gone up to her room as if she had been a child having a tantrum. Georgia had come up to apologize, and Samantha had then apologized as well. She had liked Eugenie. Eugenie had been open and friendly, welcoming, not acting the part of the star writer. Samantha was deeply embarrassed that she had made a scene. Something had snapped in her, but she insisted to Georgia that she was just jet-lagged and needed some time to recover. So she had stayed in her room for the afternoon, reading her book on philosophy, and gone to bed early. It was not the way she would have liked to start her stay in London.

But the next morning she was in luck. On the kitchen counter was a note from Georgia, saying that she would be out for the day and for Sam to make herself comfortable.

Samantha searched for a clean coffee mug, and thought it was impossible to be comfortable in the midst of this bomb site. It would be a good idea, a nice polite gesture as a guest, to clean the kitchen, to make it at least habitable, and she started immediately, searching for mops and cleaning fluids and dishwasher powder. It was easier than she thought – all the things she needed were in the side closet – and within an hour she had finished the job and rewarded herself with a cup of fresh coffee in a clean mug and a cigarette.

'Ah ha. My wife has finally found a new, and, dare I say it, wonderfully effective char ...' As Samantha turned around from her seat at the counter, Andrew stopped talking.

'Hello, Andrew. Sorry, I didn't know you were here. I just thought I'd do the kitchen for George. I didn't think I could face starting real work immediately.'

'Samantha, you are an immediate miracle worker. A trip to Lourdes is in order – in fact, I am so bloody impressed that I feel disinclined to have the whiskey I came down here for. Can I join you in a cup of coffee?'

'Sure.' Samantha got up and poured some coffee from the machine. 'What do you like in it?'

'Two sugars, please. This is a new and illuminating experience: I am usually told to get my own. 'How long are you staying, Samantha?' he asked hopefully. 'I'm very sorry not to have seen you last night, but I got back late.'

'Two weeks, I think. At least that's my deadline for this article. Do you mind if I open the window – this place needs airing out.'

'Fresh air may well kill Georgia's collection of germs, a collection she treasures. By all means, be my guest.'

As Samantha pushed the window up, the phone rang, and Andrew answered it. 'I'll clean the living room,' she thought. 'That will get me out of here and maybe Andrew will go back upstairs.'

Andrew's attitude, his open criticism of Georgia, even if it were a joke, put Samantha ill at ease. Tall and shaggy, with a minor paunch, Andrw was dressed in baggy corduroys and a sweatshirt. He looked the quintessential old-fashioned journalist – proudly dishevelled. His face, Samantha noticed for the first time, was dishevelled as well, as if the features were still searching for their right place and had only settled in their spots momentarily. He seemed as if he had just woken up, but, Samantha remembered, he always looked as if he had just woken up. There was a crumpled I-need-taking-care-of aspect to him which she realized must appeal to all women's mother instincts, but that was offset by his tone of voice – it conveyed a sense of anger, a feeling that everyone else on the planet was intellectually beneath him and they were all too dumb to realize it. Still, she was grateful to him for not mentioning David.

Andrew put his hand over the receiver. 'It's for you, Samantha. The fabulous Eugenie Woodrow. Apparently she is issuing a luncheon invitation.'

'To me?'

'To you.'

Andrew watched Samantha smile as he handed her the telephone. She had a sweet, gracious, self-conscious smile which matched her innocent, hurt eyes. An all-American girl who'd just been cut from the cheerleader squad. David had no doubt, been brutal, and Andrew found himself wishing he could comfort her. And then wishing she was wearing a cheerleader's outfit while he *was* comforting her. Lucky Eugenie, he thought, then got up and headed for the whiskey bottle.

'Aha, hold up a minute, it's probably for you again.' Samantha had finished talking to Eugenie and was halfway out the kitchen door when the phone had begun to ring. 'No one ever rings me in the morning if they can help it.' Andrew picked it up with an exaggerated swoop.

'Hello. The answering machine is not home at the moment, but leave a message with the person and it will get back to you shortly.'

Samantha smiled again and watched Andrew take a quick sip of his drink.

'David?' Andrew looked over at Samantha with raised eyebrows. She stood perfectly still. 'Isn't it early for you to be ... Right, yes, well, actually she *is* here. Do you want to ... I see. yes ...' Sam was transfixed, she couldn't take her eyes away from Andrew. He shrugged and made drinking motions with his glass. David drunk. David drunk at crack of dawn in the Caribbean with the model asleep in bed beside him. But why was he calling Andrew?

'She's fine, David. Actually, she's looking bloody beautiful. No, she's not. No. She hasn't even mentioned your name. She's just about to go out to lunch. I don't know. No. She's perfectly all right and she is *not* being nasty about you to anyone. Quite. But she hasn't. Listen, old fruit, why don't you ring me again sometime when you're sober and *I'm* drunk, then we'll have a proper conversation. Quite. Goodbye, David.'

'How did he know I was here?' Samantha asked. Her voice was preternaturally quiet.

'I gather a friend of yours in New York told him.' Andrews wigged down the rest of the whiskey.

'And he was worried that I was hysterical and ranting and telling you horrible stories about him?'

'That's the gist of it, yes. I'm sorry, Samantha.'

'Don't be. And thanks for defending me. Boy –'

Samantha looked down at the floor. 'When love dies, it goes stone cold dead, doesn't it?'

'It has that nasty habit, yes. But don't worry. Think about that Frank Sinatra song – "Love is Easier the Second Time Around".'

'What *is* it with you people and Frank Sinatra?' Samantha burst into tears and rushed out of the kitchen. Andrew poured himself another shot of whiskey.

'Did I say something wrong?' he asked his glass.

Eugenie Woodrow hung up the telephone and stared at her computer screen. What she had was not writer's block, it was writer's nausea. She didn't care about any of the characters, about the rich businessman and his frigid wife and his bimbo girlfriend, and if she didn't care about them why should anyone else? If only this lunch with Samantha would help. She could imagine a lot of people caring about Samantha, the vulnerable, sad-eyed, pale-faced Samantha, as they had obviously cared for the aging, engaging, idealistic Storm. Creating Storm had been immensely therapeutic, he had distracted her, made her forget about Duncan. Storm – the handsome kidnapper with a heart. Why weren't there any Storms in real life ports?

She was supposed to be happily successful, she knew that. But she also knew she was a fake. The book had been a fluke, a lucky shot in the dark which had gone straight to the public's heart. Why did everyone expect a follow-up? Why couldn't she forget about it? But then what would she do? Go back to the fashion world? Work nine to five on Bond Street? Maybe she could get away with faking her way through life for a while.

Most people were accomplished fakes, she thought. She'd just have to work at it. She was a middle-class girl from the suburbs of London who was suddenly appearing on *Wogan* and *Donahue* with celebrities who treated her like a celebrity. All because of one book. As well as, she suspected, her looks. It had helped that she'd learned, over the years, how to talk with a reasonably posh accent, how to eat with the right spoons, forks and knives at posh dinner parties, how to stop herself from saying unposh words like 'toilet' when she needed to pee, or 'pardon' when she hadn't heard someone correctly. She was a quick study in social mores, all of which came in handy when fame had hit. But her looks, she suspected, were the biggest help of all, and how long would *they* last? A few more years, at least, she decided, then chuckled, remembering Georgia's attempt at an instant facelife. She could just imagine herself going on television with her hands up to her temples the entire interview.

Georgia was the person closest to her now, the one who knew her the best, and Georgia would stand by her, even if her next book failed. Eugenie suddenly caught herself wondering. *Would* Georgia stand by her? She wasn't altogether sure. After all, Georgia profited from Eugenie's success. She wished she had a female friend who wasn't connected in any business way. Those kind of female friends could be counted on. Actually, it wasn't fair to question Georgia's loyalty – she might be a sharp operator, but she wasn't a bastard. Women could be bitches sometimes, definitely, but they weren't bastards.

Eugenie smiled at the thought. It sounded ridiculous, but any woman would know what she meant.

Mrs Duncan Darrell's mind became unhinged in the middle lane of the M4 as she drove back from a country weekend in Wiltshire. She saw a marked police car travelling slowly on her left and something went dreadfully wrong in her thinking.

'How bored the police must be,' she decided,

'watching everyone slow down for them.' At which point, drawing level with the authorities, she stepped on the accelerator of her Land Rover. Within twenty seconds a siren was screaming and flashing and she was signalled over to the breakdown lane.

'Did I do something wrong, officers?'

'You were speeding, ma'am.' Two medium-sized men with forgettable faces were staring at her through the open window.

'Yes. Oh dear. I thought I might cheer you up.'

The officers glanced at each other, then back at her.

'Yes, well, you see, I thought you might be bored.'

'Bored?' The larger of the middle-sized pair spoke. He sounded remarkably like her gardener. Clarissa quickly snapped to attention. She was in trouble. She had broken the law for the first time in her life.

'Oh dear. How silly of me,' she started to say, then found herself crying. The crying rapidly escalated. 'I wasn't thinking properly,' she sobbed 'Something, oh, I don't know, something horrible has happened.'

'An accident, ma'am?' The gardener sound-alike had taken over the questioning.

'Not exactly. No.'

'No children ill, I hope.'

'Not exactly. No.' Clarissa continued to cry. What could she possibly say to get out of this?

'Is it your husband, then?'

'Yes, yes. It's my husband. It's definitely my husband.' She looked at the officer with relief.

'He hasn't died, then?'

This man had a truly macabre streak, Clarissa thought.

'No, not quite. It's just he –' she floundered.

'Walked out on you?'

'Yes. Yes. That's it. Oh dear. The nasty man just walked out on me and abandoned his family – can you believe it, officer?'

'That's not for me to comment on, madam. But I suggest you calm down and drive slowly. We won't book you this time, but see that you don't do it again.'

'I won't. Thank you so much.'

The policeman retreated and Clarissa started up the engine, amazed at her blatant deception. Duncan hadn't left her, Duncan hadn't behaved any differently this weekend than he behaved every weekend of their married life. He *would* behave differently if she had been fined for speeding. MP's wives weren't supposed to speed. They weren't supposed to do much of anything, really, except be supportive and entertain well. Clarissa was good at entertaining, she was good at being an MP's wife. The daughter of a rich stockbroker father and a charity committee chair-woman mother, she was at home in an upper-middle-class world of country weekends and Tory politics. She had never put a foot wrong – except now, when she had placed it heavily on the accelerator.

She would have to watch herself from now on. Something bizarre was definitely happening in her psyche. Yesterday afternoon she'd had a strange desire to break into her next-door neighbours' house and steal their silver. As a joke. She would have given it back, of course. But she'd even been crazy enough to suggest the idea to Duncan.

'Some bloody joke, Clarissa. Do you want us on the front page of the *Sun*?'

Clarissa saw the speedometer go marginally over seventy and quickly hit the brake. She would have to put the brakes on mentally as well, she decided. Go back to being the stalwart society matron.

Still – it would have been quite amusing to rob the Stewart-Pilkingtons.

Sizing Samantha up quickly as they sat down to lunch, Eugenie did what she always did when sitting across the table from a woman – checked her out from top to bottom. Looks counted for Eugenie – how a woman chose to dress, what she made of herself physically fascinated her. When she had worked for an upmarket English designer, she'd been amazed by what rich women bought, what they thought flattered them. Ridiculously expensive dresses were snapped up because of labels, without any regard to what they actually looked like on. Clothes were, in the end, an elaborate con job. She had decided a long time ago that women dressed to impress each other, wore makeup to impress themselves, and put on perfume to impress men.

Glancing up and down at Samantha, she made a mental list of pros and cons. Samantha hadn't done a thing to impress anyone. No makeup. No jewellery. Frumpy grey dress. Flat, sensible black shoes. And not a waft of perfume in the air. But ... Good clear skin. Small wrists. Big blue eyes. Thick blonde hair. And a babyface. A babyface, Eugenie had learned, can hide a multitude of sins. And whims. She wondered whether, in Samantha's case, it hid anything at all.

For Samantha seemed to be one of the walking wounded, a casualty of marriage. The disappointment showed clearly in the slump of her shoulders. Eugenie felt as she often did when she saw a divorced woman: like a soldier who watches one of his buddies go over the top and get blown away.

'I'm sorry if I inadvertently hurt your feelings yesterday. That's one of the reasons I asked you out to lunch. I wanted to apologize.'

'Don't worry, really. I was jet-lagged and my nerves were a little on edge.'

Samantha's nerves were still on edge. They were in Le Caprice, a trendy restaurant off Piccadilly, and Samantha felt out of place. She was pleased to have been invited by Eugenie, but she was feeling inconsequential. And she was still smarting from David's phone call.

The women in the restaurant all looked glitzy. She was used to New York, where woman walked to work in gym shoes and practical suits. They didn't wear what Eugenie was wearing – a white, parachute-silk shirt with a black snake curling over it, sticking out a red tongue. And matching snake earrings. And a snake bracelet. Samantha saw that the red of Eugenie's nails matched perfectly the colour of the snake's tongue.

This is the kind of woman, she thought, that I should be interviewing, not having a friendly lunch with.

'Well, I didn't mean to offend you, but I really was writing about a man who leaves his wife for a model, and Georgia told me when you left the kitchen that that's what happened to you. I know it sounds morbid, but I'm curious about how you feel, whether you were hurt or disgusted or what. There, I said it. If you think I'm horrible and prying, please leave and tell everyone how monstrous I am.'

The waiter came up and asked them what they wanted to order. Samantha was thankful for the time he gave her to think as she pretended to study the menu. Should she tell Eugenie about David's infidelity? Should she give her material for a book which, she suspected, she wouldn't want to be caught reading?

'I'll try the salmon cakes,' said Eugenie, smiling at the waiter. 'I don't like fishcakes generally, so it's a gamble. It could be a major mistake.'

Major mistakes. Samantha thought her whole life so far seemed a series of mistakes. Mistakes which happened *to* her as she sat dully watching. Her marriage had been mediocre, her life had been mediocre. The word mediocre was beginning to churn in her mind, as her eyes focused on Eugenie's blouse.

'I'll have the salmon cakes too, please,' Samantha said. 'It's my turn.'

'Your turn for what?' Eugenie asked, puzzled.

'My turn to make a major mistake.'

Eugenie re-examined Samantha. Yes, she did look frail and done-in, but she had a little edge to her, a little fight still in those eyes. Give her a massive amount of money, a fucked-up relationship with a strong father, and an evil older sister – possibly a movie star – and she'd be a good heroine for her. Maybe she could go ahead with this book after all.

'Excuse me for a minute, Samantha, I'm just going to the loo.'

Samantha was making mental decisions quickly. Yes, she would tell Eugenie about David. Finding him in bed with a model in the middle of the afternoon when she had come home from an assignment early. She'd tell her how embarrassed she had been, how she had walked into their bedroom, seen them and immediately apologized. 'I'm sorry,' she had said, conscious only that she had interrupted, had intruded on someone's privacy. How then she had left her own apartment and gone to sit in Dunkin' Donuts at the corner. And proceeded to buy a pack of cigarettes for the first time in her life.

It would be a good story for Eugenie. Eugenie, no doubt, could adapt it for her book. The wife who is such a wimp that she apologizes to her husband for interrupting when she catches him in *flagrante delicto* and leaves him to get on with having sex with another woman in the marital bed. How pathetic can you get?

Samantha watched as Eugenie stopped and talked to a pretty woman on her way back from the loo. She'd tell Eugenie about that afternoon, yes. But she'd have to think of something else to tell her as well. To startle her. She didn't want to see the look of pity in Eugenie's eyes. She'd seen it already. She had seen it in Georgia's eyes, Andrew's eyes, even David's eyes. And she could imagine the readers pitying the poor dumb wife in the book.

No, she wanted to see Eugenie's blue eyes sparkle. Because of something she, Samantha, said. Or did. Or planned to do. She would make a major impact on Eugenie. And Georgia. Somehow. She would gamble, take a risk.

Aha, Eugenie Woodrow thought to herself, as she ate her salmon fishcakes and listened to Samantha's story of betrayal. The fishcakes were a good choice after all. And I *will* use the scene in my book. It would be better, of course, if the heroine walks in on her husband in bed with her sister, the movie star. That would make it a bit more hard hitting. But it's good stuff. Poor Samantha.

'Samantha, that's a horrible story, but there are worse ones, if it makes you feel any better. You see that woman over there I just stopped and talked to? Jilly? She's a very sweet PR lady for a publishing house and she fell desperately in love with a doctor – a gynaecologist, come to think of it'. Eugenie paused and smiled. 'There *must* be something about those men. Anyway, they were going out together for a few months, quite seriously according to Jilly. And Jilly had to go to America for a few weeks. He took her to Heathrow to see her off, and as they were walking to the plane, he turned to her and said, "Do you picture us going down the aisle together?" She took that as a proposal. Wouldn't you?'

Samantha thought for a second, then nodded.

'So would I. *She* certainly did. So she smiled up at him and said, "Yes, I do." And you know what he said? He smiled down at her and said, "Well, *I* don't." At which point she had to go through immigration control, get on the plane and of course she ended up crying the entire trip. The stewardesses thought someone had died in her family. Can you believe it? What a bastard.'

'That's horrible.' But was it worse than finding your husband in bed with another woman? Samantha wondered. Both Eugenie and Georgia seemed to think her divorce a very minor tragedy. Unable to stop herself, Samantha looked over at Jilly again. She was tossing her long blonde hair behind her shoulders. She's nervous, Samantha thought. She's just as nervous as I am. She probably thinks everything is her fault too.

'Isn't that awful? I've found out more about him since from various friends. He's a real Lothario, in fact his nickname is Doc Juan.'

'Eugenie, now that I've told you about David, can I ask you something?' Eugenie's attention had shifted from her, and Samantha felt herself becoming irritated. Here was the big story of her life, the most emotional moment, and Eugenie had changed the subject within seconds. 'What would *you* have done if you had found your husband in bed with another woman?'

'Let's see ...' Eugenie took a sip of wine and pondered. 'I would have gone downstairs, called Georgia and asked her what she'd do. No, seriously, I would have screamed bloody murder and hit them both with any suitably blunt instrument close at hand.'

'I suppose I should have done that.' Samantha sighed, deflated. It seemed so easy when Eugenie said it. *Do* something, for God's sake, don't just slink away like a whipped dog. Why hadn't she done something? 'I'm like your friend Jilly, just crying on the plane. These men walk all over us and we just lie back and let them. At least I do.'

'Oh, we all do.' Eugenie shrugged. Duncan, she thought. Goddamn Duncan Darrell.

They were both caught up silently in their separate thoughts until suddenly, Samantha sat up straight.

51

'You know, I saw this movie once where three women kidnapped a man who'd been cheating on them all. They kept him locked up in an attic, seducing him in turns all the time. At first he thought it was great, but gradually he realized they weren't feeding him or anything, they were killing him. Which they did, in the end. Kill him, I mean. Somebody should do something like that to that doctor guy. I'd like to.'

'Samantha? Are you all right?'

'What?'

'That story sounds like the reverse of *Let Yourself Go*. Do I take it that you want to kidnap Doc Juan and kill him in an attic? That would make for a good slide-show for friends when you get back. I can imagine it now: here's Buckingham Palace. Click. Here's Windsor Castle. Click. Here's the body of the gynaecologist I murdered. Click.'

'I don't want to kill him.' Samantha saw a look of relief in Eugenie's eyes. She actually thought I might, Samantha decided. It's easier than I thought to stop being a wimp. 'No. The point was, those women were treating him the way he had treated them. Of course they took it a little far, but that was the idea. And that's what I think somebody should do. Treat that doctor the way he treats women, make a conquest of him and then just walk out.' Samantha paused and looked at Eugenie. She had her attention, definitely. She plunged on. 'Do you think *I* could do it?'

'Do what exactly, Sam? Seduce him in his rooms – or as you Americans put it, his office?'

'Yes – why not?' Samantha began to chew on her thumbnail, then quickly pulled it out of her mouth 'Like you said yesterday. You want a scene like that for your book, don't you?'

'I wish I knew what I wanted for my book. But I'm sure that could fit in somewhere. I definitely want some sex.'

'Then, you see, I'd walk out. Wham, bam, thank you Sir. I'd walk out and never see him again. It's not perfect, I know, but it's different. You have to admit that.'

Eugenie laughed, lifted her thinned eyebrows and drummed her red nails on the table. Well, she thought, what's happened here? Here's one for the books. Here's one for *my* book.

'I have to say, Sam, it's an intriguing prospect. I think I understand what you're getting at. Men survive on the comfortable belief that women aren't like them, that they can't have one-night stands and just walk away. If you *did* do it, he'd expect you to want something else, he wouldn't be able to believe that you were using him for your own purposes. His ego would be flummoxed.'

'Yes, but do you think *I* can do it? I know I'm not stunning looking or anything, but do you think I could seduce him?'

'I think you could, absolutely. You're a very pretty woman, Sam – it's time you learned that.' Samantha's face had transformed at the prospect of her hare-brained scheme, Eugenie realized. She needed to do this, for some reason of her own, obviously to recoup in some way from her humiliation with David. Eugenie didn't see the plan as working, but she didn't want to discourage her. If she did, she could imagine Samantha leaving the lunch and hiding for the rest of her life in some corner, the hurt look intact. Samantha should act out whatever drama she had to, and this, Eugenie sensed, was the make or break moment. The best way to stiffen Samantha's resolve at this juncture, she figured, was to challenge her.

'I'm sure you could, but I can't see you actually going through with it. I'll bet you you don't. I'll bet you our next lunch.'

'You're on.' Samantha was beaming like a girl who had gotten an A on all her final exams.

The two women clinked their wine glasses. Samantha felt a surge of adrenalin. She was going to be crazy. She was going to be bold, crass and crazy. David wouldn't believe it. Samantha stopped with a mental skid on that thought. David wouldn't believe it. That's what had made her think of this loony plan. David's call. David's assumption that she was going to spend the rest of her life whimpering about him. The last thing David would be able to imagine was his ex-wife in a gynaecologist's office, seducing a seducer. Especially since he obviously thought she was lousy in bed. That damned 'things you don't know' phrase was going to torture her for the rest of her life. Unless she did something about it. Well, David didn't know everything after all. Samantha imagined picking up a phone and calling him. 'David,' she would say, 'sometimes I'm amazed by the things *you* don't know.' Then she'd hang up.

'So tell me,' she addressed Eugenie. 'What's my victim's name?'

'Rankin. John Rankin.'

## Chapter Four

On the next Monday morning at 11 am Samantha sat in the waiting room of John Rankin's office in Harley Street and tried to stop herself from having a nervous breakdown. The room was large, dingy and old-fashioned, with two leather chairs taken up by pregnant women, and a small round table to which she had been ushered by Rankin's secretary. Hung on the wall was a series of prints depicting men shooting various species of birds.

The pregnant women were looking resigned, and occasionally shifted their weight uncomfortably. Samantha, as she sat on her straight-backed chair, wished she had a weight to shift. What she had was a satin suspender belt, bra, underpants, and silk stockings, covered by a short, tight blue leather skirt and a diaphanous white silk blouse.

Eugenie had taken her shopping the week before, saying 'If you're going to do this, do it right. I don't want to lose my bet, but you should have a fair go at it anyway.' So Eugenie had taken it upon herself to co-ordinate Samantha's outfit, and Samantha had dipped into her savings to pay for it all. They had shopped at all the stores on Beauchamp Place – the area, Samantha knew, frequented by Princess Diana and Sloane Rangers.

Eugenie had insisted on bringing Georgia into the picture. 'You can't not tell her,' Eugenie had said.

'She'll adore the idea, and she can help as well.'

Samantha had been quietly pleased. To be the centre of Georgia and Eugenie's attention was a novel experience and one which she enjoyed. The two older women took over. While Eugenie advised on clothes, hair and makeup, Georgia delved into more intimate areas.

'It's all very well to be dressed to the nines – Cinderella at the ball – but you'll only get to *his* balls if you have the complete look. I'm talking designer nude here. You need a leg wax, underarm wax and bikini wax. And you need a tan, sweetheart. It's time to hit the sunbed.'

Samantha felt as if she were taking an intensive course in sex appeal. After one session at the sunbed, she was reassured that it wouldn't crush her to death, but the bikini wax was an altogether different matter. She'd never had one and squirmed at the thought.

Lying on the table at the beauty parlour, as the beautician swirled a stick in a small bowl of hot wax, she almost called the entire game off. She felt like a sacrificial maiden on a South Sea island, being prepared for ritualistic torture. And she was right.

Whoever thought up this process was a sadist, Samantha concluded. Hot wax smeared over your private parts with a wooden stick was bad enough, but when the beautician then applied a sheet of sticky paper and ripped off the first batch of pubic hair, Samantha screamed.

'Don't worry, love, it'll all be over in a jiffy.' The torturer, whose name was Doris, seemed to derive some satisfaction from Samantha's cries. 'I'll just finish this bit off, and do the sides. Brace yourself. Is the wax too hot?' she asked, while anointing her with burning liquid. Samantha screamed again.

'Listen, Sam,' Georgia said over a cup of coffee and croissant in a brasserie in the Old Brompton Road.

'The waxing routine is painful, sure, but it's like initiation rites. You know how men have to drive cars fast and get arrested at least once and pretend they like to arm-wrestle – well, women have to have hair forcibly removed. It's female macho. Buying nice clothes and lingerie is fun. But, as always, you have to suffer for perfection.'

Georgia was wearing a short denim skirt and a T-shirt fronted by a woman saying, 'Oh my God, I forgot to have a baby.' Samantha's description of the bikini wax had made Georgia laugh, and Samantha was beginning to feel as if she belonged.

'But if you think waxing is bad, you should try cosmetic surgery. I actually had my tits done last year. I couldn't stand having nothing up top anymore – it was fine in the Twiggy days, but now every damn magazine cover features deep cleavage. I began to get so obsessed I couldn't even try clothes on anymore, so I decided to help myself to a little silicone. I told my surgeon that he should write a book and call it *Great Implantations*.'

Georgia depressed about her looks? It was difficult for Samantha to imagine. Was there any woman in the world who could look at herself naked in a full length mirror without wanting to smash it?

'Tell me something, Sam.' Georgia brushed the croissant crumbs onto the floor. 'I love this plan of yours, but how will you know if it has worked? I mean, if you seduce him, walk out and never see him again, how will you know whether he feels like a woman – used, abused and discarded? He might just get a kick out of the whole thing.'

'I hadn't thought of that.' Dumb, dumb, dumb, Samantha said to herself. What's the matter with me? She lit a cigarette. 'You're right. I should call it off.'

'Hold on a second, I've got an idea. You tell Eugenie every little detail afterwards, she writes it in her book, and we send him a copy when it comes out. He reads it and *knows* he's been used, that it was all a game at his expense. We could even convince Eugenie to dedicate it to him. Brilliant. You can't back out now.'

Sitting in John Rankin's waiting room, however, Samantha wished once again that she *could* back out. But Georgia and Eugenie had spent the morning dressing her as if she were a bride and they were the bridesmaids. Or best women. Backing out now would be like not showing up at the altar. She had to go through with it.

Both pregnant women had already gone into Rankin's office. He was running forty-five minutes late and Samantha, flicking through a two-year-old copy of *Tatler*, thought she'd soon start sweating.

When the secretary, an elderly woman with glasses and very little hair, finally came in and said, 'Miss Lewis, this way, please,' Samantha stood up on her high heels and remembered what Georgia had said when she dropped her off: 'It can't be worse than a bikini wax, sweetheart. And it *can* be a whole lot better.'

John Rankin leant back in his chair. 'What can I do for you, Miss – or is it Mrs – Lewis?'

'It's Ms, I guess. Lewis is my maiden name. I was married, but I'm not now.' Samantha looked at Rankin and saw a killer shark of a man. He was dressed in a city suit with a Liberty print tie and looked thoroughly professional on the surface. But his blue eyes had no chance of hiding a gleam of wilfulness. They made him look absolutely confident of getting his own way.

A blond Jack Nicholson, thought Samantha, with a lot more hair and an attractively menacing smile. He was waiting for her to continue, to answer his question; and the longer she hesitated, the more he smiled.

'Well, Ms Lewis, I don't want to push you, but I'm behind schedule. What would you like me to do?'

Samantha felt as if she were on a high diving board.

58

She knew she had to plunge headfirst into the pool, but she had a sneaking feeling that there wouldn't be any water when she landed. What did men find seductive? She had dressed and primped for this moment, but she wasn't certain what to do next.

The only thing she knew for sure about men was the fact that they loved to be asked questions about themselves. In many of the interviews she had done as a journalist, she could sense an almost sensual excitement in a man as he told her his life story. Pretend you're doing an interview, she thought. Pretend he's an assignment, pretend he *is* Jack Nicholson and you're doing a cover story for *People* Magazine. She crossed her legs and looked directly at him.

'If you were a crime, what crime would you be?'

'Excuse me?' Rankin leant back in his chair, looking puzzled.

'I mean, if you were to choose a crime which exemplified your character, what crime would that be?'

Rankin put his hands behind his head and stared back at Samantha. What is she on about, he wondered. An attractive young woman comes into my rooms and wants to know what crime I'd be. This is a new one.

'Well, Ms Lewis, that's an unusual question. So it deserves an anwer. I'd be a hijacking.'

'A hijacking for profit or for political reasons?' Samantha continued. If only she had a tape recorder – then she would feel entirely at ease.

'Neither. A motiveless hijacking.'

'And if you were a piece of furniture, what would that be?'

Rankin didn't hesitate. 'A bed,' he answered, smiling. 'A huge, brass, four-poster bed with satin sheets.'

'And if you were one of the great lovers of history, which one would you be?'

'Now, that's a tricky question. Of course Casanova springs immediately to mind. But I don't think I'd be

Casanova. Or Don Juan. Nothing so obvious. No, I think I'd be Cyrano de Bergerac.'

Samantha looked into his eyes and nerved herself to take a risk.

'You're lying.'

'You're right.' Rankin laughed. 'Maybe I'm more obvious than I like to think.' His laugh, Samantha decided, was less menacing than his smile. They continued to stare at each other across the desk. Rankin leant forward and put his head on the palm of his right hand.

'I'm afraid you have the advantage of me. You know that I'm a hijacking bed and an obvious liar. I don't know anything about you or what you're doing asking me these questions.'

'Have you ever been in love?' she asked, genuinely curious about his reply.

'I don't see why I should answer that if you refuse to answer me. But no one has ever asked me that before, so I will. No. Have you?'

Samantha suddenly felt that she had ventured onto dangerous ground, but wasn't sure how to retreat. Renkin had tipped his chair on its back legs, balancing himself against the panelled wall behind him. His hands were now crossed in front of him, and he looked at her as if he were about to make a diagnosis. Samantha stared at the floor.

'You don't seem very keen on answering that one, Ms Lewis. If you're going to initiate a game, you should be prepared to play it. Is something the matter? Are you pregnant? Is that why you've come to see me? Or do you have something else in mind?'

'No, I'm not pregnant.' Samantha felt paralysed. She could sense that the verbal foreplay had interested him, but he was the one asking the questions now; and as he sat tipped back in his chair, looking at her expectantly, he seemed to have gained the upper hand.

She remembered a trick she had learned from a fellow journalist in New York: if you are interviewing someone important, make sure you stay on an even footing by copying his or her body language. If they moved forward, move forward as well, if they retreat, do the same. Samantha had found the advice particularly helpful when interviewing powerful men. One business executive had been totally thrown off stride when he stood up during an interview and found her rising to her feet too. He was so surprised that he said things he normally never would, and she got a good article out of it.

So Samantha proceeded deliberately to copy Rankin. She tipped back on her own chair, balancing herself with her high heels against the front of his desk. Her arms were crossed underneath her breasts. At least we're on equal terms at the moment, she thought, and she lost some of her nervousness.

'Yes, I did have something else in mind,' she said quietly, trying to imitate Eugenie's deep voice.

'And what would that be?' he asked, his blond eyebrows raised.

Rankin was, Samantha felt, enjoying this game. And he was going to force her to make all the running, even though he obviously knew exactly what she meant.

'What do you think it would be?' she asked, with as much sexual suggestion in her voice as she could muster.

'To use your own terminology, I'd say that if I were a thought, I would be a thought that didn't have a clue. Why don't you spell it out for me?'

This man *has* been in love, Samantha said to herself, and he still is in love. With himself. She could just hear him saying, 'Do you imagine us walking down the aisle together?' to Jilly, then taking great delight in pulling the dream out from under her feet.

They both sat for a moment, staring at each other.

'You want me to spell it out?' Samantha was the one to break the silence.

'I'm aware that English and American spelling differs on certain words, Ms Lewis, but I'll do my best to undertand.'

Boy, he *is* arrogant, Samantha thought. This scene was turning into a battle, and at that moment she wanted very much to win.

Staring straight at him, Samantha uncrossed her arms and undid the top button of her blouse.

'Does that spell it out for you?' she asked angrily.

Rankin didn't move, nor did he say a word. Sam undid the next button, then as he continued to watch, all the others. Her pale pink bra was now partially exposed. Still tipped back in her chair, as was he in his, she reached down to pull her blouse out from her skirt with a defiant gesture.

The movement threw her – and the chair – off balance. It hung for one second in mid-air, then crashed over backwards, throwing Samantha to the floor, her legs outstretched in what was close to a split position, her high heels pointing skywards, her blouse up around her arms, and her neatly blow-dried hair sprawling on the rug.

Rankin's secretary came scuttling into the room, her glasses hanging around her neck, a look of horror and concern on her face when she saw Samantha spreadeagled on the floor, like a helpless tortoise turned on its back.

'Oh, dear, are you all right? Can I help? Oh, my dear, what a fall. I heard it in my office.'

Rankin and his secretary were on either side of Samantha, trying to disentangle her from the chair.

'I'm fine. I'm fine,' Samantha repeated, shaking free of them both and standing up, all the time telling herself: don't cry – whatever you do – don't cry.

'You poor thing,' said the secretary, as she pulled

Samantha's leather skirt back down from where it had hiked up around her hips, 'I do hope you're not pregnant. What a nasty little shock for a poor little –'

'I'm *not* pregnant,' Samantha practically screamed, wildly trying to do up the buttons of her blouse, but getting them all muddled up. By now a deep blush had overtaken the sunbed tan. 'I throw up on airplanes and I fall over in chairs but I am not pregnant. I'm just stupid.'

'She'll be all right, Miss Merton. Just a slight accident. I'll take care of it. You can go now,' said Rankin, picking up the chair and putting it back in its original position.

Miss Merton, before retreating, patted Samantha on the shoulder.

'Let me make you a nice cup of tea. What a shock to your system. It's the chair, you know. These chairs are a menace. The chair in my office is a disgrace, really –'

'Thank you, Miss Merton,' Rankin said firmly, motioning her away.

'Now, Ms Lewis, I suggest you sit down again. I would also suggest that you refrain from any more acrobatics on the chair. You are a very stupid young lady indeed if you thought I was going to have sexual intercourse with you in my rooms.'

Samantha, tucking her blouse back into her skirt, was furious with herself as she sat back down on the chair in front of Rankin's desk. Why couldn't she be like Georgia and Eugenie? Why was she such a hopeless case? Then her anger turned on Rankin. Why was he so damn arrogant and dismissive?

'What's wrong with me? Am I so unattractive? So unappealing?'

'No is the short answer to that question. But I am a member of the medical profession and it is strictly unethical to have sex with a patient. What did you think, that I put my patients in the stirrups and make wild love to them on the examining table?'

'Something like that,' Samantha mumbled, chastened by his professional tone.

'And that's what you came here for?'

Samantha breathed deeply. Her anger had disappeared and was replaced with a deep sense of failure. The game was up and she had lost. She should just give up trying to be wacky and wonderful. The only major impact she had made that morning was on Rankin's floor.

'I came here on a bet. I bet two friends of mine that I could seduce a gynaecologist in his rooms, and they suggested you. I mean one of them did. She needs material for her next novel. Oh, it's too complicated. I'll leave now.' The back of her head was beginning to throb.

At that point, Miss Merton re-entered with a tray.

'*What* a nasty fall. If you don't mind my saying so, I think it's the high heels too. I know people make fun of sensible shoes, but I've never had a fall in these shoes. They may not be the height of fashion, but –'

'Miss Merton, Ms Lewis was sitting down as you may recall. I don't think her shoes can be held accountable. Thank you for the tea.'

Samantha, after the secretary left, stood up again. Rankin came over and pushed her back down onto the chair, gently.

'You have to have the tea, or she'll be offended. You know,' he continued, sitting now on the edge of his desk, 'women have tried to seduce me before. It's a hazard of the trade. Women often fantasize about their doctors. And when I get one of those, the warning bells go off, and I steer well clear. You can make a lover into a patient, but never a patient into a lover. Most of them are frustrated middle-aged ladies, though. I've certainly never come across a young woman doing this on a bet. Can I ask what the bet was?'

64

'Lunch.'

'One free lunch?'

'Yes.'

'Is that all I'm worth? The Casanova in me is deeply disappointed.'

'Sorry,' said Samantha, sipping her tea. She felt a little better. Even though she had made a fool of herself, he wasn't laughing. And a large part of her was immensely relieved that she hadn't had to go through with it.

Rankin looked thoughtful for a moment, then the mischievous gleam returned to his eyes.

'You know, I might be able to help you win this bet of yours. Technically, since you came here strictly for the purpose of having sex with me, you were never my patient. So why don't you come by my flat this evening and you can seduce me there. You may even end up on the floor again. But in a more comfortable position.'

Samantha looked at him to see if he was serious. He was. The tables were turned. Now he was propositioning her. She began to think that he wasn't so arrogant after all.

'Thank you, but that won't work. It has to be something outrageous for Eugenie's book. It's silly, really. Just forget it.'

'Do I take it that you don't want me for my body or my soul, but only for the novelty factor of my rooms?'

'That sounds horrible, but yes. I was using you.'

'And you won't use me tonight?'

'No. It's not the point. Oh, please, just forget about the whole thing.'

'Why? What's wrong with me? Am I so unattractive, so unappealing?'

Samantha laughed and stood up.

'I deserved that. But I should go now. I've taken up a lot of your time. You must have patients waiting.'

'Screw the patients.'

'I thought you weren't supposed to.'

Now he laughed.

'As it happens, you were my last appointment before lunch. And since I've done you out of a free lunch with your friends, the least I can do is to take you out myself. We'll pour the rest of your tea down the sink so Miss Merton feels useful, and I'll fulfil my personality by hijacking you. Come on, doctor's orders.'

He picked up Samantha's cup of tea and went over to the sink, his back toward her.

'But before we go, I think it would be wise if you got the buttons of your blouse sorted out.'

Langan's Brasserie on Stratton Street is a capacious, ever-crowded restaurant pandering to actors, the media world and the smart set. John Rankin was known there, and given a table downstairs, the place to eat and be eaten by other people's celebrity-hungry eyes.

Within minutes of their sitting down and ordering a cocktail – Samantha had a Campari and soda, Rankin a small bottle of Perrier – a curvaceous woman with a deep tan, dyed blonde hair, bright pink lipstick and a black Valentino suit rushed up to their table.

'John, how heavenly to see you, and how immaculate you're looking. Quite the chic consultant.'

'Hello, Sarah, it's nice to see you too. Sarah Frawley, this is Samantha Lewis.'

'Hello, Samantha. John, you know we have some unfinished business.' Sarah turned from Rankin to Samantha and Samantha thought she had seen this woman before, but couldn't remember when or where. 'The dashing doctor and I were having a lovely time one evening, and just at the crucial moment his beeper went off. Unfair, wasn't it, John?'

'Bad timing, yes.' Rankin was eyeing Samantha. This

kind of thing had happened to him before, and he enjoyed watching the woman he was with pretend not to care about previous conquests flaunting themselves. This time he saw curiosity rather than jealousy in Samantha's eyes. It surprised him.

'Sarah,' he continued, 'you're so tanned, and it's only June – a wet one at that. Where have you been?'

'Antigua, darling. With all those natives in immaculate white coats waiting on me.'

Samantha remembered where she had seen Sarah before. She had come out of the sunbed as Samantha was going in.

'Why don't you come by my flat tonight and we can catch up?'

Rankin was oozing charm now, Samantha noticed. He had assumed what must have been his favourite position, his chair back, his arms crossed as they had been in his office, and his eyes displaying a mixture of insouciance and flirtation. He casually ran his hand through his blond hair. Was that to emphasize, Samantha wondered, that he had plenty of it?

How old was he? Late thirties-ish? It was hard to tell exactly. But it was immense entertainment, Samantha thought, to see Doc Juan in action. He was much slicker than the Yugoslav in the white suit. Sarah Frawley shot Samantha a look of triumph.

'I'll be there at eight. And I'll make sure to hide that nasty beeper of yours. Or throw it off the balcony.'

Rankin laughed, but then he saw Samantha laughing too and stopped abruptly. Sarah, content with her exit line, walked back to her table, where she was sitting with another woman.

'I'm glad you found someone for tonight,' Samantha said, without looking up from the menu.

Rankin was beginning to believe that she meant it. He pretended to study the menu as well, but he was formulating a plan. He wanted Samantha now, but he knew he would have to make more of an effort than usual. Something about that act of hers in his office had struck him. She was a strange mixture, this one. Why had that botched seduction attempt affected him? Why hadn't he stopped and dismissed her as soon as he knew what she was after? Why hadn't he felt like laughing when she fell over? Because of an innocent quality to her, yes, and also, his feeling that he'd quite like to be the one who made that innocence blossom.

He hadn't had a real challenge in a long time. True, the threat of AIDS had slowed him down somewhat. There had been that embarrassing first time using a condom when he hadn't been able to get it on properly. His conquest had thought that ineptitude hysterical in a gynaecologist. But he was over that now, almost as agile in putting them on as he was in taking off bras.

Rankin realized intinctively that getting through to Samantha would require a new approach.

Samantha looked across the table at Rankin and wondered what it would be like to fall for him, then instinctively recoiled from the idea. He was too smooth, too aware of his charm. He had had countless women, she could tell, and she would hate to be just another notch on his sexual belt. Another Jilly. As she thought of Jilly, Samantha could feel herself blush. It was embarrassing, as soon as he'd asked her out to lunch, how quickly she'd forgotten about Jilly, about the whole purpose in seeing Rankin. But he had become a person now, not the token man to take vengeance on.

Trying to seduce Rankin in his rooms had been a one-off crazy dare. It was a silly idea to prove to herself that she could change, could be a different person. All because of David's call that morning. But how much could a person change in one week? She would have probably chickened out when the crunch came anyway. Now she would never know. She did know that John Rankin would be a nightmare as far as emotional involvement was concerned. He was, she decided, what Americans call a tough cookie. And she didn't see herself as the one who could make that cookie crumble.

They ordered lunch and John Rankin began to tell Samantha about the success of his new *in vitro* fertilisation method. Samantha listened and asked questions. By the time the coffee arrived, Rankin was still talking earnestly about his work. He hadn't even noticed when Sarah Frawley tried to catch his eye to wave goodbye. Poor Sarah, Samantha thought watching her walk out. As Georgia would say, there goes another tale of impending human misery.

Georgia Green knocked on the door of her husband's study and went in. Andrew was sitting at his computer, and didn't bother to swivel his chair around to greet her.

'Sorry to interrupt you, scumbag,' Georgia said, taking a seat on the sofa beside his desk.

'Georgia, your terms of endearment grow more affectionate every day. Why don't you try "Oh, light of my life" or "Beloved one"? That would be nice for a change.'

Andrew hadn't taken his eyes off the screen in front of him.

'Right. Listen, beloved light of my life. I'm about to go out to Eugenie's for the evening. Girls' night out. I probably won't be back till late, so don't worry about me.'

Andrew turned around. He looks thinner all of a sudden, Georgia thought. And why is he wearing a tie?

'Don't worry about me, either. I'm fine. Have you phoned the takeaway pizza place or is it a pub supper for me?'

'Neither. Samantha cooked some casserole thing yesterday, and it's in the fridge, all set to heat up. You *can* turn the oven on, can't you?'

'Possibly.' Andrew swivelled his chair to the side and looked out the window. 'But Samantha will be back, won't she? I know she's working this afternoon, but she should be finished soon.'

'Sam's meeting me and Eugenie. She's one of the girls.'

'Oh, I see. She's one of the girls, is she? She seems to have become our housekeeper as well. The kitchen's spotless. So is the sitting room. I have to assume it isn't your work. Are you paying her?'

'Don't be silly. Sam likes that domestic stuff.'

Andrew, have you lost weight in the past week? You're looking fucking smart. In fact,' said Georgia, moving over to him and pulling his shirt out from his trousers, 'you've made me feel like fucking. I think strange new feelings could course through our bodies. I have ten minutes. Come on.'

'Georgia, I think I'll pass on that. I don't want you to be late for your night out. And perhaps you could attempt to be a little less crude than usual with Samantha. It might damage her career if she goes back to New York punctuating every sentence with the word "fuck".'

'Well, fuck you, sleazeball. Sam can take care of herself. She may well have taken very *good* care of herself this morning.' Georgia took a step back from Andrew and picked up her shoulder bag.

'What exactly do you mean by that?'

'You pass on ten minutes of sexual thrills and I pass on telling you my secrets. You'll never know what you're missing. See you later, beloved. I'm out of here.'

Eugenie's house in Hampstead was small, but high tech. Large sliding glass doors opened into a tiny

70

garden which was cleverly lit by strategically-placed spotlights, making it look dense and tropical at night. Two big leather sofas flanked a glass table in the living room, the walls of which were covered by bookshelves and a very sophisticated stereo system. The kitchen and dining room were combined, a few steps up from the living room. And a staircase led to one vast bedroom and en-suite bathroom above.

'I've always said this looks like the perfect bachelor pad,' said Georgia as she swept in and placed two bottles of champagne on the round glass dining-room table.

'And I've never understood how you can have such feminine tastes in clothes and such masculine tastes in decor.'

'Well, now that you mention it, George, I've never understood how you can have such masculine tastes in clothes and such non-existent tastes in decor.'

Eugenie took one of the champagne bottles, put it in the fridge and took out three glasses from the cupboard over the sink.

'Sam should be here soon, shouldn't she? I know she was seeing someone at the American Embassy this afternoon about that article of hers. I'm dying to find out what happened this morning. She hasn't called you, has she?' asked Eugenie.

'Nope. But it's seven, she should be here any minute. Unless she fainted in Rankin's rooms and he had to take her to the hospital.'

'Georgia, you really are a drama junkie. Poor Sam, I feel a little guilty about this whole thing. At first I thought she *had* to do this to get her own back on that husband in some twisted way, so I encouraged her. But now I'm not so sure. I'm beginning to think she's just doing it to impress us, to show us she's not a frigid little heroine. I think that scene in your kitchen really got to her.'

'Maybe she's doing it for us, maybe she's doing it for herself – it doesn't much matter. Whatever she's done, it's done by now.'

The doorbell rang and both women jumped.

'You open the bottle, and I'll let her in. I think we all need a drink,' Eugenie said, going over to the glass door.

'Hi,' said Samantha. 'Gosh, this place is fantastic, Eugenie. Hi, George.' She immediately noticed that Georgia was in her inevitable jeans and T-shirt, while Eugenie was dressed in a white linen suit, fashionably crumpled, with what seemed a massive amount of gold bracelets on each arm and large hooped gold earrings.

The white and gold set against her dark hair was striking. They're a funny pair, thought Samantha, Georgia with her red hair which doesn't look like it has been combed all day, and Eugenie looking closer to Cleopatra than Elizabeth Taylor ever got.

'Before you both jump on me, no, nothing happened. I tried, but it's unethical for a gynaecologist to have sex in his rooms. So I'm afraid I don't have much of a story to tell. I'm sorry.'

'Sam, sweetheart, don't apologize. Here, have a drink,' said Georgia, managing to uncork the champagne bottle without any fuss, pouring it into the glasses. 'Come on down to Eugenie's plush living room. You deserve a toast for the effort. Bloody British wimps, so concerned with their ethics.'

Samantha followed the other two down, and sat back on the leather sofa. She wasn't sure how it had happened, but she began to feel at home with them.

'He might have lost his job. You can't blame him for that,' she said, taking a large gulp of champagne.

'Why didn't we think of that?' Eugenie asked. She was sitting beside Georgia, on the sofa opposite Samantha. Kicking off her heels, she curled her legs up

72

underneath her. Georgia unlaced her sneakers, took them off and put her feet up on the glass table.

'Well, that explains it,' said Georgia. '*That's* why my gynaecologist has never made a pass at me. Of course he's dying to. It takes all his self-control to keep his hands off me even when one of them is inside me, but he doesn't want to lose his job. And the same must be true for Eugenie and hers. Sam, you've made our day.'

'Was he as attractive as everyone says?' Eugenie wanted to know.

'Yes. I mean, he's kind of too attractive, if you know what I mean. He knows it. When we went out to lunch, a woman named Sarah something – I think it was Sarah Frawley – came up and practically threw herself at him and he took it in his stride. He's very sure of himself. But he can be really nice, especially when he's talking about his job.'

'Sarah Frawley? Did she bear any resemblance to a blonde vampire?' asked Georgia.

'A little. I guess. Do you know her?'

'Sarah Frawley is the original social astronaut. Any time I see her it reminds me I should take out the trash.'

Samantha was very glad to be on the right side of Georgia's tongue.

'Where did he take you?' Eugenie asked.

'Langan's.'

'Oh, that's posh. He was obviously trying to impress you. But wait a minute. Haven't we all forgotten something? Why did he take you out to lunch, anyway? I thought you were going to love him and leave him, teach him what it's like to be a woman.'

Samantha took her high heels off and crossed her stockinged legs. There was no point, she figured, in telling them about the chair debacle.

'I don't know. That all seemed absurd soon after I got there. Besides', Samantha was struggling to justify her actions, 'I was his last patient before lunch and he thought it would be a good idea.'

'I'm sure he did.' Georgia poured herself another glass of champagne. 'I bet he thought he could get your pants down somehow – maybe not in his office, sure, but somewhere, somehow.'

'He *did* proposition me,' Samantha said, unable to hide feeling coy and pleased with herself.

'You bet your sweet bippy he did. I hope you told him to fuck off.'

'George, I don't understand. I thought that you *wanted* me to have sex with him.' Samantha was confused. She had turned him down, but she thought Georgia would think she was a coward for doing so. It didn't make sense.

'Seducing the guy in his rooms on your own terms is one thing. But becoming yet another string to his bow in his little love nest is another.'

'That's funny. That's just how I saw it.' Samantha had finished her glass of champagne as well. Eugenie reached forward with the bottle and filled it for her.

'That's how any intelligent woman would see it,' Georgia continued. 'I'm all in favour of good dirty fun, but men like the doc shouldn't always get what they want. I've known a few in my day, and they're all the same. They think they're doing you a favour if they condescend to sleep with you. Then, after they've satisfied their egos, not to mention their libidos, they say, "That was terrific, but whatever you do, don't get involved with me." '

Georgia pulled her legs off the table and sat upright.

'And you know what that's like? That's like saying, "Go into a corner and whatever you do, don't think about a white horse." You had no intention of thinking about a white horse, but you go into a corner and what comes into your mind? Herds and herds of white horses.

'You probably had no intention of getting involved with this shmuck, but he tells you you can't and suddenly it's the only thing you can think about. So you sit by the telephone waiting for it to ring.'

'You pick it up every five minutes to make sure it hasn't gone dead …' Eugenie chimed in.

'And you become obsessed. It's real teenage stuff. But men like that reduce you to a sixteen-year-old even when you're fifty-five.'

'Why does someone like Sarah Frawley get involved, then?' Samantha wondered.

'Because Sarah Frawley is seriously stupid, like that Jilly woman you feel so sorry for. That type of woman thinks to herself: just let me have one more night with this vision of manliness and I'll be the one who changes him. I'll succeed where all others have failed. Besides, they're English, so they're used to men treating women like shit.'

'Georgia, I object,' Eugenie exclaimed. 'I'm English.'

'True. And where is your Prince Charming? I don't see him here tonight.'

'You know I'm still recovering from Duncan.' Eugenie looked slightly offended.

'And what is Duncan? Latvian? Duncan is a Brit. He's worse. He's an upper-class Conservative MP. I bet when he goes to his house in the country, he pulls on his plus-fours and tells interminable stories about Eton. I bet when he gets pissed he starts singing, "Why can't a woman be more like a man?" I don't think there's an Englishman living who hasn't sung that song at least five hundred times in his life.'

Georgia was really getting excited, Samantha noticed. Her eyes had narrowed, and her hands were waving in the air as if they were birds let out of a cage, a sign, Samantha had come to learn, that Georgia was going to pursue a subject with vehemence. It was like watching a gambler on a winning streak – Georgia was not to be interrupted.

'At first I thought that they are all latently gay, you know – boarding-schools, mother complexes, all that stuff. But that's not right. Gay men usually like women. I mean, you can talk to a fag.

'No. Straight Englishmen think women are a pain in the ass. It's the only sentiment which reaches across all class barriers. They think women are out to rip them off, ruin their fun and generally be a nuisance. You should see all the television sit coms and commercials about badgered, henpecked husbands with gorgon wives. Dealing with men in this country is like dealing with British Telecom.'

'What?' Eugenie and Samantha asked in unison.

Georgia stood up. 'I'm going to break out the next bottle and while I'm doing that I'll figure out what I meant.'

Eugenie and Samantha looked at each other and smiled as Georgia went off to the kitchen. Eugenie took out a pack of Silk Cut and offered one to Samantha.

'Watch out for Georgia when she's in a mood like this,' Eugenie warned. 'If she has stopped thinking all men are kind of cute, she must be getting serious, and that can be hazardous to your mental health.'

Samantha wanted to ask Eugenie more about this man Duncan, but wasn't sure if it was the right time. Coming back with the bottle in one hand, her handbag in the other, Georgia returned to her seat on the sofa. She poured more champagne into all three glasses, then reached into her bag and took out a small white rectangular-shaped packet. Opening it up gingerly, she then fished in her bag again and brought out an American Express credit card and a pocket-sized mirror.

'Everyone thinks I'm on coke all the time anyway, so I indulge myself a few times a year,' she said, taking some white powder from the packet with the credit card, placing it on the mirror, and fashioning it into three separate lines. 'Do you two want some? We should be celebrating. I've got some good news.'

'No, thanks,' said Samantha, watching as Georgia took a ten-pound note from her pocket and rolled it into a straw shape.

'I think I'll stick to the bottle,' answered Eugenie. 'Coke gives me a headache. But what's the good news? Are you pregnant?'

'Fat chance of that.' Georgia leant over the table, pushed her hair back, placed one finger against the side of one nostril and swept up the coke with the other. She sat back and sniffed for a moment.

'Andrew's gone off sex. Or else he's gone off me. I used to think it was because of my tits being small, but then I had the operation and that only worked for a few months. Maybe he got off on the scars. Once they faded, so did his interest.'

'Georgia, that's ridiculous.' Eugenie lit a cigarette. 'You've been married five years. He's probably just going through a bad patch.'

'Sure. But it's not as if I don't make an effort to keep things interesting. I mean, I heard from a friend that if you go down on a man and take his balls in your mouth and start to hum, it drives him crazy. So what do I do last night?

'I get dressed up in some slinky number and I crawl under the duvet and it's hot down there, let me tell you.' Georgia sniffed loudly again. Her eyes were starting to look wild.

'And I'm practically suffocating and I think – oh, fuck, what am I supposed to hum? Name that tune. The only one I can think of is "The Star Spangled Banner". There I am, really getting into the National Anthem, and you know what the shit does?

'He falls asleep. His snoring interrupts me on "gave

proof to the night that the flag was still there''. *His* flag hadn't even gotten to half mast.'

Eugenie started to laugh. So did Samantha.

'Maybe you should have tried "God Save the Queen",' Samantha said, surprising herself. The champagne was beginning to take effect. Georgia laughed as well.

'You think *that's* bad,' Eugenie began, still giggling. 'I'll tell you an even worse one. But first I think I'll change my mind and have a line of that stuff. I'll have a headache tomorrow anyway. so why not start now?'

Georgia went through the same process with the coke, and handed Eugenie the ten-pound note. Eugenie got down on her knees over the glass table and snorted it as demurely as possible. She stayed seated on the floor, her legs stretched out under the table.

'I heard about a trick once where you drink iced water, then suck the man's prick for a while, then drink hot coffee, and go down on him again. It's supposed to send him on a one-way trip to paradise. Anyway, I decided to try it out on Duncan.

'The iced water part was fine, but when I sipped the coffee and started it again, Duncan leapt out of bed screaming. I'd almost burned his prick off. Honestly, I didn't know it would be more sensitive than the inside of my mouth. He thought I was trying to castrate him.'

'Where,' asked Samantha, helping herself to her third glass, 'do you find out about these tricks? Is there a book or something? My sex life with David might have been different if I'd known about things like that. He once said I didn't – I mean, I would have liked to have tried one of those on him.'

'Sure,' said Georgia, standing up and starting to pace around the room. 'And maybe you would have burnt his prick off or hummed him to death.'

She stopped pacing and stared out into the garden.

'Listen, there's no way to win. In the end it doesn't matter what you do in bed. You finish up either with an interesting bastard who makes you yearn for a predictable nice guy, or with a predictable nice guy who has you dreaming about interesting bastards.' She turned around to face Eugenie. 'That's a fair description of Duncan, isn't it? An interesting bastard?'

'A married interesting bastard would be more to the point. I'm cold, I'm going up to get a jersey.' Eugenie got to her feet quickly and vanished up the spiral staircase.

'Poor Eugenie, she's still hung up on that guy. She was his lover for two years, and I think, until the end, she really believed he would leave his wife. Didn't you, Eugenie?' She had reappeared in the living room, pulling a black cashmere jersey over her head.

'I suppose I did,' she answered, her voice even lower than usual.

'That's because he gave good romance.' Georgia was now standing directly behind Samantha.

'What?' Samantha craned her neck around to see Georgia's face.

'He gave great romance, you know, like some woman give great head. He wrote Eugenie poems and gave her meaningful presents and discussed Shakespeare with her. He was a great mind-fucker, and from what you say, Eugenie, a good body-fucker too.

'But a mind fuck done the right way is ten times as powerful. The problem is that it doesn't last. Men can concentrate on romance only for so long. Pretty soon the poems turn into scribbled notes saying, "See you tomorrow", the presents show up only on birthdays, and Shakespeare takes a long walk off a short pier.'

'You're right, George, but you're so depressing. Can we get off the subject of Duncan for a while? I was just

79

getting a nice buzz.' Eugenie, Samantha thought, looked vulnerable for the first time. It was hard for Samantha to believe that any man would turn away from Eugenie.

Georgia started pacing around the room again, then honed in on the stereo system, fiddling with various knobs. Finally she pulled out an album from the shelves underneath.

'Wait for it, girls,' she said, putting a record on the turntable. Suddenly the Supremes were singing 'Baby, baby, I'm aware of where you go/Each time you leave my door'.

Georgia began to dance – a Motown routine, rolling her hands from side to side in time with the music until Diana Ross sang 'Stop, in the name of love' – at which point Georgia put her hand up like a policeman halting traffic; on 'Before you break my heart', she placed both hands under her left breast, a pleading look on her face.

Eugenie leapt up and pointed her forefinger to her head as the line 'Think it o-o-ver' played. And Samantha sat watching as the two joined forces, dancing to the music and miming away to the words.

'Fantastic!' Samantha cried, clapping as Eugenie and Georgia collapsed on the floor with a flourish at the end of the song. 'You two are great.'

'That's nothing,' replied Georgia, 'you should see our synchronized swimming.'

Samantha picked up the second bottle of champagne, poured some into Georgia and Eugenie's glasses, then polished off the rest. 'But wait a minute, George. You haven't told us why all Englishmen are like British Telecom.'

'Right.' Georgia lay on her somach, and put her hands under her chin. 'Let's see. One: you can never get any information out of them. Two: you're continually getting crossed lines. Three: when something goes wrong, they don't have any idea how to fix it.'

'And four,' added Eugenie, standing up, 'you shut up and pay the bills no matter what the complaints, or else they cut you off.'

'Now I'm going to put some spaghetti on. You must be hungry, Sam.'

As Eugenie went up to the kitchen, Georgia lifted herself from the floor and went back to the sofa, drinking her champagne and fixing some more lines of cocaine.

'This is terrific. This is like a pyjama party. I need more nights like this. Andrew can really dampen my spirits sometimes. He even told me tonight that I shouldn't say fuck all the time. I felt like telling him that he should marry Amy Vanderbilt or Mrs Debrett, if there is such a thing.'

'George,' said Samantha, looking around for more champagne, then realizing she had finished it, 'I think I'm getting tipsy. Fucking tipsy.'

Across London John Rankin sat up in bed, turned on the light and reached for the glass of champagne on his bedside table. This isn't happening to me, he thought. This is absurd. This *can't* happen to me.

Sarah Frawley sat up as well.

'John? Is there something else I can do? Is there anything special that you need?'

'I don't need anything *special*, Sarah. For God's sake, you've tried just about everything. I'm tired, that's all. I've had an exhausting day.'

'You didn't look so tired at lunch, as I remember. Quite the contrary. There's nothing wrong with me, is there?'

'Aside from the fact that your hairspray asphixiates me, no, there's nothing wrong with you.'

He must really like me, Sarah decided, snuggling up to his side. I read in a book that men are only impotent when they feel absolutely serious about a woman. I think I've broken through the veneer. I'm different from the others.

She stretched her hand underneath the duvet and grabbed his cock.

Oh, no, here we go again, Rankin thought to himself. I feel like a battered piece of meat. I wish my bloody beeper would go off.

Georgia, Eugenie and Samantha were all gathered around a pot of water, watching strands of spaghetti boil.

'Is it ready?' asked Samantha.

'Hold on.' Georgia grabbed a fork from the kitchen counter. 'This is the only thing I know about cooking. I can tell when spaghetti's done.' She put the fork into the pan and extracted one piece of spaghetti, then flung it against the wall opposite. 'Nope. It didn't stick.'

'Gosh, that looks fun. Can I have a go?' asked Samantha, trying very hard to concentrate.

'Me too, please.'

Eugenie and Samantha both grabbed forks and all three women hovered over the spaghetti.

'It's tough to get just one piece,' complained Samantha as she lifted her fork and the spaghetti fell off back into the pan.

'Watch the expert,' Georgia commanded.

She began to fish around, then emerged with a huge forkful of spaghetti and hurled it against the white wall behind the stove.

'Look, it stuck. It's done.'

'You cheat. That was a big bunch,' cried Eugenie. 'Anybody can do that. Watch me.' She pulled out another mass of pasta and flung it. It landed just above Georgia's. 'See. Come on, Sam, you show her too.'

Samantha had enough physical co-ordination left to pull out the spaghetti, but she couldn't aim it properly. It ended up splattered over the kitchen cupboards.

'Great shot, Sam.' Georgia got some more out of the pan.

'This spaghetti reminds me of Andrew these days – limp. Take that, you bugger.' She threw it against another cupboard.

'And it reminds me of Duncan – wet and soggy.' Eugenie reached in and hurled some more. It stuck to the glass frame on a picture of Venetian gondolas hung on the wall over the dishwasher.

'I wish I'd thrown David against a wall. I never even got angry with him. This one's for him and his model,' Samantha said, taking out a forkful. With a feeling of real liberation, she spun around like a discus thrower and flung it in the air. It landed on the brick-tiled floor.

The three took turns hurling the pasta until the pan was empty and the entire kitchen was dotted with pale strands of spaghetti. When they had finished they looked around at the mess and began to laugh hysterically.

'This is it,' Georgia managed to get out between paroxysms of laughter. 'We've got it. We can all be even more rich and famous than we are now. We can market this. Instead of tupperware parties, we can have pasta-throwing parties for pissed-off housewives.'

'That's wonderful, George,' Samantha giggled. 'But what about the mess? Poor Eugenie. Who's going to clean this up?'

'You don't understand, dumb-bag. It's part of the service. Express your anger and redecorate your kitchen at the same time. The Italian look.'

'It's a good way to diet too,' said Eugenie. 'Throw your food against the wall, then you won't be tempted to eat it.'

'You know, I keep meaning to ask you two a question.' Samantha was wiping the tears from her face with her sleeve.

'Fire away,' said Georgia.

'Well, I don't get propositioned by strange men that often, and I don't know how to handle it. I mean, like that Yugoslavian guy on the plane. I wasn't very good at saying no. What's the best way of telling a man you don't want to sleep with him?'

'It depends.' Georgia sat up on the kitchen counter, in the one area free of spaghetti. 'If you don't want to hurt his feelings – let's say he's a nice guy, but he's married – then you can say, "Fred, I couldn't possibly sleep with you because I know if I did, it would be *so* fantastic that I'd fall desperately in love with you and both our lives would be ruined." That gives him an ego boost, and it lets you off the hook.'

'If he's a nice guy, unmarried and available but for some reason totally unfanciable, you can say, "Sorry Fred, but I've been fucking my brains out all day and I just can't fuck anymore." That would shut him up, believe me. *Or* you can say, "Sure thing, Fred, but I have to warn you, I'm into really kinky sex." Ninety-nine per cent of the time, they'll turn tail and run a mile. The other one per cent might cause you trouble, though.'

'That's great, that's wonderful – I wish I'd thought of all that. You know what I did?' Samantha put her head in her hands. 'I threw up. Literally. Do you believe it?'

Eugenie, who had been searching the refrigerator for food, turned around.

'I think that's the best of all, Sam. I love it. If some nasty little Yugoslav propositioned me, that would be the perfect line. "I'm terribly sorry, Sacha, but I have to be sick." '

'She's right, Sam.' Georgia jumped down from the counter. 'Just think how many assholes would be scarred for life if that happened more often. God, I'd love to use that.'

'I may throw up now if I don't eat something, even

84

though that's the last thing I want to do.' Eugenie was opening all the cupboards. 'Are you very hungry, Sam? I think I have some cheese and biscuits somewhere.'

'I'm fine,' answered Samantha, 'I'm great. I feel terrific.'

Andrew Green finished the casserole in front of him, stood up and rubbed his stomach. He picked up the bottle of claret on the table, and a glass, and moved into the sitting room.

'Right,' he said out loud, 'I'll try one. Just one. I have to build up to this slowly.'

Putting the wine bottle and glass on the table, he lay face down on the floor. He stayed that way for a few minutes, then placed his hands, palms down, at either side of him.

'Right. Just one,' he repeated, arched his toes and struggled to raise himself. His upper torso stretched up in the air like a seal waiting to be fed, but that was the only movement he could manage.

'Bloody hell,' he swore, collapsing. He lay there for another two minutes, then tried again. This time he managed to lift his entire body off the floor, and a smile spread across his face. Then he slowly lowered himself back, trying to touch his chin to the ground. But his legs and stomach came into contact with the carpet long before his chin, and his arms swiftly folded underneath him.

Standing up, he poured himself a glass of claret, then turned on the cassette player on the shelf behind him.

Bing Crosby started to sing "I love you, Samantha", and Andrew pushed the stop button immediately.

Who had put that tape on and why was he fantasizing about Samantha every minute of the day? If he could just have some time alone with her, without Georgia, without any interruptions. They could talk, or even take a walk in the park. Hold hands. How long had it been since he had held hands, since he'd felt, as he did now, like an excited teenager? He wanted to take care of her, to protect her and guide her through life. Her vulnerability was what made him ache for her. Georgia was so tough, so independent. She hadn't cried for years. Not that he had liked it when she did. The sight of Georgia in tears was an irritant, it was a demand: I'm crying, you have to help me. Samantha was something else altogether. She didn't expect anything from him. But he would be glad to give it, he could succeed where David had so blatantly failed. Bright boy David had finally ballsed things up – it was typical of him to go for a showy model in the end. Depth had never been his stong suit. Samantha deserved a real man, Samantha deserved him.

But Samantha was out of his reach – off with Georgia and Eugenie for a girl-talk session. Georgie was probably even now detailing the paucity of their sex life. Would Samantha understand why he'd been so turned off lately, or would she think he was a failure in the sack? It wasn't fair – these women shouldn't be allowed to rabbit on like that.

'It's a bloody conspiracy,' he mumbled, grabbing the bootle of wine and trudging upstairs.

'I don't know about you, but when I have an orgasm I sound like Donna Summer on a bad night.' Georgia was lying on one of the leather sofas, her head resting on her hand. She had just put the 'Bad Girls' album on the stereo and they were listening to 'Love to Love You, Baby'. Eugenie and Samantha were sitting opposite her, legs up on the table.

'I think *I* sound like a bat caught in someone's hair,' laughed Eugenie. A half-empty bottle of white wine was on the floor beside Samantha.

'You couldn't possibly, Eugenie, your voice is too low. Come on, I'll do mine, if you do yours,' Georgia said, in a schoolgirl-daring tone.

'All right. You first.'

'Oooohhh,' Georgia began to murmur quietly, then built up the volume. 'Ooohhh. Ooohh oohh ooh ooh.' She put her head back, closed her eyes and started to pant. 'Oh, oh, oh.' Then she sat straight up and screamed, 'Aahhh.'

'There you go, that's the shortened version.'

'That doesn't sound *anything* like Donna Summer. You sound like a witch trying to spook people on Hallowe'en.'

'Ok, smart ass, let's hear you.'

'Mmmm ...' Eugenie's voice was at its normal low register, then she closed her eyes also, her face in a squint and her mouth turned downwards in what looked like an expression of pain. The "mms" gradually became higher and higher pitched until she ended with a sustained squeal and flopped back against the sofa.

'I've never heard a bat, much less a bat caught in someone's hair, but that sounds to me like a dog that's been run over. God, poor men. Think what it must be like for them to listen to us. How about you, Sam?' Georgia looked across at Samantha who had been sitting quietly sipping her wine.

'I don't know.' Samantha's words were beginning to sound slurred.

'You don't know what?' asked Georgia.

'I don't know what I sound like having an orgasm because I've never had one. Or at least I think I've never had one. I don't know.'

'Sweetheart, you'd know if you had. Jesus. Maybe we shouldn't have dismissed old Doc Juan so quickly. You could be having one right now, you little sweetheart. No wonder I didn't like David.'

'Sam, haven't you ever –' Eugenie stopped in mid-sentence.

'What she wants to say, Sam, is haven't you ever done it yourself? But obviously you haven't.'

'No.' Samantha was blushing and reached down to the wine bottle to hide her face.

'Well, that's cool,' Georgia said. 'Look on the bright side. Think about what you have to look forward to in life. It's like I save books that I want to read now to read when I'm fifty, so I'll have something to look forward to. For God's sake, don't be embarrassed. Listen, even when men know what to do to get you off, they end up not bothering. They can be real selfish in bed. Oh, Christ, I'm droning on. I better take a sleeping pill or I'll talk all night.'

No one spoke as Georgia reached into her bag and pulled out a bottle of Mogadons. Donna Summer was singing 'Someone found the letter you wrote me on the radio'. Eugenie, after the spaghetti-throwing incident, was looking more dishevelled than Samantha had ever seen her. Her eyes weren't as wild as Georgia's, but her white linen suit was as crumpled as a used paper bag. Georgia's hands were shaking slightly as she chased the Mogadon down with some wine.

'Can I have one of those, too?' asked Eugenie, and Georgia handed the pill bottle across the table.

'Oh, my God, I almost forgot. I can't believe it.' Georgia leapt up and narrowly avoided knocking over her glass. 'I had some good news, remember? I can't believe I haven't told you. Listen Eugenie,' Georgia went back to her pocketbook and took a piece of paper out. 'Listen to this fax I got just before I came. It's from my old friend Rick, the producer I told you about.' Georgia began to read out loud.

'Honeycrunch,
  Let Yourself Go on a binge, sweet thing. We're on for a mini series, or should I say, mega series. And it

looks like Mickey Rourke may be our Storm. With Kathleen Turner, Charlotte Rampling and Jodie Foster as his kidnappees. All that heaven will kill any man. I'll be in London next week and expect you to kiss my feet. Judging Miss Woodrow by the picture of her on the book's back cover, I think you should introduce us. It might change my luck. I haven't done too well in the dating game recently.

The last little cutie I stepped out with left me, saying, "The trouble with the world, Ricky, is that women get older and men never grow up."

I thought you'd like that.'

Love and kisses
Rick.

Eugenie remained seated. She swallowed her Mogadon and looked at Samantha, beside her.

'I only wrote Let Yourself Go to get back at Duncan when he refused to leave his wife for me. I quit my job in a Bond Street boutique, and I was determined to write something which would be sold in every bookstore, and every airport, so he'd have to see my name every damn place he went.'

'Oh, Eugenie, I'm sorry. That's awful. You've been so nice to me. I wish I could help.' Samantha reached over and put her hand on Eugenie's.

'Hey, you guys, this looks like a sob scene from Little Women. Just think, Eugenie, Duncan will have to see you on the cover of TV Times now. He'll suffer even more. So cheer up. I think we should have a party to celebrate. Next Thursday is the Fourth of July: let's have an Independence Day Party for Rick and the book. We can have a bash. I'll even invite Mr Rankin. What the hell, I'll even invite Sarah Frawley. I'll invite Duncan and his wife too. We can reduce her to a snivelling wreck. This will be fun.'

'How can you invite Rankin? You don't know him.'

Samantha asked. The room was beginning to dance, she noticed. She picked a lamp out and tried to focus on it to stop it from moving, but it quickly spun away.

'I'll call him up and suggest I become his agent for his autobiography. I've got a great title: *John Rankin – My Life Below the Belt.*'

'But I will have finished my article. I'll be back in New York by then,' Samantha mumbled, then passed out, her head landing in Eugenie's lap.

'She's not going anywhere,' said Georgia, 'except to bed. I don't think I should drive back tonight. Can we crash here?'

'Of course. Help me carry her upstairs.'

The two women lifted Samantha to her feet and, standing on either side of her, with their arms around her waist, managed to drag her slowly upstairs and tuck her up in Eugenie's double bed.

'I think that pill is working. I'm too tired even to change into my nightdress,' Eugenie said, climbing under the duvet beside Samantha. 'I've never slept in my clothes before. You won't tell anybody, will you?'

'Mum's the word.'

Georgia went downstairs to turn off the lights. She looked at the spaghetti on the kitchen walls and laughed to herself. By the time she had gone back up, Eugenie and Samantha were sleeping peacefully, Eugenie's arm lying across Samantha's stomach.

I wish I had a camera, she thought, they look like two schoolgirls. I suppose I might as well join the crew.

Georgia took off her jeans and crawled into bed beside Eugenie. On the front of her T-shirt, just showing above the duvet, was a picture of a woman saying, 'Well, if we can send one man to the moon, why not all of them?'

# Chapter Five

Clarissa Darrell was annoyed. A famous cousin of the royal family had come into the hairdresser's at the same time as she, had been swept into a private room downstairs, and had commandeered all the attention that Clarissa was used to getting herself. As a result, she was not satisfied with her hair – the chignon on the top of her head, she could see, was slightly off centre. And she had had another one of her strange turns at the salon. She had thought she'd put an end to them after her encounter with the police.

'So. A chignon as usual, dear?' the lithe little male hairdreser had asked.

'No, Robert. This time I think I'll have a punk cut. You know, something spiky.'

'Ha, ha, ha,' he'd snickered 'Aren't we being amusing today.'

'I mean it, Robert. Why do I have to look the same all the time? It's tedious. I want a punk cut with a green streak.'

'Ha, ha, ha. What, pray tell, did we eat for lunch? Or should I say drink? Very naughty, but I won't tell a soul. The chignon as usual, then. Deborah, take Mrs Darrell to the sink, please.'

Clarissa dutifully followed Deborah, who did have a punk cut, to be shampooed. What is happening to me? she wondered as she was rinsed and re-rinsed. I said that without thinking. But I meant it. I must get a hold of myself.

On the drive back to her house in Chelsea, other motorists kept beeping their horns at her. Clarissa smiled self-consciously. Perhaps her hair was perfect, after all, or perhaps it was her profile which was attracting their attention. She liked her Roman nose and above-average cheekbones. She didn't blame the men for beeping, but she wasn't about to acknowledge them.

Staring straight ahead in her Range Rover, she continued driving. Until another horn beeped so insistently that she looked over towards the noise. A woman was pointing to the front of Clarissa's car. It was then she realized her tyre was going flat.

She pulled into a garage, where, after a few minutes, a mechanic informed her that her spare tyre was flat as well. And she had to wait forty-five minutes in a reception room smelling of petrol for a call-out vehicle to put it all right. By the time she arrived back, she was ready to yell at the nanny, and the housekeeper. She was even more ready to yell at her husband.

'Can you tell me exactly why we are going to this frightful party? And what are we supposed to wear?'

Duncan Darrell was carefully placing into his shirt the cuff-links Eugenie Woodrow had given him for Christmas two years before.

'We are going to this party because we were invited, and because it is being given by one of the more successful literary agents in London. If my political career stalls at any point, I thought I might like to write a book, and it would be helpful to cultivate a good agent.'

Duncan looked over at Clarissa. Lord, the perks of having a gullible wife. Clarissa wasn't stupid, she was just smug. Self-confident. It wouldn't occur to her that he might want something more in a woman. Something different. Insecure wives – they would be difficult to fool.

'As for my dress, well, it's a Fourth of July party, so I'll wear my white linen trousers, blue blazer and red and white striped shirt. Why don't you dress festively?'

Clarissa gave a contemptuous smirk, but then she always gave a contemptuous smirk when she had to do something she didn't want to do, Duncan thought, unfazed. He began to button his shirt.

What was Eugenie up to? She hadn't called or written for two years, and suddenly an invitation for the 'Let Yourself Go Fourth of July Party' arrived. That book which stared up at him from bookshop windows, and seemed to be mandatory airplane reading for any woman between the ages of twenty and fifty.

'But it is not just a Fourth of July Party, Duncan.'

Clarissa was still standing, arms folded, with her smirk. She hadn't moved toward her closet. She was on the edge, Duncan knew, of becoming truly difficult.

'It's for that horrible book. I don't see why we should give any credence to that rubbish. What if we are photographed there? It's too embarrassing.'

'Clarissa, please relax and get dressed. I doubt very much that the *News of the World* will have spies positioned around the room. I accepted for us. So we're going. You don't want to be rude, do you?'

Clarissa never wanted to be rude.

'No.'

Clarissa decided not to make an issue of this party. If she went willingly to this, she could use it later. The next time Duncan complained about going to one of the dinners *her* friends had organized, she could remind him of her own ability to sacrifice. After fifteen years of marriage, she felt she knew how best to win matrimonial skirmishes.

Choosing a brown silk dress with a round collar and puffed sleeves, she lay it on the bed, along with a matching Hermes scarf. She had a sudden vision of herself in fish-net stockings and a black leather mini-skirt. It vanished instantaneously as she began to pull a pair of tights up around her hips.

She looks like her mother. Why do all women have to look like their mothers? Duncan wondered, as he combed his hair artfully to conceal his bald patch. She didn't look like her mother fifteen years ago. Her ankles are thickening by the minute. Eugenie has the thinnest wrists and ankles I've ever seen. She could slip free of any handcuffs known to man.

Husband and wife continued to dress in silence.

'Darling, get a move on. You look splendid.' Duncan was impatient. He was beginning to get the same rush of adrenalin he had when a general election was called. He was ready for action. He wanted to see Eugenie. He especially wanted to see if Eugenie had another man.

'I'm ready,' replied Clarissa, finishing with her customary two layers of pancake makeup.

But really, she thought, why does he make that pathetic attempt with his hair? The bald patch will show by the end of the evening anyway. And in those clothes he looks like the little queer who delivers the flowers.

'You look splendid too. What a smart couple we make.'

Clarissa picked up her Gucci bag and headed for the door.

Sarah Frawley stood in front of her compact disc player with a disc in each hand. Should she dress to Beethoven or Mozart? Beethoven, she decided. Mozart was a problem. All his works were numbered with a K – how was she supposed to remember which music went with which number? She didn't have a head for figures, and she knew she would get confused. Beethoven was easier. The Kreutzer Sonata – she would put on the Kreutzer Sonata and listen carefully. She was better with names.

John Rankin hadn't called since that night she had spent at his flat. John Rankin's flat had shelves filled with classical music. Sarah Frawley knew it was an age-old gambit to make 'his' interests your interests, but it was a gambit she felt worthwhile. After all, how many attractive unmarried heterosexual men were there left in the world? And classical music was better as a passion than stamp collecting. So she had begun to educate herself. When John Rankin called – and she felt sure he would – when John Rankin asked her around to his flat again, she would know something about music. She wouldn't be too blatant about it, of course. But she could drop a few names, beginning with the Kreutzer Sonata.

She put the disc in the player, turned the volume up, and went back to her bedroom, a frilly haven decorated in pinks and greens, with a big four-poster bed and plenty of closet space for all her clothes. As the violin played in the background, she opened up the closet doors and chose black satin pants and a scooped-neck sleeveless red blouse, then searched for her large red leather belt and red high heels.

She finished dressing, put on her makeup from Cosmetics à la Carte and set her answering machine. It would be a good idea if she was out when John Rankin called. God knows why she was invited to this Fourth of July party, or who would be there. She had only met Georgia Green a few times socially, and had found her to be a typically brash American. But she wasn't one to turn down an invitation. And she had quite enjoyed that book *Let Yourself Go*.

As she was leaving her flat in Notting Hill, Sarah took the tape she had bought that afternoon to play in her car. Schubert's Unfinished Symphony – that should be an easy one to remember. But why, she wondered, wasn't it finished? Had he died in the middle of it? Had he gone deaf? No, Beethoven had gone deaf. Mozart had been poisoned. What had happened to Schubert? Maybe he had killed himself. She would have to look that one up when she got back.

What was the matter with him? John Rankin, standing on his balcony on a hot summer's evening watching the river police cruise down the Thames, was worried. The plain fact of the matter was that he was impotent. He couldn't get it up. Not with Sarah Frawley that night. Not with six different girls the following six nights. They had tried, he had tried, but the damn thing wouldn't work. He had never in his life endured such humiliation. If this continued he would have to see a doctor. No. He slapped his hand on the balcony wall. He *was* a doctor. What could a doctor tell him that he didn't already know?

He picked up a glass of wine, put the Mozart Requiem on the CD player and went into his bedroom. Relax, he told himself. A good doctor would tell you to relax. This is just a momentary hiccup. Many men go through this. It's normal, perfectly normal. Relax. Get ready for the party. He unloosened his tie, unbuttoned his shirt, took them off, took off his trousers and boxer shorts and sat down naked, on the end of his bed, facing a mirror.

Looking at the reflection of his genitals lying peacefully on the duvet, he suddenly stood up, took them in his hand and shook them.

'What's the matter with you, you lazy sods? Can't you do a good night's work anymore? Tonight. You better bloody well do your stuff tonight.'

He was bound to find somebody at this party, although, thinking about it, he probably wouldn't know a soul there. Georgia somebody had rung him up and introduced herself as a literary agent.

'You may want to write a book some day. Come along and meet some literary types,' she had said, and he'd been quite flattered.

Perhaps what he needed was a new body to spur him on. He had been with names from his past those six nights, sticking to the tried and tested formula. Branching into new territory might be the answer.

John Rankin finally relaxed and began to get dressed. He put on a clean pair of boxers and started to select a shirt. He stopped, his hand on a pale blue shirtsleeve. How had this woman Georgia thought of him? And why? What was familiar about her? The American accent. Where had he last heard it? He thought carefully. Ms Samantha Lewis. Ms Samantha Lewis who has a friend who is an author. Ms Samantha Lewis who is, undoubtedly, up to another trick. He grinned. And then that old familiar feeling came back. For just two seconds he didn't believe it, couldn't trust himself to believe it. Then he looked down, and he saw his pink boxer shorts begin to make room for his horizontal-climbing-to-vertical member.

Rankin went down on his knees and kissed the floor.


Eugenie Woodrow wished that she had never agreed to this party. It was all Georgia's idea. Georgia was trouble. Georgia would enjoy watching Eugenie's face when Duncan and his wife arrived. What was she supposed to do – pretend she didn't know Duncan? Throw her arms around him and tell his wife to stop standing in the way of true love? And what did she feel for Duncan now? Fascination.

She was fascinated. She had so many questions to ask him. How dare he choose his silly wife over her? How could he have managed to keep her so entertained for the two years she was his mistress? How could he be so romantic and so practical at the same time? And, the most important question of all: why wasn't there any other man like him?

Duncan, when Eugenie had given him the ultimatum – Clarissa or her – had simply put one forefinger to his head, the other forefinger to hers, and made as if to blow out both their brains.

'When the horse starts to limp, shoot it,' he had said. 'Put it out of its misery. It will kill me and it will kill you, but instant death is better than prolonged suffering.'

'Does that mean you love Clarissa?'

'No. It means I love you but I'm going to stay with Clarissa. And it means that if you can't accept that, we should stop seeing each other.'

'I can't accept that.' Eugenie said.

'You know,' Duncan said, sweeping Eugenie's dark hair back with both his hands, and looking at her quizzically, 'Your face has always puzzled me. You look like a horse. But not in the way that most Englishwomen look like horses – all long angular faces, flaring nostrils and wide mouths. You look like an Arabian thoroughbred. A delicate pony's face.'

'A dead pony's face. You have just shot me. So please, Duncan, do me a favour and leave right away. I would like to cry by myself.'

'So would I.' Duncan picked up his coat from the sofa and left, without touching her again.

Two years later Eugenie studied her face in the mirror. What do I look like now? she asked herself. I look like a nervous woman. I look like a nervous woman still hopelessly in love. I'm supposed to be beautiful, but Duncan says I look like a horse. What should I wear – stirrups and a saddle? Maybe someone at the party will take pity on me and give me a horse tranquillizer. Why is Duncan coming to this party? And why, why did I let Georgia invite him?

Samantha sat uncomfortably perched in the middle of the back of Georgia's MG. The roof was down, the sun was shining, Andrew was sitting in the front; and Georgia, as she drove, was singing, 'Heaven's just a sin away'.

'I should have been a country and western singer. I wish I had been born in Tennessee.'

'I wish you had too. Then we wouldn't have to go to the Bronx on our American holidays.'

'Vacations, Andrew, not holidays. Holidays are holy days. Like Christmas. Or Martin Luther King Day. They are specific. Vacations are general. Right, Sam?'

'Right.' Sensing that she was about to be pulled into a family disagreement, Samantha tried to sit back in her seat, but found it impossibly cramped and resumed her position, her head between Andrew's and Georgia's seats in the front.

'Is the Fourth of July a holy day?' Andrew had turned toward Samantha as he asked his question.

'It's both,' replied Georgia. 'It's a holy day and a vacation, an endless vacation from the Brits.'

'Georgia, I'm getting slightly fatigued with your rabid Americanism. You don't like this country, you don't like the British people, but you live here and you're married to a Brit. Don't you think it's time to sign a peace treaty and gave us all a vacation from your barbs? Look at Samantha – she doesn't complain.'

Samantha squirmed, and looked down. She saw that her suspender belt was showing on her left thigh, and quickly pulled her skirt over it.

'I can't look at Samantha. I'm driving. Anyway, she's only been here two weeks and she knows she's going back sometime. I have to stay and wage my own guerilla war.'

'You don't *have* to stay. You're perfectly entitled to go back to the Bronx and live with your crazy anarchist father. You'd probably be very happy there.' Andrew paused. 'Much happier than you are here with me. You should consider your options.'

Georgia swung the car over to the side of the street, turned off the engine and faced Andrew.

Samantha sat wishing she could disappear, or leap out of the car. Instead, she pretended to have dropped an earring and put her face down to the floor, where she counted five chocolate-bar wrappings and saw a vast array of English coins.

'Is this the end? Did I understand what you just said? Are you telling me you think I should leave, that it's over between us?' Georgia asked this quietly, but Samantha heard it. She began to pick up some twopenny pieces. The blood was rushing to her face. This can't be happening, she thought. This just can't be happening.

Andrew leant forward in his seat and put his head in his hands.

'This isn't the time or place, Georgia.'

All three occupants of the car fell silent. Samantha thought she was going to faint. She straightened up, gripping the change in her hand, and found herself looking into Georgia's eyes in the rearview mirror. Georgia was smiling. And then she was singing.

'Our D-I-V-O-R-C-E becomes final today,' sang Georgia. 'Me and little J-O-E are going away.' She turned the key and started up the engine. 'I love him so and this has been pure H-E-double-L for me.' She moved back into the traffic.

'See, I could beat Tammy Wynette hands down. Now cheer up and stop being so stupid. I promise not to say another word about the quirks of this raj-forsaken race. You better promise too, Sam.'

Feeling as if she had just averted a head-on collision, Samantha smiled back at Georgia in the mirror.

'I promise. Look' – she opened her hand – 'I found some money on the floor.'

'Brilliant. Let's buy some drugs at Sainsburys.'

Georgia drove on, one hand on the wheel, the other tapping the side of the car. Her hair was even wilder than usual, having been professionally 'scrunched' that afternoon. She was wearing a low-cut emerald green dress with a badge on the front, between her breasts, stating 'Bored Teenager'.

Samantha didn't understand what this penchant for badges and T-shirts with slogans meant to Georgia. Nor could she understand how Georgia had managed to turn that scene with Andrew into a joke. She never seemed to lose control. Even on that night of drink and drugs at Eugenie's, Georgia was somehow in control. Samantha wondered whether Georgia ever cried, whether she ever became a 'helpless female'. Eugenie, she felt sure, was capable of breaking down, of collapsing.

But George? Maybe it had something to do with that crazy anarchist father Andrew had just referred to. She would have to ask George about him. But not now. Andrew was maintaining a grim expression in the front. He was staring out his side of the car, and Georgia was still tapping away on her side. And then she started to sing again.

'Oh, England swings like a pendulum do, bobbies on bicycles two by two. Westminster Abbey, the tower of Big Ben ...'

'Georgia. Spouse dearest. You can say whatever you like about this country, but please promise to stop singing.' Andrew turned his head to the front and switched the radio on.

Samantha relaxed. Everything was back to normal.

Georgia Green did not give many parties but, when she did, they were unusual. For her birthday the previous year she had organized a caravan of friends for a tour of Milton Keynes, and had delighted in pointing out the concrete cows, the Hiroshima Peace Pagoda, the shopping mall planned along ancient Druidic principles. 'Isn't it great?' she had exclaimed. 'On Midsummer's day, the sun rises right above McDonald's.'

For Eugenie's party, Georgia had taken over a trendy church off Picadilly, known for its memorial services for media people. Not one of the hundred or so guests had ever been to a book party in a church before. As they mingled among the pews with glasses of wine in their hands, they conducted their conversations in lowered tones – feeling, as they exchanged literary gossip, slightly blasphemous.

By eight o'clock, however, when the party had been officially going for an hour, voices were rising and any respect for the surroundings had dissipated amid stories of advances received, editors axed, affairs suspected.

Committed smokers, not allowed a cigarette inside the body of the church, had congregated in the entrance hall, where they mingled with tramps off the street, used to seeking shelter there but not to receiving free wine for their troubles. One of the girls pouring out the booze from the impromptu bar at the back had asked Georgia what to do about the tramps, whether to serve them or try to kick them out.

'Serve them, by all means,' Georgia had replied. 'Who knows, maybe they'll get drunk enough to buy a book.' Paperback copies of *Let Yourself Go* were on sale behind the bar.

Eugenie Woodrow had spent the last forty-five minutes talking to gossip columnists. She was tired of selling herself, and sat down in an unoccupied pew for a break. 'Yes, of course I love the idea of Mickey Rourke playing Storm,' she repeated to herself. 'Yes, I am busy on another, even racier novel. No, there is no "man" in my life at the moment.'

She had chosen, finally, an off-the shoulder white dress randomly festooned with dark blue stars, and matched it with dark blue heels. 'I'm supposed to be a star,' she'd said to herself, 'so I'll dress like one.' Then she had put on red lipstick and red nailpolish, purposefully. Duncan hated red on lips and nails. He had told her they were a signal to men that a girl was available. Well, she *was* available. If he *did* come, he would see that she had changed. That she would no longer do only what he wanted her to do.

'Please turn to hymn number 142.'

Eugenie heard the whisper in her ear and all her muscles tightened. Picking up a hymn book, she turned to the designated number. 'All Things Bright and Beautiful'. Typical Duncan. She turned around. He had vanished.

'Really, if I have to hear one more person in publishing here whinge about American takeovers, I'll kill. We've saved your asses.' Georgia was busily haranguing an editor in the back pew of the church when she was tapped on the shoulder from behind.

'Excuse me, but are you Georgia Green?'

Georgia turned to see a vision of male beauty. She took a rapid gulp from her glass.

'Yes. I am.'

'Sorry to interrupt, buy my name is John Rankin, and I just wanted to thank you for inviting me tonight.'

'Oh, my God.' Georgia stood looking up at him. He was indescribably delicious. 'Are you sure you're not an actor? I mean, are you sure you don't want a part in the mini series? I'm sorry, but would you excuse *me* for a minute? There's someone I have to see immediately.'

'Of course. I'll just get myself a drink.' Rankin strolled toward the bar, and Georgia quickly scanned the crowd. Seeing Samantha in the centre of the aisle, talking to Andrew, she pushed her way over to her.

'Sam, I have to talk to you. Now.'

'Georgia, Sam and I were just discussing Dan Quayle. Would you be so kind as to let us finish our conversation?'

'I don't care if you've just discovered Dan Quayle in bed with Jesse Jackson. I've got to see Sam alone. Come on!' Georgia grabbed Samantha by the elbow and guided her upstairs, to the church balcony. They sat down next to the organ.

'You nutcase. Are you out of your tiny mind?' Georgia took Samantha by the shoulders and shook her.

'Georgia, what's going on? What's this all about?'

'What's this all about? It's about God's gift to women. It's about a gynaecologist named John Rankin. It's about the fact that you were invited to his flat and you didn't fucking accept. Listen, Samantha. I have names of good shrinks in this country. I'll call them up tomorrow. You should go see one. See all of them. Something is seriously wrong with you.'

'Georgia, we've had this conversation. I've told you, he's too smooth. And I'm sure he's had thousands of women. I don't want to be another notch on his belt. Don't you remember? Remember Jilly?'

'Remember Jilly? Is that a battle cry? Samantha, forget Jilly. There are belts and there are girdles of heaven. Oh no, look!'

'What?' Samantha turned her head in the direction Georgia was looking.

'Look. There he is. At the altar. And there's Sarah Frawley talking to him. This is horrible. Go down there now. Get him into the vestry or something. Just get him.'

Clarissa Darrell stood at the bar with as much composure as she could muster. Where was Duncan? And who was this filthy old man with the torn shirt and stench of alcohol standing beside her? A writer, no doubt. They were all such unattractive people, with no sense of decorum. This one was particularly scruffy. But, she thought, he was probably some prize-winning journalist. One has to make an effort on these occasions. She turned to him.

'And whom do you work for?'

He seemed surprised.

'Myself,' he answered, grabbing two glasses of red wine from the tray going by.

'That must be fascinating. Should I know who you are? I'm terribly ignorant about people in your world.'

He finished both glasses, picked up two more, and squinted at the top of her head.

'Don't mind me saying so, love, but you have a terribly ignorant hairdo.'

Clarissa watched in rage as he shambled off toward the doorway of the church. Really, she thought, I must find Duncan and get out of this frightful place immediately.

Eugenie stood in the vestibule, smoking a cigarette, and watched as Samantha came towards her. Samantha had changed dramatically in a short time. There was only a remnant of that wounded look left, and the slumped shoulders had straightened. Eugenie re-evaluated her. Samantha would no longer qualify as the put-upon heroine. In fact, she looked enviable in her pink skirt and white silk jacket. She looked as though she had a future. Eugenie lit another cigarette and handed it to Samantha.

'How are you doing? You look fantastic.'

'Thanks. I feel as if I were in a madhouse. So I came over here for a break.' Samantha inhaled and laughed. 'I found myself in the middle of some soap opera. Georgia's taken one look at John Rankin and wants me to go seduce him again. It's crazy.'

'Georgia's crazy, haven't you noticed yet? But you're right about the soap opera. You know what would really make her happy? It would make her happy if your brother, who had been reported missing in action in Vietnam, came into town having lost his memory and undergone plastic surgery. You and your brother could then fall in love without knowing you were siblings. Even better, you're not only his sister, you're also a nun. Georgia would be over the moon.'

Samantha and Eugenie started to laugh together.

'Maybe that should be the plot of my third book.'

'Third? I haven't seen the second yet.'

Samantha looked up to the voice and saw a man with brown hair not quite covering a bald patch. Her immediate thought was that he resembled Basil Rathbone playing Sherlock Holmes – tall, hawkish, thin, with a face which showed a combination of worldly-wisdom and world-weariness and a starched, upper-class voice. He was staring at Eugenie.

'Samantha Lewis, this is Duncan Darrell, Conservative MP for Chudley.' Samantha shook his hand, then put her cigarette out on the floor.

'It's nice to meet you. Excuse me, you two, but there's someone I'm supposed to see at the altar.' Samantha thought she couldn't leave the two of them alone quickly enough, and began to back off. 'That sounds romantic,' she heard Duncan say. 'Speaking of which, Eugenie ...'

As Samantha turned and walked away, she noticed a woman moving towards Eugenie and Duncan, a woman with a funny hairstyle and a mouth set in a pout.

Georgia sat for a while surveying her guests, her party, from the balcony. There were the usual groupings – the old drunken hacks who were telling each other how Fleet Street had died and how journalism wasn't what it used to be. The young hacks were discussing how boring and out-of-date the old hacks were. The old editors were telling each other how much publishing had changed and literary standards had declined, while the young editors were discussing which were the hot new books for the autumn. But where was Rick? Late as usual.

There was one circle of women who were most likely talking about salaries and possible promotions, while another, off to the side, where probably detailing the rigours of school runs. Some wives were clinging, limpet-like, to their husbands, while others were circulating freely.

Parties, Georgia decided, were all about showing off. Everyone was saying how wonderful they used to be, or how successful they are now, or how amazing they *will* be when the time comes. Some women could, if they didn't have a career themselves, show off their husbands, or their children. Others could simply show off by looking great. All of them, male and female, were busy building or maintaining a reputation, even if it was simply a reputation for being good listeners.

Down on the left, Georgia spotted a well-known female author who, she knew, was in the midst of a Self-Improvement course. Seventeen hours at seventy pounds a go, and you were supposed to develop social skills, confidence and the ability to communicate your new-found persona to the world at large, including television audiences. The horrible truth was, it had worked. This woman was more relaxed, more self-assured, friendlier than she had ever been; she could now consistently sparkle, even at an ungodly hour on Breakfast TV. What was this world coming to, Georgia asked herself, when Self-Improvement courses actually worked?

Turning her gaze away in despair, Georgia picked out a silver-haired television producer standing in the middle of the aisle, flushed and looking defeated. He was lousy, so word had it, in bed. And, what was worse, he knew everyone knew. An old girlfriend had done the dirty and spread the word in a not-very-well-disguised first novel. Georgia watched as he chatted up an attractive young woman. Maybe she hadn't read the book. Maybe she didn't care. Georgia felt immense pity for him. He may have been the only person there out to *destroy* his reputation.

Then she spied Samantha's blonde head walking toward the altar. 'About time, kiddo,' she said to herself. 'It's about time people at this shindig stopped talking about advances and started making them.'

Sarah Frawley knew competition when she saw it, and now it was standing beside her in the shape of that blonde woman Samantha Lewis. John Rankin's eyes had narrowed when Samantha approached and he had cut off his conversation in mid-sentence to give Samantha a kiss on the cheek.

Before Samantha's arrival, Rankin had apologized to Sarah for not calling her. But it hadn't sounded very genuine, and Sarah hadn't had enough time alone with him to make the impact she was hoping to when she had so unexpectedly run into him at this party. Damn that girl, she thought. Why do they let so many American women into this country? There should be laws against them. She certainly wasn't going to yield her ground.

'Isn't the architecture of this church breathtaking, John? So old, yet somehow so relevant.' Rankin nodded his head, but he was looking at Samantha. Sarah began to feel slightly desperate. She looked up to the balcony and saw the organ pipes.

'It reminds me of the Kreutzer Sonata, the same intricate and immaculate structure.'

'Oh, I love the Kreutzer Sonata as well,' said

Samantha, and Sarah grimaced. 'Tolstoy is unbeatable as far as I'm concerned.' The grimace turned to a catlike grin. She doesn't know what she's talking about, the little fake, thought Sarah. I've caught her out.

'Beethoven, dear.'

Samantha met Sarah's eyes and felt a powerful animosity, like a tennis ball hit straight at her.

'Both,' said Rankin. 'Beethoven wrote the music and Tolstoy wrote the short story.'

'Oh, I see,' Samantha smiled. 'I'm fine on literature, but I don't know much about classical music.'

Sarah took a step closer to Rankin and put her hand on his arm.

'John has a magnificent collection of classical music in his flat.'

'And, Samantha, if you would change your mind and come to my flat, I could play The Kreutzer Sonata for you. Then you can tell me if the words have any relation to the music.'

Sarah looked at Rankin as if he had knifed her in the back. How outrageous, how insensitive could this man be? He was a bastard – there was no other word for it. If he thought he could humiliate her through this American bimbo without paying for it, he was wrong. She pushed her bracelet up her arm with her free hand. The other remained on Rankin's sleeve. She tightened her grip.

'What a good idea, John. I'm sure Samantha would love your flat, every stick of furniture in it, down to the bed. And Samantha, while you're admiring his bed, I think he should play Schubert's Unfinished Symphony for you. Because poor John has problems finishing things himself. In fact, he has problems starting things. He's a non-starter, our doctor here.' With that, Sarah let go of Rankin and walked off down the aisle.

'What was that all about?' Samantha asked, wondering how she managed to get involved in triangles she didn't want to be involved in: David and his model, Georgia and Andrew, Eugenie and Duncan. Now John Rankin and Sarah Frawley.

'Nothing at all. Sarah has a few problems.' Rankin was seething, but calmed down as he looked at Samantha. The wicked grin appeared on his face, and he passed his hand through his hair. 'So what's this party all about, Ms Lewis? Don't tell me. Let me guess: you're going to try to seduce a rector in his pulpit. At least you can't fall over in a pew.'

Watching Samantha talk to the man at the altar, Andrew felt sick. He was classically good-looking, that man, well-built, tall and blond. An *homme fatal*. He probably had a country house with fishing rights. He would shoot off to Scotland in August to kill the first grouse of the season. While he, Andrew, had nothing to offer her. An overweight married man with the occasional, as Georgia would say, good line. He knew he should feel guilty about falling in love with Samantha, but he didn't. How could he be blamed for those pale blue eyes of Samantha's? They lingered on. They promised understanding, tenderness, compassion. They said she would cook him lovely meals and listen to his anecdotes without trying to top them or make cracks. They understood that he was meant for better things in life than cranking out all these books; her eyes knew that he was trapped in trivia, and they would help him break out. Become the serious person he had been too lazy, as yet, to be. He would make sure Samantha kept her eyes open when he made love to her.

Everthing in the world was a joke to Georgia. If he told her, undoubtedly his passion for her friend would be the source of a lot of funny quips. He couldn't stand that. Georgia was so damned exhausting. They hadn't had a normal conversation in three years.

Andrew made his way to the bar, picked up a glass of wine and surveyed the crowd. It was beginning to thin out, this bunch of wankers. Wankers away. Then he saw Georgia walking on the other side of the vestibule, talking to Rick Holland. Oh, wonderful. That fabulously funny Rick Holland. Andrew sighed. The thought of the repartee between Rick and Georgia tired him to such an extent that he went over to the door of the church and sat down on the floor. Right beside the tramp with the torn shirt.

'Do you think people invented morality to try to stop themselves from falling passionately in love all the time?' asked Andrew, staring straight ahead.

The tramp coughed loudly, then began to roll a cigarette.

'You know what Tarzan said to Jane, guv. It's a fuckin' jungle out there.'

Just my bloody luck, thought Andrew. Another joker.

'Hello Georgia – you didn't tell me your father was in town.'

'Rick, you creep. You're late. And what do you mean my father's in town?'

Richard Holland motioned towards the tramp with the torn shirt lying up against the church door.

'He's looking great, Georgia. And so are you. Bored teenager? We'll have to do something about that, you little chicken.'

As she studied Rick Holland for a moment, Georgia knew that if she were diagnosed as having a terminal disease, she would want him in the doctor's office beside her. Unorthodox looking, with eyebrows which met in the middle of his forehead, forming one straight bushy black line, and a blunt nose which broadened

111

further whenever he smiled, Rick had been the best friend of her lover in university days, and the one man Georgia knew was guaranteed to make her laugh. She hugged him, then stepped back.

'It's terrific to see you. Let me get you a drink.'

'The drink can wait. I want to meet the author of this sex-filled, love-torn saga I'm producing, this metaphysical treatise. I want to discuss the future of existentialism with this broad. I want to get into her pants.'

Eugenie was trying to signal to Georgia to rescue her. She was standing between Duncan and Clarissa, and for the past ten minutes they had been discussing who might win Wimbledon. A few more seconds and Eugenie thought she might lose her control. Having never met Clarissa before, Eugenie was appalled by Duncan's choice. An uptight, frosty woman with a chignon and a Hermes scarf, prattling on about Boris Becker and how much her Wimbledon debenture was now worth.

Duncan was standing there, nonchalantly, in his red, white and blue outfit, acting as if talking with his ex-mistress and his wife were an everyday affair. Georgia was, thank God, walking towards them with her arm around a strange man. He had one extraordinary eyebrow and a distinctive lope – it was unlike any walk he had seen – aimless and purposeful at the same time.

'Excuse me for mingling,' announced Georgia, as she and Rick broke into the circle formed by Eugenie, Duncan and Clarissa, 'but Eugenie, you must meet Rick. Richard Holland. My old buddy and also the producer of the *Let Yourself Go* mini series.'

'I'm in love,' said Rick, shaking Eugenie's hand. 'But don't think I'd cancel the project if you weren't nice to me, Miss Woodrow. All I ask is that you worship me from up close.'

'Rick, Georgia, this is Clarissa Darrell and her husband Duncan.'

The four interchanged handshakes, but no one spoke for a moment. Georgia was trying to gauge the situation by studying Eugenie and Duncan's eyes. Rick was staring at Clarissa.

'Mrs Darrell,' Rick began, 'Mrs Darrell. May I compliment you on your hair. I've always thought that hair should reflect life. That's why I'm considering buying a toupee. I heard Maurice Chevalier's toupee is up for auction. Thank heaven for little rugs. Really, that is spectacular. I love it.'

'Thank you.' Clarissa beamed. What an interesting, perceptive fellow. Movie producers were obviously a cut above writers. 'Do you know,' she continued, addressing Rick, 'Some frightful man insulted me when we first came in.'

'No. Where is the fiend? I'll take care of him.' Rick, Georgia could see, was enjoying himself immensely. The crowd had thinned to such an extent that Clarissa had a clear view of the church entrance.

'There he is, over there.' Clarissa pointed. 'Sitting at the door with some other *louche* character. Who *are* those people? Should I recognize them? Are they famous writers? Is that their excuse? People take such liberties these days.'

'One of them is my husband,' said Georgia. Clarissa flinched.

'And the other is her father. He must be working on the sequel to *Being and Nothingness*.'

Eugenie regarded Rick with relief. He was a diversion from Duncan, from Clarissa, from this uncomfortable menage. She hadn't dared to look Duncan in the eye since Clarissa had so swiftly interrupted their tête-à-tête.

'How fascinating.' Clarissa began to straighten her scarf. Every person in the group around her noticed that it bore traces of makeup. 'Duncan, dear, look – there's Hughie Campbell. What's he doing here? We must go and speak to him.'

As he followed Clarissa away from the group, Duncan glanced back at Eugenie with a wink. She returned it with a look entreating him to leave her alone, hoping all the while that he wouldn't.

'So, darling one' – Rick put his arm around Eugenie – 'None of life's little nuances gets past me. I see I have some competition from Mr Darrell. We'll have to wean you away from the married man syndrome. Not that I'm against it *per se*. But a man who winks, well, as you English say, it's simply not on.'

Samantha knew, after a few minutes of converation with Rankin, that she was in danger. All her worries about being just another conquest were evaporating as Rankin listened to her account of her journalistic career. He knew how to listen, he knew what questions to ask, and he *was* good looking. Besides, he probably wasn't as much of a womanizer as everybody said. People liked to exaggerate other peoples' lifestyles.

They had moved from the altar to the first pew of the church, and the sun was still shining through the stained-glass windows, creating rainbows of light. Rankin had one leg up on the wooden pew. He had wrapped his arms around his knee, and rested his chin on top of his right wrist. The pose made him look like a sculpture – Man in Concentrated Ease, Samantha would have named it. And his face had softened. He reminded her of a young boy who had just changed into pyjamas.

Samantha felt childlike as well. She was, she realized, free to recreate herself. Rankin knew nothing of her past, of her failure with David, and she didn't have to tell him. All he knew was that she had tried to seduce him for a bet. She could, if she behaved like a strong, self-confident woman, actually become one. She could be a different person entirely. There were no old friends around to say, 'Sam, this isn't like you – you're not being yourself.'

She had, as she thought about her possibilities, stopped talking. Rankin straightened up and put his hand on the back of her neck.

'It's a perfect night, Samantha. A rare event in this country. I know I've invited you to my flat before, but would you reconsider this time? I have a balcony that overlooks the river. We could get a takeaway curry and sit under the stars. I know that sounds like just another proposition, but it's different this time. Isn't it?'

'Yes, I guess it is.' Samantha realized that she'd never met such a handsome man. Had she ever met even a normally handsome man? She considered the question. A lot of men were *nice* looking, David being one of them; a lot of men were seductive because of their power or their mental agility or their sense of humour, but she'd only seen really *handsome* men in the movies. Now she understood what a man must feel like, having a stunning woman by his side at a party. It was undeniably heady.

'Well, come on then, let's sneak out.' Rankin took Samantha's hand, stood up, and managed to avoid Georgia, Eugenie and Rick as he led her to the door. Samantha didn't notice Andrew as she stepped over his outstretched legs into the night.

'Whoa, babycakes. When one woman calls another woman a cunt, you know something bad has gone down. To whom are you referring, you gorgeous creature, you little bitch?' Richard Holland kept his arm around Eugenie and gave her shoulder a squeeze.

'I'm talking about that cunt over there. Vanessa Ritter. The one who came to interview me, arrived one

115

hour early, and then wrote a truly dreadful review. The worst I got.'

'Darling, if she spelt your name right, who cares?'

'I do.'

Eugenie had had a lot to drink. She felt entitled to get drunk after her meeting with Clarissa. And Clarissa was still there, still in sight. She and Duncan were a few feet away from Vanessa Ritter, speaking to some ugly Hooray Henry. Duncan had his arm around Clarissa's waist.

'But Eugenie, look at Vanessa ...' Georgia was enjoying herself. She had given up on her attempt to coax Andrew away from the church door and returned to Rick and Eugenie as the party meandered to its finish. 'She's wearing a fake leopard-skin dress with a plunging neckline which reveals what? I mean, look at her cleavage – it looks like recycled Nancy Reagan.'

'Georgia, you're so adorable when you're trashing someone. Your little face lights up like Shirley Temple with an ice-cream cone. Steady girls, here comes Vanessa in our direction.'

'And here come the Darrells.' Georgia was worried by the approach of the Darrells. Eugenie was drunk. Highstrung and drunk – not a good combination when the old lover and his wife are around.

Duncan, Clarissa and Vanessa Ritter arrived simultaneously – Duncan and Clarissa to announce their departure, Vanessa to make her apologies.

'Eugenie, Georgia – it's so nice to see you both. Eugenie I just had to say how sorry I am about that review of mine. But it had to be said by someone, you must admit. I'm afraid it fell to me. You must hate me.'

'I do.'

The Darrells could not intrude on this exchange to say their farewells. They were caught silently looking on. Duncan still had his arm around his wife's waist.

'You do what, Eugenie? Accept my apology?'

Vanessa was essaying a smile which mixed contrition and superiority, and emerged as slightly lopsided.

'No. I do hate you.'

'Oh, dear.' The lopsided smile remained. 'I *am* sorry. I suppose I should leave.'

'We must be going too,' Clarissa cut in. 'You know nannies these days. They want to go out every night, even if it is midnight and they're working the ...'

'No. I don't know nannies. I do know that I'd like to give Vanessa a little tip.'

'Duncan,' Georgia said immediately. 'Being a Liberal myself, I could give you Conservatives a tip ...'

'Georgia. Don't interrupt me. *I* was giving *Vanessa* a little tip. When you review a book, Vanessa, try your hardest to get it right. I know it's difficult, especially if you haven't read it. *Let Yourself Go* was not, I know, *Pride and Prejudice*. Jane Austen is not moving over in her grave to make room for me. But it was not a shopping and fucking novel either, Vanessa. There wasn't a designer name in the book. How were my characters supposed to shop, and where? They were kidnapped, for God's sake.'

'You know what I meant, Eugenie. It is of the genre. Three rich women and a hero named Storm? What else could it be? A low-grade rip-off of the Patty Hearst story, as I said.'

Eugenie found herself looking to Duncan for help. His eyes refused to meet hers.

'Darling, have I told you?' Rick tightened his grip on Eugenie. 'Patty thinks it was the best. She said to send her love and admiration. She's so adorable, *I* could kidnap her. Do you think I should change my name to Storm. Or Typhoon? I could have a whole new career. The Last Typhoon.'

Staring at Vanessa, Eugenie could feel herself unravelling. *Let Yourself Go* deserved criticism, she knew that. But not of Vanessa's sort. The next novel, yes. The next novel would doubtless be a calculated shopping and fucking book. She couldn't think of anything else. But *Let Yourself Go*, despite being written for all the wrong reasons, had some merit. It was her baby, her child, and there was Vanessa standing like a schoolteacher, giving her child bad marks without knowing what the hell she was talking about. Searching for a verbal weapon to wound Vanessa, Eugenie fell back on the physical; it was the only area in which she felt secure at the moment.

'I'd like to give you another tip while I'm at it, Vanessa. A little cosmetic tip. Something you can benefit from. You know, women with skin like yours, as they get older, develop little lines around their lips, little cracks. And if you wear lipstick, as you do, it smudges and gets caught in those lines. See?' Eugenie reached out and moved her forefinger over Vanessa's upper lip. 'There. See how it has spread into the cracks. What you need is a lip liner. If I ever *do* write a shopping and fucking book, I'll tell you where exactly to go to get one.'

'Isn't that fascinating?' Clarissa began, oblivious to the contortions suffusing Vanessa's face 'You know I heard Jerry Hall saying exactly the same thing on *Wogan* last night and I –'

'And, Vanessa, I also know there's a wonderful cream on the market to hide those nasty red marks you have, the ones men and women get from a lifetime of hard drinking. Tiny little blood vessels bursting all over your cheeks.'

'Uh oh,' groaned Georgia.

Vanessa Ritter, looking as if she were in the first stage of an epileptic fit, took the glass of wine in her left hand and threw its contents at Eugenie Woodrow's face. With no result. She had forgotten that she'd finished it. Seeing the empty glass, she turned from epileptic to apoplectic.

'You third-rate little hussy,' she screamed. 'How dare you? You write drivel. And you can't take it when someone dares to tell you so.' Vanessa stopped. Words were not enough. She took a step toward Eugenie, grabbed her right nipple with her thumb and forefinger and tweaked it with a vengeance.

'Jesus!' Eugenie yelled in pain. 'Ouch!'

Everyone in the church looked over at Eugenie. Vanessa stomped off in her leopard skin, like an animal who has just devoured its prey. Eugenie stood massaging her breast, tears in her eyes.

'Honey, let me do that for you,' Rick said. Eugenie managed to smile. Duncan frowned.

'I'll take care of it, Rick. I just cannot believe how much that hurt. It *really* hurt. Where did she learn how to do that?'

'Mud wrestling?' Georgia suggested.

'Or an advanced course in tit-for-tat diplomacy.'

Everyone, especially Clarissa, laughed at Rick.

'I would hate to see her in the House of Commons,' said Duncan. Nobody laughed. Duncan decided that he didn't like this man Rick. He didn't like him one bit.

'How embarrassing.' The other partygoers were still staring at Eugenie's group. 'I hope no one saw what happened. I'm afraid I lost it. I went right over the top.' Eugenie had sobered up quickly.

'I've never seen such a rude woman. Really. You were simply offering her some advice. As I was saying, I heard it on *Wogan* last night and I went out to buy some lipliner today. It's very sensible, really. There was no need for her to be so rude.'

Eugenie shut her eyes for a moment. The idea of Clarissa Darrell defending her made her feel guilty, angry and profoundly tired.

'Duncan, darling,' Clarissa continued, 'We really must be on our way. Thank you so much for a lovely party.' Clarissa turned to Georgia. 'It was wonderful to meet such interesting people. I do hope your husband and your father are feeling well. And I enjoyed meeting you, Mr Holland. I think it's so fascinating that you know people like Patty Hearst. I'd love to hear more about her. You must all come and visit us sometime soon.'

Rick leant over and kissed her on the cheeks in the French fashion, three times. Clarissa blushed.

Duncan grabbed her and guided her to the exit. Georgia watched as Clarissa bowed down to shake hands with Andrew, then the tramp.

Rick adjusted the left shoulder pad on Georgia's dress.

'Why don't we three party animals go to my hotel? We can leave Andrew at the church door as a sacrifice to the gods.'

'No thanks, Rick. I think I better see this party to the end as it was my idea in the first place. And then I'll sweep my husband off the floor.'

'Strike one. Eugenie?'

'Oh Rick, you're sweet, but no. I need to go home tonight. I need to be by myself.' Eugenie hugged Rick and kissed him on the cheek. She felt very alone and very miserable.

'I'll be getting along then. Really, you women are passing up a golden opportunity. You don't know how unique I am. My mother never understood how I could have turned out black from the waist down.'

'Here we are.' Rankin was laying one chicken tikka, one prawn bhuna, one lamb madras, one pilau rice and a large quantity of popadoms on his balcony table. Then he went back to the kitchen to fetch the plates, knives and forks. Samantha looked out over the River Thames and wondered what it would be like to sleep with another man. Would she be able to relax with John? Would she have an orgasm? What would he expect of her? And could she ask to borrow his toothbrush after this curry? How embarrassing. Why were intimate encounters such minefields of embarrassment?

Rankin returned, looking cool in his blue shirt. He looks like a man in a cigarette ad, Samantha decided. Come to Marlboro Country. Samantha reached into her purse and pulled out her cigarettes. She heard Phil Collins begin to sing 'One More Night'.

'I thought you were a classical fan.' She sat down at the table as Rankin poured the wine.

'I am. But I'd like to be Phil Collins. I'd like to be a sassy little guy with a tough face and a tender voice.'

'You're lying again, John.'

'You're right again, Samantha. I have no desire to be Phil Collins.' Rankin smiled.

'But is it difficult for you to be so good looking?'

'Samantha, you ask some of the strangest questions. I suppose you want an honest answer.'

Samantha nodded.

'OK. No, it's not difficult.'

'Is it easy?'

'A piece of cake.'

Samantha laughed and bit into a popadom. That was an honest answer, she had to hand it to him. And then an alien but enjoyable feeling surged through Samantha's psyche: John Rankin was a more attractive man than David's model was an attractive woman. Yes, the model had been long-legged, big-breasted and sexy, but she didn't have the equivalent of Rankin's wicked grin, or, more importantly, his class. There were a lot of women out there like the model, but there weren't a lot of men like Rankin. She had won a battle she hadn't even been aware she was fighting, and the sense of victory eased the absurd hangover of loyalty she felt for a cheating ex-husband.

They sat talking and eating for what seemed like

hours, until Samantha began to shiver as the night set in. Rankin put his jacket around her. The competition between them was no longer evident – she wasn't trying to seduce him, he wasn't trying to seduce her. They were both naturally seducing each other. On equal terms. He hadn't been dominating the conversation, nor had she. The balance of power was perfect. Samantha caught herself wondering how long that could last, how long before one or the other of them got the upper hand and the battle between the sexes began again. Was happiness like this momentary or could it be indefinite? If she made a wrong move, if she showed a weakness or let him know how captivated she was, would he exploit it?

They had finished two cups of coffee each. Samantha pulled Rankin's jacket tightly around her and fell nervously silent. Rankin looked at her intently, and was quiet as well. Then he leant forward.

'I like Elvis Presley,' he said.

'Really?' Samantha asked.

'I especially like that song: "It's Now or Never".'

Samantha lit a cigarette.

'And it's now or never now, Ms Lewis.'

Samantha put her cigarette out. Rankin stood up, and she followed suit. He took her hand and led her into the bedroom. All the while Samantha was worrying about her breath. Would the nicotine mask the curry? Did two curries cancel each other out like two meals with garlic in them? Here was the third man in her life, the third man who would make love to her, and she was panicked about the thought of kissing him.

'Now make yourself comfortable on the bed. I'll be back in a jiffy.'

Rankin disappeared into what was obviously the en-suite bathroom and shut the door. This is unfair, she thought as she heard the tap start to run in the sink.

He's brushing his teeth. How could she make herself comfortable if he had brushed his teeth and she hadn't? When Rankin reappeared, Samantha, who had been sitting on the end of the bed, stood up.

'Excuse me for a second, please, John,' she said, and headed straight into the bathroom he had just vacated. There were the toothbrush and toothpaste living beside the sink. She picked up the toothbrush. Would he mind if she borrowed it? She looked at herself in the mirror. And heard Georgia's voice in her brain saying, 'Don't be an asshole. He's about to screw you. His tongue's about to be in your mouth, dummy. Other places as well, if you're lucky. Why would he care about a toothbrush?' Samantha brushed her teeth quickly, then rubbed the bristles dry with a towel. Then realized that they were wet to begin with, so turned on the tap again and ran the toothbrush under it. I'm a neurotic, she thought. I'm a nervous wreck. How can I perform in bed when I'm such a shambles?

'Just get the fuck in there,' Georgia's voice cut in again. 'Don't be so wet. Remember – it's now or never.'

Samantha came out of the bathroom to find Rankin sitting on the bed with a glass of champagne in each hand. He had changed into a white bathrobe. She took an involuntary step back.

He no longer looked like a blond Jack Nicholson. He looked like a blond Rock Hudson in a Doris Day movie, and Samantha's mind wandered. She thought of AIDS victim Rock kissing Linda Evans in *Dynasty*. She wondered whether that rumour about Rock marrying Jim Nabors in Las Vegas was true.

'Samantha.' Rankin said, 'Come back. You've gone somewhere. Where are you?'

'In Las Vegas,' replied Samantha, trying not to look at his hairy knees.

This is a bizarre, unpredictable woman, thought Rankin. There we were on the normal flightpath to bed, and she had diverted to Las Vegas.

He handed her a glass of champagne and she sat down beside him on the bed.

'Do I remind you of Doris Day?' Samantha asked.

John Rankin put his glass down on the floor, and stared at Samantha. She has a strange ability to throw me off balance, he decided, trying to think how to answer her and wondering what the hell Doris Day had to do with anything.

'I haven't thought seriously about Doris Day for a very long time, Ms Lewis. What is her connection with Las Vegas?'

'John, could you take off your bathrobe, please?'

First she wants to know whether she's like Doris Day, now she wants me to strip. Rankin undid the belt of his robe.

'I'd be delighted to.' At least I'm back on familiar territory now, he thought, taking off the bathrobe. And look here – there won't be any problems tonight.

Standing up naked, Rankin pulled Samantha up from the bed. He unfastened the buttons of her silk jacket and slipped it from her shoulders. Then the blond doctor unzipped the blonde journalist's skirt and let it fall to the floor. They stood facing each other – she in her underwear, he wearing only his wicked grin.

'Come on,' said Rankin, moving to the lightswitch and turning it off, 'let's get into bed.'

Under the duvet, Rankin pulled Samantha to him and started to kiss her. She was still wearing her bra, her underpants and her suspender belt and stockings. As his tongue delved further into her mouth, Samantha tried to loosen up, tried to disassociate her mind from her body, tried to relax.

She moved her stockinged foot up and down his bare leg. With one hand she tickled the back of his neck, with the other she reached down for his penis, found it easily and began to massage it gently. At that point they were both on their sides, facing each other. She could feel the condom he was wearing and was briefly disconcerted – did he think she'd had hundreds of partners? Would he be disappointed? Should she have asked for a cup of coffee and some iced water before they'd gotten into bed?

After a few minutes of Samantha's stroking, Rankin turned her over, pushed her underpants to the side and entered her quickly, moving up and down with some urgency.

Samantha caught on to his rhythm and began to move with him. This is like a dance, she thought with relief. All I have to do is follow his lead. And forget whether I'm being sexy or not.

Abruptly, he shifted his movement and went from side to side. She couldn't quite catch on to the shift, and felt, if there was such a thing in sex, as if she were stepping on his toes. She tried quickly to adjust her rhythm to his, but then her Janet Reger underpants got in the way. They moved to the side when he moved to the side. And she couldn't spread her legs very far apart without ripping them. What was she supposed to do about that? Hold them clear? Stop and take them off? Let them rip? Or did he like the feel of them against his penis? Could he feel them through the rubber anyway? Samantha was confused.

Rankin stopped moving altogether, and Samantha's confusion deepened. Had he had an orgasm? Was he disappointed in her? She lay, frigid, as he pulled out of her. Reaching out in the dark, he grabbed something from the bedside table. It was the bottle of champagne, she realized. Had it been so bad that he needed a drink?

She took the opportunity to slip her underpants off, but as she was deciding what to do with them, whether to toss them onto the floor or not, he was inside her again, his body pinioning both her arms beneath it. Before she understood what was happening, he pressed his lips on top of hers, and let loose with a huge mouthful of champagne. It wasn't a trickle, it was a deluge, and Samantha began to choke. Her body started to thrash, as if she were drowning, one hand trying to push him off while the other, still holding her underpants, ended up desperately clutching his balls. As she was struggling to swallow, champagne running out of the sides of her mouth, she heard him groan loudly and felt him shudder to a halt inside her.

Releasing her grip on him, struggling to breathe, and coughing all at the same time, Samantha managed to move Rankin to the side and sit up in the bed. still holding her pants.

'That was amazing, Samantha,' Rankin sighed, now lying on his back. 'I suppose I shouldn't ask where you learned to do that? It felt wonderful.'

Samantha didn't know what to say. Learned to do what? *That* was wonderful? She had almost choked to death. Men were supposed to have orgasms when they were hung, were women supposed to have them when they drowned? She certainly hadn't. And he wasn't making any moves toward her now. Was that all there was?

Eugenie saw Duncan surreptitiously look at his watch.

How Duncan had managed to sneak out out of his house that night. Eugenie neither knew nor cared. He had rung her doorbell at midnight as if the two intervening years had not existed. Neither of them spoke about their separation.

As soon as she heard the bell, Eugenie knew it was Duncan, knew that they would go up to her bedroom, knew they would make love like maniacs for an hour, and knew that Duncan would then look at his watch. It was all so predictable, and, for Eugenie, so impossible to stop.

She considered him as he retrieved his clothes from the floor. The only change in his appearance were extra lines around his eyes – but those were laugh lines, not worry lines, and as soon as she understood that he had lived without her and managed to smile, all those questions she had wanted to ask him melted away.

Intense love was like a mental disease, she decided. When she and Duncan had first found each other they were like two inmates running rampant in an asylum. They were almost literally insane about each other. But as the two years of their affair went by, she'd begun to notice a change. He was getting better. So she had made a stand, forced him to choose between Clarissa and her, hoping he was still crazy enough to choose her. He hadn't been. And now, she could tell, he had *fully* recovered. He was paying a visit to her in the madhouse, he might continue to pay visits. But he had a clean bill of mental health. If she wasn't careful, his health would make her crazier.

'How is book number two going? Will it be another bestseller?' He was sitting fully clothed now, on the side of her bed, stroking her hair.

'How much time do you have for an answer?'

He looked at his watch again.

'About fifteen minutes.'

'Duncan?' Eugenie took a deep breath and sat up in bed, not bothering to pull the sheets around her. She had the rash on her chest which always appeared after an orgasm. She reached for a cigarette from her bedside table, and Duncan lit it for her.

'What?'

'Did you read *Let Yourself Go*?'

'No. Eugenie, you of all people should know I don't read books like that. Even if they are written by the most wonderful woman in the world. I think you are absolutely amazing to have succeeded to such a degree and I'm very happy for you.'

He bent his head and began to lick her nipple. She looked down at his bald patch and willed herself not to get excited again, but it was a losing proposition. Instead she took his head in her hands and pushed it away from her.

'Had we but world enough, and time, this coyness, lady, would be no crime.' He winked. Again his head bent down, this time to the other breast.

'Duncan,' she shoved him away. 'That's the tit Vanessa got. It's still sore. By the way, does every married man in the world misquote that poem to his mistress?'

'I wouldn't know. I don't sleep with married men.' Duncan pushed the sheets away from Eugenie's body and separated her legs. Then he burrowed his head between them.

'I thought you didn't have enough time,' she moaned. And moaned, between puffs on her cigarette, some more. Until she started to sound like a dog being run over.

Georgia was awake at 1 a.m. For a moment she wondered how Samantha was getting on. Andrew had described Samantha's exit from the party, and Georgia could tell from the description that she had gone off with John Rankin. She hoped the doctor was doing well. She hoped it was Samantha's lucky night. It certainly wasn't her own.

Why had Andrew consistently showed no interest in her?

She had been amazed, leaving the party, that, despite his sprawled position next to the tramp, Andrew hadn't actually been drunk. They had seen Eugenie off in a taxi, and driven home alone at 11 p.m. Then he had disappeared into his study for an hour while Georgia got undressed, took a bath and waited for him in bed. Appearing at midnight, he stripped and climbed in beside her, but hadn't even kissed her goodnight.

Diary of a sex-starved housewife, she thought, what a lousy title for a book.

'You're cruising for a bruising, sweetheart.' Georgia addressed this to Andrew's sleeping form, then disentangled herself from him and got out of bed. Walking into the bathroom, she turned on the light and studied herself in the mirror. This is absurd, she thought. This is chronic *Woman's Own* stuff. My sense of humour needs a jump start. Don't lose it, don't be like Eugenie tonight and make a scene. Don't do what you want to do – don't shake him, wake him up and demand some attention. Just calm down. Be rational. What would a man do in the same circumstances?

That was the question Georgia's father had always asked her when she was having difficulties. What would a boy do, George? Do whatever you think a boy would do and you'll improve your position. Later on in life, it became what would a man do? Her father was a tough old committed anarchist, and she loved him. Briefly, she considered calling him. But would a man call his father to whine about lack of affection from his wife? Would a man stand staring at himself in the mirror searching for split ends? Hardly. Why *can't* a woman be more like a man? No wonder she hated that song so much. Her father wanted her to act like a man. Andrew wanted her to act like a man – all the men she loved wanted her to act like a man. But did men, in the end, fall in love with women who acted like them?

No. They fell in love with sweet young things with adoring eyes, those females who managed to feed a male ego twenty-four hours a day. But what about her ego? How long had it been since Andrew had bothered to ask her a question about herself, about how *her* psyche was? He'd asked those kinds of questions at the beginning. Maybe she should have another beginning with someone else, have an affair. That seemed to be the only time men paid attention – at the start of a romance. Perhaps she should have an affair with Rick.

Continuing to pick through her hair, Georgia discarded the notion of Rick.

'Why not?' she asked her reflection 'Why not Rick?'

'Because' she answered, reaching for the bottle of Mogadons beside the sink. 'Because it wouldn't change the fact that my husband seems to be in love with someone else, and the thought of him with that someone else is killing me.'

'John, excuse me for a second. I've just got to get a cigarette out of my bag.'

'The post-coital cigarette? You should stop smoking, Sam, but I guess you're allowed one now.'

Samantha slipped her underpants back on, went into Rankin's bathroom, found a towel and wrapped it around her, then proceeded to the living room where she had left her bag. As she searched for her Silk Cut, she decided her first reaction had been too harsh. So what if she hadn't had her first orgasm? She had built her hopes up too high. Maybe next time he would go slower, pay more attention to her, forget about the champagne. It was bound to be better.

Lighting up, Samantha caught sight of her watch and saw it was now 1 a.m. Georgia hadn't seen her leave the party with John. She might be worried. She should call her and let her know where she was staying the night. Georgia would probably still be up. Then Samantha realized that she had forgotten Georgia's number and didn't have it with her. She'd brought an evening bag to the party, not her normal one with the Filofax. She would have to look it up.

John Rankin's desk stood in the corner of the living room, a large mahogany one with many drawers. The telephone directories were flat on top of it, by the desk lamp. Samantha looked at them and thought how much nicer the London directories were, split up alphabetically, compared to the one huge, impossibly heavy yellow one for Manhattan. She went over and pulled out the pink E-K, to find Andrew Green's number.

As she opened the cover she saw a sheet of lined paper with names on it and a varying number of asterisks beside the names. She picked up the sheet. There were three more sheets underneath, all with names and asterisks.

Approximately six seconds elapsed before Samantha figured out what these papers amounted to. She examined each page carefully. There were Joannas, Carolines, Stephanies. Bindys, Susies, Sallys. Rosies, Janes, even one Athena. And, inevitably, Jilly. The highest score seemed to be a tie between a Natalie and a Charlotte, who, for their efforts, had earned four stars. Samantha found herself wishing that he'd put their last names down as well – she could call and congratulate them. Had they all been through baptism by champagne?

She stood paralyzed for the moment by the desk, every competitive intinct in her awakened. Where would she fit in on this hit parade? What kind of rating was she going to get? The war was on again, with a vengeance.

Rankin called out her name from the bedroom.

She pulled a pen out of its holder on the right of the desk.

Samantha, she wrote at the end of the list. Pausing, she debated whether to place no asterisks beside her name, or five.

She put five.

# Chapter Six

Georgia walked into her kitchen the next morning, poured herself a cup of coffee and sat down opposite Samantha at the counter.

'Sorry it didn't work out for you last night,' she said.

'How do you know? Did you hear me come in?' asked Samantha, abashed and surprised.

'No, I didn't. I don't need to know what time you got back. All I have to do is look at your eyes. If a woman's had a good fuck in the last twenty-four hours, her eyes shine in a certain way. I can tell.'

'Really?' Samantha wished she had a mirror.

'Absolutely. It's one of my many talents. I can tell when Princess Di's had a good one, Maggie Thatcher, even the Queen. Sometimes I think I should market it. Get a spot on TV AM and tell the world about famous women's sex lives.

'And sometimes I'm really naughty and I tell people at dinner parties. That always causes a stir. All the woman with shining eyes blush, all the ones without frown, and all the men look really self-conscious.'

Georgia was wearing Andrew's plaid dressing gown with the sleeves rolled up. Her face was a little groggy with the after-effect of the Mogadon and she was cradling her mug of coffee close to her with both hands.

Samantha looked at Georgia's eyes. There was no hint of a sparkle. Georgia, aware of the scrutiny, frowned and shook her head.

'Me neither. So what happened with the doc? Does he whisper medical terms while he's going at it and shout "Cystitis!" when he comes? That would be enough to put even me off.'

'He was, I mean, we did but I don't know, it wasn't, you know – I didn't –'

'Samantha, take a deep breath and please translate that for me.'

Samantha did breathe deeply. She was still getting used to talking about sex.

'I mean we went to bed but nothing special happened – you know, the earth didn't move or whatever they say.'

'They say orgasm, sweetheart.'

'Right. Anyway, then I found a list he had of all the women he had ever slept with and that did it. I just got dressed and walked out and he kept asking me why, but I wouldn't say anything and he had a horrible bathrobe and I think he's a jerk.'

The doorbell rang, but Georgia didn't move.

'Andrew can get that. This is too much. He has a *list*?'

'Yes, it's pages long and it's hidden in the telephone directory. It has stars rating the women. I couldn't believe it. Anyway, I added my name to the end and gave it the highest rating then put it back where I found it.'

Georgia took an elastic band off her wrist and pulled her mass of scrunched hair into a pony tail.

'Whew. Ratings and all. The Egon Ronay of the bedroom. Did he have them divided geographically as well?'

Before Samantha could answer, Andrew came into the kitchen with an armful of white tulips and handed them over to her.

'These are for you. It seems you have an admirer.'

As Samantha opened the paper wrapped around the

tulips and took out a card, Andrew studied her eyes. Georgia had told him about women's eyes and sex ages ago, but he'd never bothered to look before. Now he was relieved to see that Samantha's eyes seemed normal. Occasionally Georgia's little insights came in handy.

'Andrew, could you leave us alone, please? Sam and I were in the middle of a serious discussion.'

'Nuclear disarmament? Your upcoming trip to Greenham Common? Of course, I wouldn't dream of interrupting. I was just the delivery boy.' He poured himself a cup of coffee and left.

'Oh, God, they're from John,' Samantha groaned. 'He wants to thank me for a delicious evening. And he wants to see me again. I don't want to see him. I just want to forget about the whole thing.' Samantha threw the flowers down on the counter.

'Well, sweetheart, if the world's most handsome gynaecologist isn't that hot in bed and he's dumb enough not to keep that list under lock and key, I'd say that you *should* forget about him. He'll chase you like crazy, though. Be prepared. He's probably not used to women walking out on him.'

'No, he's probably not. You know what bothers me the most? He's so predictable. If I had stayed, I would have become just one more name for the list. He wouldn't have sent flowers, he'd be busy right now calling another woman. Where can I throw these things away?'

'Hey – don't look a gift-horse gynaecologist in the mouth. I love tulips. Let's put them in water, then I'm going to do some work. *Then* I'll call Eugenie and we three can have lunch.' Georgia stood up. 'I have a problem and you two might be able to help.'

Samantha watched as Georgia stuffed the tulips in a teapot. Typical Georgia not to have a vase. Untypical Georgia to need help with a problem. Rankin's card lay in front of her on the counter. 'Thank you for a delicious evening,' it said. 'But you left me feeling voracious. When and where can we continue? I'll ring today.'

'Nice try, sunshine,' she murmured to herself, picking up the card and stuffing it in her pocket. 'But you're history.'

Clarissa Darrell walked down to her kitchen in her tracksuit to make her first cup of tea for the morning. There, gathered around a portable colour television at the breakfast table, sat her nanny and housekeeper, watching the American soap opera *Santa Barbara*. She was about to ask them if they had nothing better to do, when she saw a male figure on the screen, a young man wearing tight jeans and a work shirt. She forgot her tea and sat down beside them.

'Who's he?'

'That's Brick,' the nanny answered, amazed that Mrs Darrell had joined them. She had been working there for four months and this was the first question not directly related to little Rupert Mrs Darrell had asked. The change in routine gave her some courage. 'Isn't he dishy? He's the chauffeur for an old lady named Minx and Minx has some secret plan for him, but nobody knows what it is. Meanwhile he's falling in love with Amy, Joe's sister. But I don't think Amy's pretty enough for him.'

'Brick,' Clarissa smirked, not taking her eyes off him. 'Who would name a child Brick? It's too ridiculous.' Still, she thought, he's really quite attractive. He looks a little like that man last night, Rick. I wonder if Rick knows Brick. She smiled, then stood up as Brick's scene ended.

'Can I get you a cup of tea, Mrs Darrell?'

'Yes, please. And could you bring it up to my bedroom?' She had to admit she'd enjoyed herself at the end of the party. Women attacking other women's breasts was common and undignified, but it was quite exciting entertainment. And there was something else she had enjoyed immensely about last night. What was it? Something that was eluding her. A dream – that was it. A dream featuring Richard Holland performing underwater sexual acts on her in a hot tub. Clarissa reddened at the memory and turned away from her staff, walking quickly upstairs.

How old was Rick Holland? He couldn't be *that* much younger than she, could he? It must be quite glamorous to live in Hollywood. To make mini series.

Clarissa found herself going past her bedroom, up the stairs and into the nanny's room. Her hunch had been right. There, on the second row of the bookshelf was a paperback copy of *Let Yourself Go*. Clarissa took it back to her bedroom, peeled off her tracksuit, got under the covers and began to read.

Eugenie, sitting beside Samantha and across from Georgia at the Ho Sai Gai restaurant in Soho, considered what Georgia had just said. The table was silent as she drank a half a glass of Perrier. She wanted a little time, but they were waiting for her reaction.

'So who's the lucky girl?' she finally asked.

'I don't know. I can't even explain how I know he's in love with someone else, I just do.' Georgia attempted to spear a dumpling on the plate with her chopsticks, but it slithered away.

'Perhaps he's just "in lust",' Eugenie put down her chopsticks and put her hand on Georgia's arm. 'Tell me honestly, would you mind if he had a fling, just a fling, mind you, not a full-blown affair?' Eugenie, Samantha noticed, asked this in a calm, matter-of-fact tone. Her knees nudged Samantha under the table and Samantha returned the pressure.

'Yes, I'd mind. I'd mind a lot.' Georgia was working

herself up. Her hands were clenched on the table, but her head was bouncing from side to side like a boxer's.

'Why should he have fun with some other woman – why can't he have fun with me? And what if it starts out as a one-off fling, but they have so much fun it develops into an affair? And I'm buying new dresses and tarting myself up and maybe even trying to cook for him while he's telling her in bed how desperate I'm getting and how I don't understand him. Yes, I'd mind.'

'Georgia, don't forget, you're speaking to the "other woman". It's no fun for her either, let me tell you.'

Eugenie's deep voice was soothing, but Georgia wasn't in the mood to be placated.

'No fun for the other woman? Bullshit, Eugenie. That's bullshit. The other woman gets to play the interesting, sympathetic soulmate who is such a relief from the dragon wife. *And* she gets good sex. Don't pretend otherwise. I can see *your* shining eyes today.'

Samantha was torn. She sympathized with Georgia, she knew how she must feel. Hearing Georgia was like listening to a tape of her own unspoken thoughts not so long ago. But Georgia had no right to take it out on Eugenie. Eugenie wasn't to blame. Eugenie was just a woman – they were all just women trying to figure out an impossible puzzle – men.

'George, sex is not what it's about. It may be for the man, yes. A new piece of crumpet, or –' Eugenie looked down at her plate, 'a dumpling. But women don't get involved with men for sex – they should, but they don't. They want much more.'

'What *do* women want?' Samantha wanted to know. She also wanted to divert the conversation, to stop Georgia from escalating her argument with Eugenie.

Eugenie and Georgia exchanged a look and a short, sharp smile.

'Your turn to answer that question, Eugenie,' said Georgia.

The three had given up any pretence of eating. So had the table of businessmen positioned beside them. Four men who had gone out for a working lunch abandoned talks of property deals and were riveted by the conversation. Eugenie, Georgia and Samantha carried on oblivious.

'Women want to be preferred.'

'Eugenie,' Georgia picked up her chopsticks and pointed them at her friend. 'For a best-selling authoress who is supposed to appeal to the lowest common denominator, you talk a lot of pretentious crap sometimes. Women want to be *preferred*? What is that supposed to mean?'

'Men just want to be men, but women want to be perfect. The perfect girlfriend, the perfect wife, the perfect mother, the perfect person who can't be lived without. They want to be so perfect that they are preferable to anyone else. Irreplaceable.' Eugenie shrugged as she said the last word.

Georgia slumped back in her chair. She looked old, tired, sad. That's what happens, Samantha thought, women who are on the defensive begin to look like presidents in the second term of office – they age dramatically before your eyes.

'Irreplaceable? I'm not so sure, Eugenie. You know, my father once told me that women were like market forces – unpredictable, ultimately powerful, and capable of bringing out all the baser instincts of men.' Georgia stopped speaking and was quiet for a moment. Then her face relaxed and she smiled, the first real smile Samantha had seen all day.

'He also told me that he married my mother because she was so easy to undress.'

'Is she still?' Samantha asked.

'I wouldn't know – she ran off with an insurance broker when I was five. My father said he knew there was trouble brewing when she began to come home wearing dresses covered in buttons and zips and hooks. He's kind of a clumsy guy. It would take him hours to get them off. He figured she was trying to tell him something. I guess he was right. Anyway –' she had sat up straight again, and her head had stopped bobbing.

'My father and mother are beside the point. What the fuck am I supposed to do about Andrew and this low life, whoever she is? He obviously prefers *her*. I bet she's five foot ten tall and wears short skirts.'

'Georgia – you're what? Five foot seven? Hardly short. And would you please look under the table and see what little there is of *your* denim skirt.'

'All right. So she's a brazen hussy.'

Eugenie grinned. 'And you're not?'

'Well, I might be brazen, but I am not a hussy. This may come as news to you, but I haven't ever cheated on Andrew.'

'Whoever she is, she's probably not married. Are you telling me you never had a fling with a married man before you became Mrs Green?'

'OK, OK, Eugenie. If you're trying to tell me that she might be a decent human being like you and me and Sam, forget it. I bet she's eighteen years old. When I turned thirty I decided that there's not an eighteen-year-old girl in the world who is a decent human being.'

Eugenie put up her hands in a gesture of surrender. Georgia pressed her point.

'For all I know she's a dwarf who wears Elizabethan costumes and never swears and wouldn't dream of having oral sex. But it doesn't matter because she's *eighteen* years old. And there is absolutely nothing I can do about that, is there?'

'I think you're overreacting a little, George,' Samantha said.

'Am I? I like sex, I'm funny. I make money. What

139

reason could he have for falling for someone else? Age. I wish Michael Jackson and Cher would set up a plastic surgery place – like the Betty Ford Clinic. I could meet famous people while I was having my face lifted. Christ – why do men have to fuck younger women when they get old? It's so unfair.'

'Well –' Eugenie nudged Samantha under the table again and Samantha felt that she was just beginning to understand friendship between women. It was a lot more complicated than she had ever imagined.

'There is no point in whinging on about men and their egos and appetites. Let's take that as read. What you need is some practical advice. If Andrew has fallen in love with someone else, there's not a damn thing you can do about it.'

'Thanks a lot, Eugenie. That's terrific advice. That's just what I need to hear. Maybe the guy who did my tits can do my face too. Maybe I'll get a discount for having had two operations.'

'Belt up, George. What I mean is, there's nothing you can do about *him*. Men with sex on the brain are on a roller-coaster ride. They can't get off until it stops. But you *can* do something about the woman.'

'What? I don't even know who the jailbait is.'

'Find out.'

'Great. Hire a private detective? Put on sunglasses and hide behind pillars? And what if I do find her? What do I say? "I'm frightfully sorry, but if you don't lay off my husband I'll kneecap you"? That's just great.'

'Hey,' Georgia continued, looking down at the tablecloth. 'Do you think it's possible to commit hara-kiri with chopsticks?'

'Georgia, you can be a real trial at times,' Eugenie grimaced. 'Will you please listen to me? I don't care how you find her, just find her. And then make friends with her. Without letting her know you know, you make friends. Invite her to lunch. She'll be too curious not to come. Then be unbelievably charming – she'll get a heavy case of the guilts.

'The next step is to talk her through how you and Andrew first got together and how romantic he was – men are really creatures of habit, they repeat themselves. Chances are he will have said and done the same things with her as he did with you and she'll feel miserable. Like second-hand clothes.

'*Then* you let it slip how wonderful a time you have in bed together. You can be very offhand about that. When she goes to bed with him afterwards, she'll be thinking about you the entire time. Even if she suspects you, even if she's clever enough to think you might be doing this to put her off, she won't be sure. The doubt will be corrosive. She'll wonder if he does the same things to her as he does to you. And she'll begin to resent the fact that he's still sleeping with you.'

'He isn't.'

Eugenie's face assumed an air of angelic sweetness.

'So lie a little.'


John Rankin picked up the telephone on his desk and dialled Georgia's number.

'May I please speak to Samantha Lewis?'

'She's not available.' Too true, Andrew thought, sitting in his swivel chair. Too true, mate.

'Oh, I see. Perhaps you could help me. I sent her some flowers this morning. Do you know by any chance if they have arrived?'

'Yes.'

'Yes they have?' This man was tiresome, Rankin thought. A pain in the backside.

'All present and accounted for. Two dozen white tulips are drooping their weary heads downstairs.'

'Could you leave a message for her? Would you tell

her I called and ask her to ring me? John. She has my number.'

'Fine,' Andrew said and put down the phone. I've got your number too, smoothychops. You're as shallow as glass.

Rankin, as he hung up, buzzed for Miss Merton. In she came, wearing the tweed jacket and skirt which was her uniform, summer and winter.

'Would you arrange to have a bottle of Louis Roderer Cristal sent to Ms Samantha Lewis – the same address as the one you found in the files this morning.'

Miss Merton nodded, and left.

Rankin was left alone again, wondering. Why had Samantha departed so abruptly last night? Hadn't he performed well in bed? Of course he had. He always did – when he got it up. Women had told him so. And they wouldn't lie, would they?

Yes, they would. They lied to men all the time about orgasms – he knew that. Plenty of his patients had felt the need to tell him that. But his ladyfriends wouldn't lie to him. Why would they lie and keep coming back if they weren't satisfied? QED. Of course they were satisfied.

He took a comb from his back pocket and ran it through his hair.

All right, perhaps he had been a bit selfish with Samantha the first time around – he had been so pleased to get it up that he'd rushed things a little. He couldn't exactly explain that to her, now, could he? And he would have made up for it. There wouldn't have been a problem if she hadn't walked out.

Well, if she didn't respond to the flowers and the champagne, he'd simply wait. He would play it cool, distant. She'd come running to him. They always fell for the mysterious, aloof figure. It couldn't possibly matter that this time he didn't feel particulary cool or aloof, that he was feeling twitchy and unusually sensitive.

Rankin paused and looked at his comb. There were hairs, but not too many. It wasn't falling out. He would take a full head of hair with him to his grave. But his mother's brother was bald. Baldness was hereditary and it passed through the mothers' genes. He physically shook off the thought as a dog shakes off water after a swim.

He would call Samantha's bluff, if he had to, and she would lay all her cards on the table for him. Nothing could be simpler.

'God, the effort involved in all this. I have to find this sap, make friends with her, invent stories about my fascinating sex life, probably even pay for lunch. Is it worth it? Are men really worth all this plotting and scheming?'

'Come on, George. Of course they're not worth it. But you have to admit, it keeps things interesting,' Eugenie said.

'That's true.' Georgia nodded.

'I don't understand.' Samantha had the sensation of a deep-sea diver who had gotten lost and didn't know which way was up. 'Is the whole male-female thing a game to keep everyone from being bored? Everyone's so busy with strategies, scoring points. But is there anything at stake? I mean, is there such a thing as true love?'

'Oh, Sam.' Eugenie's and Georgia's voices were full of pity.

'You're such an innocent,' Georgia added quietly.

'I am not. I am *not* an innocent. I just want to know, that's all. Is there something wrong with that?'

'No. Of course not. But don't ask a woman that question. Even old cynical ones like George and me. We pretend there's no such thing as true love, but we believe in it like fanatics. We're not above using guerilla tactics to keep the illusion going because sometimes that's the only way. The person you should ask is a man. Men are the deeply devious ones on this issue.'

'I object to that.' The man whose seat was closest to Eugenie's at the neighbouring table was unable to contain himself any longer. He turned in his chair and faced her head-on. 'You're talking a load of rubbish.'

'And you're listening,' Eugenie shot back. 'You're not supposed to listen in on other people's conversations.'

'Jack, come on. We've paid the bill, let's go.' The three other men were laughing quietly and looking sheepish, as if they had been boys caught looking up a woman's dress.

'Pardon me. But these ladies are discussing men, they're criticising men, and here they have four men at the next table who can set them straight.' He took off his tortoiseshell glasses and rubbed the lenses with his handkerchief, then put them on the table and rubbed his jaw.

'If you ladies are interested, as you seem to be, I'll tell you all about true love. True love is knowing exactly how to keep your partner happy, through the good times and the bad. I don't know how a man keeps a woman happy because you're such a confused, insatiable sex, but I know exactly how a woman can keep a man happy, and it's easy. Much easier than making friends with his mistress.'

'By all means, please, enlighten us.' Eugenie gave what amounted to a royal wave in his direction.

Jack leant forward. 'First you tell him that he is, without a doubt, the best sexual partner in the universe. Then you stop complaining. You don't tell him that he has put on weight or that he spends too much time at the office, or that he doesn't pay enough attention to you. You don't utter a single word of complaint.' He replaced his glasses and smiled at Georgia.

144

'No shit, Sherlock.' Georgia gave him a mock smile back. 'And does that stop him from having an affair?'

'It won't stop him. Your friend here was right about that,' he glanced at Eugenie – she acknowledged it with a nod.

'But his mistress will start to complain. She'll complain about how little time they have together, how she can't call him at home, how he's never around when she needs him. She'll turn into a nagging wife and he'll be relieved to scamper back home.'

'Well, Jack,' Eugenie looked pointedly at the wedding ring on his left hand, 'I can see you know whereof you speak. How's the little woman these days? No complaints?'

'Not one. She knows that if she behaves herself and looks after me, I may stray, but I'll always come back.'

The three women sat staring.

'That's true love?' asked Samantha.

'As it happens,' he continued, ignoring her question, shrugging his shoulders and pursing his lips. 'I've come up from Bristol today. If one, or indeed, if all of you lovely ladies would like to keep me company tonight, I can teach you all about the ins and outs of keeping a man happy.' He gave a sly sideways look at the women and pursed his lips again.

If there was ever a moment when three people knew exactly what each other was thinking, this was it. Samantha, Georgia and Eugenie stood up in unison.

'I'm sorry Jack,' Georgia began.

'It's frightfully nice of you,' said Eugenie.

'But I think we're all going to throw up,' finished Samantha, and the three made a beeline for the ladies' room.

'No wonder you have problems with men.' Jack's face had turned explosive. He was shouting at their retreating backs. 'I think you're a bunch of lesbians.'

'Oh, God I wish we were.' Georgia's shoulders were

shaking with laughter as she leant up against the sink. 'Just think, if we were lesbians we could have one-off nights of passion and not worry about birth control or diseases or hairy hands like that King Kong had in there.'

'We could make lists of all the girls we had slept with,' Samantha put in. For the first time in her life, she pulled out her lipstick and began to apply a second layer of red in front of the mirror.

'And lesbians don't usually get married, do they? We wouldn't have to worry about being wives or mistresses. It may be the answer.' Eugenie's voice came from behind the loo door.

'There's only one problem,.' Georgia washed her hands and pressed the blower to dry them.

'What?'

'We'd have to kiss other women.'

# Chapter Seven

Sitting in the Chamber of the House of Commons at Prime Minister's Question Time, Duncan Darrell wore his 'interested and serious' look. Maggie was detailing her schedule for the next day. Duncan was planning his sex life for the next year. That would be as long as he could stretch his period of grace with Eugenie, he reckoned. One year gratis – she wouldn't ask him to leave Clarissa, she wouldn't make any non-negotiable demands. They could spend a year rediscovering each other before she began to get anxious again.

He'd had a narrow escape when he'd first started up with her. There had been affairs before, of course, but none so all-consuming or passionate. He had almost sacrificed his family, his career, everything for that deep voice and that perfect body. But he had soon recognized his obsession for what it was – a mid-life crisis. Eugenie was charming, intelligent, sexy, fun. But she wasn't, well, to put it bluntly – she wasn't his class. Or Clarissa's for that matter. That book. Clarissa wouldn't be caught dead reading that book, much less writing it. Class would always be a crucial factor in the English equation – Joan or Jackie Collins might well become stars, but they would never be ladies.

'Is the Prime Minister aware of the unemployment rate in Grimsby?'

Here we go, thought Duncan, a Labour member banging on about the poor again. What a waste of time. I won't waste any of my time with Eugenie. I'll take advantage of my year. I'll have the time of my life.

The Labour backbencher was winding up his speech.

'The Prime Minister wants to have her cake and eat it too.'

There were cheers from the Labour side of the Chamber, hisses from the Conservative. One of Duncan's colleagues leant over and whispered to him.

'I say, old man. I never have understood. What's the point of having the bloody cake if you can't eat it too?'

Duncan laughed. The lines around his dark eyes crinkled. He thought he had never heard a truer phrase spoken.


Samantha sat back in the taxi and contemplated her immediate future. She had finished her article, faxed it to New York and was at the end of her two-week break. She could leave now, go back to her apartment and resume her normal life. Or. Or she could stay a while longer – she didn't feel guilty about imposing on Georgia as long as she bought food, cooked and helped around the house. She wanted to stay, she had to admit that. She was actually having fun. But was it fair on George and Andrew if their marriage was in trouble? Maybe she could help. Maybe she could talk to Andrew, make him realize what an amazing woman he was married to. And maybe, just maybe, Georgia needed her around, just as she had, for some inexplicable reason, needed Georgia.

Besides – as the taxi drew up to Georgia's house, she searched in her pockets for change and felt Rankin's card still there – if she were to be brutally honest with herself, she had unfinished business to complete. John Rankin. Despite the flowers, despite the card, she felt at a disadvantage. Because she had reacted according to pattern: she had gotten emotionally involved and done exactly what she had done with David – walked out of a painful scene. She had been hurt and she'd run away. What she hadn't done was to rise above her emotions, to use him as he had used her. What had attracted him to her in the first place? Her blatant attempt to have a one-off fling with him in his rooms for a bet. He'd been drawn to what was a masculine exercise of power. And then, seeing those names, she had turned into a wimpish little girl again. She had bought his seduction scene hook, line and sinker; she had believed she was the one who made a difference. Until she had seen those names. Then she had bolted.

Now she wanted him to chase her like crazy, she wanted him at her feet, begging. So she could step on his face. Who cared about true love, if there was such a thing? She was in a battle and she wanted to win.

Hit by the force of her own anger, Samantha sat down on the steps outside Georgia's house and lit a cigarette. What was she turning into? What had all the clothes and the makeup and the talks with Georgia and Eugenie done to her? Turned her into an avenging she-devil? She was back to square one – trying to make John Rankin know what it felt like to be used by someone. It was a crazy plan the first time round, and even crazier now that she knew him. John Rankin would never know the meaning of the word used. He was a man born to use.

She threw the cigarette on the pavement and grabbed her ankles, hugging them close to her. She could feel the stubble growing back on her legs. Soon it would be time for another waxing session, time for another sunbed. Time to stop chewing over her problems and just get on with life. Play it by ear when Rankin called, be spontaneous.

Standing up, Samantha suddenly smiled. Oh my

God, she thought, I'm even plotting to be spontaneous. There's no end to the games. But Eugenie's right. It's not boring.

Andrew was ensconced in the sitting room when Samantha entered, lounging on the armchair, reading the *Independent*, a bottle of champagne and a half-full glass at his side.

'Samantha,' he called to her as she passed by. 'Come in and join me. What a nice surprise. I thought you were Georgia.'

'Georgia's having tea with Rick.' Samantha stood in the doorway. 'I just have to check what's in the fridge for supper. I'll be right back.' This could be it, Samantha realized as she walked into the kitchen. Maybe I can talk some sense into him. I'll have to be careful, though. He's an awfully prickly man.

Andrew stood up as she returned and held out a glass of champagne.

'Louis Roderer Cristal. I hope you like it – it's the best.'

'Gosh.' Samantha took a sip and sat down. 'It's wonderful. This is really nice of you. It's incredibly expensive, isn't it?'

'Yes, well, it fell into my lap, so to speak.' He reached over and clinked Samantha's glass. 'Cheers.'

'Cheers. Andrew – I'm kind of expecting a call. Did anyone leave a message for me?'

'Let me think.' Andrew paused. Samantha waited.

'No.'

'Oh.'

'I'm glad we have this chance to be alone, Samantha. We've never really had a proper conversation, have we? It's impossible to have a proper conversation when Georgia's around.'

'I don't think that's fair, Andrew. Georgia's one of the funniest women I know.'

'Exactly,' Andrew snorted.

'And one of the most attractive and most intelligent.' Aware that she shounded like a PR lady, Samantha stopped there.

Rising from the armchair, Andrew went over and sat beside her on the sofa. He took her hand in his.

'Please, Samantha, don't tell me you're one of her little acolytes, sitting around making jokes and talking about men as if were a species you had just discovered in New Guinea. You're above all that, you're –'

'I'm her friend.' Samantha withdrew her hand 'And I have to say that I think you should be her friend too. I know she loves you. Doesn't that count for you?'

'What would you say if I told you I'm in love with someone else. Doesn't that count?'

'Oh, Andrew –' Samantha tried to sound surprised. 'Do you have a cigarette?' Andrew fished in his jacket pocket and offered her one, then lit it. Samantha wondered how she had ever survived without smoking. Perhaps because she hadn't often found herself talking to the husband of a friend about his passion for another woman. Had everyone's life always been this complicated? The complications in her life had taken quantum leaps since she had discovered David in bed with the model.

'Yes, of course it counts. Love always counts. If it *is* love. But is this woman in love with you?'

Andrew turned his head away and looked at the fireplace.

'I don't know.' He turned back and stared at her. He wasn't sure of the best way to approach her, chose a line from his book of romantic quotes, then wondered whether John Donne would be wasted on her. She was, after all, an American. But then her pale blue eyes crippled him again and he fumbled his assurance. 'Could anyone be in love with me? Could you be in love with me?'

'Andrew –' Samantha wanted to giggle, then, looking at his expression, smothered the impulse. 'Andrew, I've just told you that Georgia loves you. Whether I could love you or not is beside the point.'

'It might –'

'OK, it might mean that this other woman could love you,' she interrupted. 'Maybe anybody could love anybody, given the right circumstances. Maybe Neil Kinnock could fall for Maggie Thatcher if they were stranded on a desert island together –'

'Is that what you're saying it would take for you to fall in love with me? Being stranded somewhere where there wasn't even the possibility of another male? That's comforting news.'

'I didn't mean it that way. Come on. This is ridiculous. If you're infatuated with someone else and she isn't with you, I suppose she's twice as desirable because she's unattainable.' Samantha, even in the midst of what she recognized was a crucial conversation, couldn't help but notice the time and the fact that the phone hadn't rung. How could she be spontaneous if Rankin didn't even call. 'God, men are hopeless,' she muttered.

'I suppose we are. I suppose I am. Hopeless.' She had slayed him with that remark about the desert island. Evidently she didn't take him seriously. No one took him seriously. What did he have to do to be taken seriously? Be Martin Amis and write books about the danger of nuclear weapons? That had been done. The Contras had been done. The Israelis. The Palestinians. The Ethiopians. They had all been done.

Andrew rubbed his eyelids with his thumb and forefinger. Samantha was starting to believe he had a penchant for the melodramatic.

'Honestly, Andrew, I don't mean to be unsympathetic. I'm sure what you're going through is difficult. But if you've gone haywire over some young bimbo and she's not even reciprocating, I think you should consider how lucky you are to have Georgia. Maybe you should try to remember how much you loved her in the first place.'

'You sound like an agony aunt. You should know life isn't as simple as that. And what if the young bimbo, as you call her, is not *that* young and is definitely not a bimbo. What if she's –' Andrew hesitated, scanning Samantha's face and seeing only a blank. He was toeing the line, but he couldn't quite bring himself to cross it. 'What if she's somebody like you?'

'What *are* you talking about?' Samantha was now genuinely surprised. 'Are you trying to tell me she's a friend of Georgia's?'

'Yes. She's a friend of Georgia's. A very good friend.' Briefly, Andrew wished he wasn't an Englishman. He wished he could fall on his knees in front of Samantha and confess. But this was as close as he could come. He couldn't even look at her as he waited for the realization to sink in. Instead he filled his champagne glass and stood up, pretending to study the piece of junk Georgia had insisted on bringing over with her from New York – a model of a small stage with little statuettes of the American presidents standing on it in different poses. Many of them were decapitated.

'Andrew,' Samantha softened her voice. 'I'm sorry, but in that case, you *are* in a hopeless position. I don't think any good friend of Georgia's would even begin to think about having an affair with her husband. I know Georgia doesn't believe in female solidarity. Neither do I, really. But one thing I've learned here is that friendship, good friendship like mine and Georgia's for example, has become irreplaceable. I know I wouldn't endanger it for the world. I don't think any one of Georgia's friends would. I'm sorry, but I think you should forget about the whole thing.'

Andrew continued to stare at the presidents, his back toward Samantha.

'I think I better go put the supper on. Andrew –' Samantha stood up, went over and put her hand on the back of his shoulder. 'I'm sure everything will work out with you and Georgia. Honestly. Maybe you've fallen for one of her friends because she reminds you of George, really. That happens sometimes. It's just misplaced emotion. Think about that.'

Samantha left the room, but didn't do anything about the supper. Instead she sat at the kitchen counter, feeling drained and stupefied.

'It's unbelievable.' She was talking out loud. 'It's absolutely unbelievable.'

She couldn't tell Georgia – it would ruin everything. She couldn't tell anybody. She could only hope that Andrew kept his mouth shut and the whole thing died a natural death.

Who would have believed it? Andrew Green in love with Eugenie Woodrow.

'Sweetie pie, what's the worst possible scenario on this one?' Rick Holland sat in the Palm Court at the Waldorf Hotel, picked up a cucumber sandwich and immediately put it down again. 'No wonder the people in this country look so miserable – are they really expected to eat these things? I wouldn't feed it to a rat. Seriously, honey, what's *your* rat? What is your worst fear?'

'I don't know. I guess the worst would be if he ran off with her.' Georgia now recognized that she was obsessed. Lunch with Eugenie and Samantha had helped, but she had told Rick about Andrew as soon as she sat down. She couldn't stop herself. On the taxi ride to the Waldorf, she had just managed to resist the urge to blurt out the story to the driver.

'Right. He runs off with her and you're miserable, depressed, suicidal. Your friends gather round you and tell you what a shit he is, what a shit he always was but they never had the guts to tell you before, and you're a little more upbeat after that. But then they get tired of talking about it and since you can't talk about anything else, they begin to avoid you. You get depressed, miserable, suicidal again. That's the bootom line, darling. I've seen it all before and that's as bad as it gets. So cheer up. Let's dance.'

The Palm Court was also the scene of a *thé dansant*, the most civilized of afternoon activities in a metropolitan hotel. A myriad group of couples was swirling around the small dance floor. As Georgia put her hand on Rick's shoulder and waited to be guided, the band was playing, 'They Can't Take That Away From Me.' Rick took her hand firmly in his and started off on a two-step. Forgetting Andrew, forgetting everything but the music, Georgia followed his lead and found herself floating. His loping gait translated, on the dance floor, into a smooth, self-assured glide.

The tune changed into 'A Fine Romance', then 'Isn't It A Lovely Day to be Caught in the Rain?' They turned and twirled and Georgia wished that she could stay there dancing forever, pretending she was Ginger Rogers in a denim mini-skirt. But the band needed a break.

'I never knew you could dance like that.' Georgia was flushed and happy, as they returned to their table.

'There is no mastery without ease, sweetheart. That's the key to dancing, the key to life.'

'Are you that good in bed too? Can we have an affair?'

'We've just had one.'

Georgia smiled at him. He's right, she thought. And that was better than sex.

'There you go, you're smiling again. You see,

darling, you can agonize over all your problems and get nowhere, or you can have some fun. I'm sure shrinks help with depression, but so do good times. If you're asking my advice about Andrew, I'd say you should face the problem squarely and do what any sane person would – get the hell out.'

Next week I'm going to St Lucia to check out the shooting of those opening scenes in *Let Yourself Go* and I think you should come too. You and that dumb husband of yours.'

'That's not a bad idea. Maybe if he's away from the object of his affections for a while he'll forget about her. Maybe he'll have some good times with me under the palm trees. You're brilliant, Ricky.'

Rick shrugged. His eyebrow arched.

'Nothing to it. But if you're going to enjoy yourself, so should I. Get your friend and mine, Miss Supreme Authoress to come along. I'd like to do a feasibility study on her while we're there.'

'Oh, Rick, do you really fancy Eugenie?'

'Let me put it this way, she's not my type.'

Georgia thought about this for a minute.

'You mean you could get serious about her?'

'I mean I could get funny about her.'

The band started up again with 'You're Easy To Dance With'. Rick stood and bowed to Georgia. She stood and curtsied.

'OK, babycakes, let's show them how the pros do it.'

156

# Chapter Eight

It was Samantha's job to make the flight reservations to St Lucia. As she dialled, with the Fodor Guide to the Caribbean in front of her, she hesitated. Was it such a good idea, this trip, or would it end in tears? Georgia had pressed her to join the party, to accompany her, Andrew, Eugenie and Rick, and Samantha had let herself be convinced. She wanted, for one, to keep an eye on Andrew while Eugenie was around. How could she suggest to Georgia that Eugenie's presence was not necessary without giving the game away? And if Georgia knew that Eugenie was the 'other woman', even unwittingly, Samantha felt sure that their friendship would unravel. Eugenie would be in a no-win position. If she had to explain to Georgia all the reasons why she had no interest in Andrew, Georgia would take it as an insult. If she said she *did* like Andrew, but not enough to have an affair with him, Georgia would still see her as a threat. No woman can be happy about her husband fancying her best friend. It was too close for comfort. Samantha felt like Fawn Hall hiding secret papers in her shoes to protect Ollie North. She would do everything possible to keep Andrew's infatuation under cover.

Also, Samantha wanted to get away from the spectre of John Rankin. He hadn't called the day afer the Fourth of July party, or the day after that and she had felt depressed and immensely angry with herself for caring. He had robbed her of the chance to get even, to behave like a cool, unfazed whatever-will-be-will-be character. To behave like him.

'He might be really busy, Sam,' Georgia had suggested, 'He might be delivering quintuplets.'

'That doesn't take two days,' she had replied.

'No. But what seems like forever for a woman waiting for a phone call, can seem like seconds to a busy working man.'

'He said he would call, and he didn't. That's the end of it as far as I'm concerned.'

'Maybe he's playing hard to get. You know, the remote, distant character.'

'Georgia, men don't have to play those kind of games. Especially a man like him. Even if he were, what am I supposed to do? Call him up and flatter that huge ego more? "When can we do it again, John? I'm just dying to be drowned in champagne." No way. I've chalked it up as an interesting experience. It was good for me – I haven't made enough mistakes like that. If I had maybe I wouldn't have made the awesome mistake of marrying David.'

'What should I do if he does ring?'

'Tell him I'm out. And ask Andrew to say that too.'

A few days later John Rankin did ring. And once he had started, he didn't stop. He rang continually; but Georgia, who had misgivings, and Andrew, who didn't, followed Samantha's instructions. She was out.

'Are you sure you don't want to relent?' asked Georgia, after another call. 'I feel a little sorry for him. Even if he does keep a list. I mean, all men probably keep lists, even if they are only mental ones. And you know something? I think women do too. Maybe his mother died those first few days. Maybe *he* had a heart attack and now he wants you by his bedside.'

'George – you're impossibly inconsistent. First you say to go for him, then you say not to, then you change your mind again. Why don't you let me handle this my way?'

'All right. OK, I admit I'm swayed a little by those devastating looks of his. But go ahead, do it your way. Did you ever hear Sid Vicious do his rendition of "My Way"?'

'No. Was it good?'

'It was different. But I hate to think about what kind of lists *he* made in his short time on earth.'

Samantha completed her call to the airlines and booked First Class seats for herself, Andrew, Eugenie and Georgia. Rick had already made his reservation on the same flight. As soon as she put the phone down it rang again, and she answered it automatically.

'Ms Lewis. You're in, finally. I was beginning to think you were avoiding me.'

'Mr Rankin. How did you know it was me?'

'You have a distinctive way of saying hello. And I've also spoken to your friend enough times to know her voice. You've been a busy girl, haven't you?'

'Yes.' Samantha picked a cigarette out of its pack, lit it and inhaled.

'I heard that, Samantha. You should stop smoking.'

It wasn't any of his business whether she smoked or not, Samantha thought, irked by his proprietorial tone. She didn't say anything and there was a strained silence across the wires.

'I just rang to see how you are,' Rankin continued. She was, he decided, the most difficult woman he had ever met. She hadn't thanked him for the flowers or the champagne, she hadn't even returned his calls after he had realized that playing the mystery man wasn't working. Had their evening together meant nothing to her? It had meant a lot to him, more than he liked to contemplate. One takeaway curry on the balcony, one brief physical encounter and he had become hooked. His interest in other women had waned to the point where he had almost given up looking at anyone else. And he felt it impossible to believe that the earthquake which had rocked his emotions hadn't even touched her.

'I'm fine, thanks, John. How are you?'

'I'm fine, thank you.' Rankin felt like screaming down the mouthpiece, but controlled his voice. 'Samantha, this is a silly conversation.'

'I don't see what's silly about it. You asked me how I was, I asked you how you were. It's polite.' I love it, thought Samantha, I love being unemotional. Let the worm squirm.

'You know it's silly. Samantha, am I way out of line in thinking we had a fun Fourth of July night? Until you departed so abruptly, I mean.'

'Yes, we had a fun night.'

'Well then,' Rankin relaxed, his tone became intimate. 'Why don't we have another fun night? Only this time a longer one?'

'I'd love to, John, really I would. But I'm flying to the Caribbean on Tuesday morning and I have so much to do that I don't think I'll have the time.'

'Not even for a drink?'

'I'm afraid not.'

Was there a medical term for a heart imploding, Rankin wondered. Was this the reason he had never fallen in love before? Because it was so painful? It didn't make sense. He should be able to dismiss her – she was pretty, but not stunning; funny but not hilarious, bright but not a genius. Why her? Rankin cradled the telephone against his head and felt for his pulse. He was surprised to find it beating normally.

'The Caribbean? That sounds exotic. Where, exactly?'

'St Lucia.'

'Will you give me a ring when you get back?' He was begging, but it was too late not to beg.

'If I come back. But I'll probably go straight to New

160

York from there. I need to get back to work. Call me if you're ever in Manhattan.'

'I'll do that.'

'Great.'

'Great.'

'Goodbye, John. And thanks for the flowers.'

'Goodbye, Samantha.'

Rankin put the phone down on his desk and swore. If she would just spend some time with him, he knew she'd change her mind. Maybe he wasn't irresistible, but he was damn close when he made the effort. Now she was leaving – he couldn't exactly abduct her, could he? He had some pride left. John Rankin sat staring at the wall in front of him. He wasn't being rational. He had met this girl only twice. He could easily forget about her, she could easily become just another to add to his list. Put her name on the list and she would become like all the others – a conquest. It would be an exorcism.

He reached for the E - K directory and pulled out the sheets of paper. Going over the names from the top, he replayed some of them, as an athlete replays moments in championship games. He did this slowly, at times trying to fit the names to faces and bodies, at others, chuckling to himself. Until he reached the end.

'Jesus wept,' he muttered, staring at her hand-writing. The little sneak. How did she find this? Rankin stood up, still holding the piece of paper. His mind was skating toward all the right deductions. Exactly when she had found it. How she must have felt. 'You're different, you silly cow,' he said to her name, 'didn't you realize that?' Noticing, for the first time, the five asterisks beside her name, he grinned. Cheeky little devil, he thought, by the time I'm through with her she'll have earned those stars.


'Eugenie, I don't understand. Why are you going away now? We've just found each other again. You're wasting precious time.' Duncan's voice was lowered as he spoke into the telephone. Clarissa was due back any minute. He must gauge this conversation carefully. If Clarissa came back and he had to hang up abruptly, Eugenie would be annoyed. On the other hand, he wanted to convince Eugenie to stay. He'd cleared his schedule for the next week in order to spend some time with Eugenie. She had no right to run out on him like this.

'I need a break, Duncan, and I feel like going to the Caribbean. You know perfectly well that I can't plan my life around your free moments anymore. I did that before and I'm not going to do it again.'

'I see.' Don't push her, Duncan thought, reconsidering his position quickly. Let her think she can be independent. It won't be long before she gives up that stance. Unless …

'Are you going with a boyfriend, Eugenie? Is there something you haven't told me?'

'No to both questions.'

'Good. One thing we've always been is honest with each other.' Spying Clarissa's car pulling up in front of the drawing room window, Duncan reckoned he had about two minutes to wrap up the conversation. 'Where are you going to be, anyway?'

'I'm flying to St Lucia on Tuesday. I think I'll be away about ten days in all.'

'Have a marvellous time, darling. I'll see you when you get back.'

'Goodbye, Duncan.' Eugenie, despite not wanting to, added, 'I'll miss you.'

'Me too.'

The phone clicked as he put it down, the front door clicked as Clarissa opened it, and Duncan's mind clicked as he thought of a way to make a supremely romantic gesture to Eugenie, the kind he'd made so often at the beginning of their affair.

Not stopping to speak to Duncan, whom she saw standing in the drawing room, Clarissa rushed upstairs to the bedroom, carrying a bag full of books. She felt like a dirty old man with a stack of porno magazines in brown wrapping. But she couldn't tell Duncan about her new passion, he wouldn't understand. He'd laugh at her. *Hollywood Wives, Hollywood Husbands, The Love-makers, Scruples, Destiny, Lace* – how could she explain her new-found infatuation with books bearing these kind of titles? She could hardly justify it to herself. Except to say that she was thirty-eight years old and she felt as if she had rediscovered her adolescent emotions. Excitement, wanderlust, sex, all the emotions she had thought she could live without, all the emotions which had ebbed away over the years without her even being aware of the loss. Until she had read *Let Yourself Go*. Uncontrollable passions, intrigue, men like Storm – they must be out there somewhere. She had even begun to tape episodes of *Dallas* and *Dynasty* to play back when Duncan was out of the house.

It's like having a sweet tooth, she thought as she hid her six new paperbacks in the bottom drawer of her dresser. Duncan would call it a trash tooth.

Clarissa walked into the bathroom and began to get undressed. As she took off her skirt, underpants and stockings and turned on the taps of the bath, she became agonizingly aware of an itch, a sexual itch. She was unmistakably randy. The image of Duncan down-stairs didn't help. She didn't want him now, his predictable lovemaking. She wanted something different. Women in the books she read had vibrators, but there was no way Clarissa could bring herself to go to some seedy shop in Soho and actually buy one. Looking at the bathtub, she wondered whether she should turn it into an ice-cold plunge. Wasn't that the time-honoured way to stop these urges? But wasn't a cold bath a little drastic?

163

Naked from the waist down, Clarissa turned off the water and stood pondering. She put two fingers on her clitoris and began to rub it briskly, up and down. For five minutes, she stood there, massaging furiously, but it didn't seem to be particularly effective. In fact, she felt stupid and her fingers were beginning to ache. She stopped, resigned to feeling randy.

Then she caught sight of Duncan's electric razor. Could that substitute for a vibrator? What if she fumbled it momentarily and ended up shaving off a patch of pubic hair? Not a good idea. But what about the electric toothbrush standing there beside the sink, re-charging its batteries? That couldn't possibly hurt her. That might just do the trick.

Grabbing it, Clarissa headed for the bedroom and jumped under the duvet. She switched the toothbrush on, reached down again, and felt the bristles moving quickly against her. Within a few seconds she knew she'd made an inspired choice. Why, oh why, she mused, as she lay back on the pillows, hadn't she thought of this before? It was heavenly. She would have to get a stock of these little detachable brushes. Then she forgot about everything and arched her back as a short, sharp, intensely pleasurable feeling hit her between her legs and she quickly jerked the brush up and away from the sensitive area.

'What *are* you doing? What's that noise?'

Duncan stood in the doorway looking quizzical and vaguely annoyed. Clarissa sat up like a shot and saw immediately that the toothbrush in her right hand was peeking its head above the duvet.

'I was brushing my teeth.'

'In bed?'

'Yes, darling. Didn't I tell you? I have the most divine little dentist now who says that it's far, far better for your gums if you brush them when you're absolutely prone. Something to do with the angle, I expect.'

'Doesn't the toothpaste get all over the sheets?'

'The toothpaste? Well, of course. I mean, of course it would if you *used* toothpaste. But he says toothpaste is out now. Toothpaste can be carcinogenic. Really, you should only actually use toothpaste once a day. In the evening.'

Duncan sighed and looked at his wife. Was she going bonkers? Would he have to put up with these fads for the rest of his life? Would he have to start eating health food?

'I just came to tell you that I'm going out for a meeting. I'll be back shortly.'

'Wonderful. Have a wonderful time.'

Out of the bedroom and halfway down the steps, Duncan stopped. Clarissa was thirty-eight now. Was that too young for the menopause?

John Rankin decided not to pack his Bermuda shorts. There was something unbecoming about a man's legs unless they were tanned. He folded a pair of white flannel trousers and placed them in his suitcase. They would be hot, certainly. But they had their advantages. He had, on a visit to West Palm Beach two years previously, worn them on the tennis courts. All the Americans present had thought that exceedingly suave and British. 'Does Prince Charles wear those playing tennis?' one young woman had asked with innocent, awestruck eyes. What was her name? SuSu. SuSu was one of the ones he had chuckled over as he re-read his list. After their lovemaking, she had turned to him and pleaded, 'Say something, John.' 'Do I have to?' he had sighed, then deciding to indulge her, had continued, 'Didn't that say it all?' 'Oh, sure. But I wanted to hear your English accent. You know, like, even after Princess Di and everything I still have real strong dreams about Prince Charles.'

Rankin delved into his drawer for a pair of white

socks. The flannels were a good idea. Should he go all the way and wear the white panama hat to the airport tomorrow? He took the hat off the top of the dresser. Samantha had never seen him in a hat. Rankin posed in front of his bedroom mirror – hat on, hat off, hat tilted to the side, hat tilted to the back, hat slouching over his eyes. He couldn't decide. What would I like if I were a woman? He asked himself. He pushed the hat back, so a mass of blond hair escaped at the front, took off his jacket and slung it over his shoulder with one hand. The other was in his trouser pocket. If I were a woman, he decided, I'd like me.

Thank God I'm not.

Samantha sat on Eugenie's bed and watched her pack. Eugenie was so organized, so precise with every object she handled. Her wrists and fingers were so thin Sam wondered how she could find watchbands or rings small enough to fit her.

'You know, you have a surgeon's hands.'

Eugenie paused and considered her hands for a second.

'So I'm told. I wouldn't mind being a surgeon, as long as I could perform transplants. I think I'd quite like tearing people's hearts out. Like Donna Elvira in *Don Giovanni*.'

'Is it that bad with Duncan?'

'Oh, Samantha, you are sweet. If I had said that to George, she and I would have had a diseased conversation about the joy of ripping up people's vital organs. No, it's not that bad. I simply have to decide whether I'm going back into the ring with him and whether I'm prepared for another knockout blow.'

'Why is everyone being so negative about Georgia all of a sudden?'

Without warning, Samantha began to cry. She had left Georgia, also packing, half an hour ago. George had been buoyant, looking forward to the trip, telling Samantha she should find some stud in a steel band who would take care of all her problems. And she had shown Samantha a hat she had bought for Andrew. A white panama hat with a broad brim. 'Do you think he'll like it?' she asked hesitantly. 'I'm so glad he agreed to come. You know I think it helped when I told him you and Eugenie were coming as well. Maybe he doesn't want to be alone with me just yet. But by the end of this vacation he will. I just wish I didn't feel so tired.' Georgia being so vulnerable was an affecting sight. Samantha had worried about her on the taxi trip to Hampstead.

Seeing Samantha's tears, Eugenie sat down on the bed beside her and put her arm around her.

'I'm not being negative about Georgia, Sam. I was just joking about her love of all things macabre. I'm sorry if I upset you. I really don't mean to be nasty. Who else has been giving her a hard time?'

'Andrew. You know he *is* in love with someone else. He told me.'

'Did he tell you who she is?'

Samantha wavered. Eugenie was staring at her, waiting for an answer as Samantha rapidly calculated the effect an honest answer would have. Eugenie would be pointedly cold to Andrew on the trip, causing Georgia to wonder why. Or Eugenie wouldn't come on the trip, causing even greater speculation. Andrew would wonder whether Samantha had told Eugenie. The layers of complication were multiplying by the minute. Her own psyche was reeling with the possibilities. Ignorance might not be bliss, but it could buy everyone involved a little time.

'He said she isn't *that* young and she isn't a bimbo.' That was the truth, Samantha thought, maybe not the whole truth, but a slice of it at least.

'Oh, well, I suppose that's relief. Georgia's not in

competition with the dreaded eighteen-year-old.' Turning her attention back to the packing, Eugenie pulled a pair of shorts from the wardrobe and held them against her. 'No. I think better not. Shorts don't do me any favours. But these might look good on you. Why don't you try them on?'

Samantha stood up, slipped off her skirt and pulled the shorts up over her hips.

'Perfect.' Eugenie walked around Samantha, sizing her up. 'Do you know what's funny? Here are Georgia and I giving you marching orders about the body beautiful, and there you are, looking terrific while neither she nor I have done a damn thing. I think it's *your* turn to take *us* in hand.'

Smiling self-consciously, Samantha tried not to look at herself in the mirror while Eugenie went into the bathroom to pack her makeup bag. A minute later Eugenie appeared at the threshold of the bedroom with an amused expression.

'Something's just occurred to me,' she announced slyly.

'What's that?'

'Maybe *you're* the mystery woman Andrew Green has taken such a tumble for.'

'Eugenie, you idiot!' Samantha laughed, grabbing a pillow from the bed and throwing it at her.

'Oh, I forgot.' Eugenie advanced on Samantha, the pillow raised. 'You *are* ridiculously young, and a bimbo to boot.'

'Didn't I tell you? Of course I did – you've simply forgotten. I arranged this trip last week and I specifically remember telling you about it over dinner. Remember? It's a fact-finding tour of the Caribbean. How the British West Indies are faring as opposed to the French West Indies. Trade. Import-export. Tourism. All those dull but necessary subjects. If I went into it all, I'd bore you to tears.'

Beaches, thought Clarissa. Palm trees. Coconuts. Limbo dancing. Hadn't the opening of *Let Yourself Go* taken place in St Lucia?

'Perhaps you did tell me.'

Clarissa was acting awfully scatty these days, Duncan decided, but at least now that faraway look in her eyes was working to his advantage. He hadn't, in fact, said a word to her about the trip. He wanted to spring it on her, not allow her any time to think up objections.

'What time are you leaving?'

'Flight Number 107 to St Lucia. 10.30 a.m. from Heathrow. Don't worry about driving me there – I can take a taxi. I suppose I should pack my shorts. It will be positively sweltering at this time of the year. What a pain. I'm not looking forward to this at all. You're lucky to be here, especially with this decent weather we're having.'

'Mmm.' Clarissa tried to focus on Duncan's lank frame, his narrow dark eyes, his long hawkish nose. Could he be described as a tall, dark stranger? she asked herself. Storm had been tall and dark, but the Storm in her mind looked nothing like the Duncan now in front of her.

Could she separate the Duncan she knew from the Duncan she didn't? He must have secrets, he must have secrets like I do, she thought. He can't possibly be as straightforward as I think. He can't possibly be as boring as I'm beginning to think.

'Clarissa!' Duncan snapped his fingers in front of her face. 'Are you daydreaming? I asked you where my white suit is.' Was there a tactful way to introduce the subject of menopause?

'It's downstairs in the hall cupboard. It came back from the laundry a few days ago. I'll go and get it.'

Downstairs, as she poured herself a glass of wine,

Clarissa's thoughts were running so quickly and jumping so many fences along the way that they could have entered the Grand National.

What kind of people went to the Caribbean in the summer? Movie actors. All movie actors had houses in the Caribbean – they must visit them sometimes. Better to visit them off-season – fewer autograph hunters. The Caribbean must be rigid with movie stars in July. If not movie stars, then at least lots of shady people. Drug smugglers, gun runners, kidnappers. Attractive kidnappers. If she wore all her best jewellery perhaps the kidnappers would think she was an heiress.

Duncan would be busy, working. She would have time to play, to have the kind of fun she read about. Hearing his voice bellowing her name, she refilled her glass and picked up the telephone. An efficient wife, she had memorized the airline number instantly. There was bound to be a seat available in First Class at this time of year.

'For God's sake, Clarissa. You said you were getting my suit. Who are you blabbering to? I need to get on with my packing.'

Clarissa covered the mouthpiece with one hand and turned to her husband standing in his boxer shorts in the doorway.

'I'm just making a reservation for myself tomorrow, darling. I thought I'd join you. Won't that be fun?'

# Chapter Nine

Amazingly, this disparate but inextricably intertwined group of individuals didn't collide until forty-five minutes before take-off. Rick, Georgia, Andrew, Samantha and Eugenie all arrived at Heathrow an hour and a half before take-off, as scheduled, and duly checked in their baggage and proceeded to the First Class Lounge. Rankin, collecting his ticket and heading for the lounge a half an hour later was followed closely by Duncan and Clarissa. The entire night before Duncan had thought up ways to dissuade his wife from accompanying him, but each time he broached a problem, she dismissed it, until he gave up and resigned himelf to what was obviously going to be the most disastrous trip of his life.

So when John Rankin was buzzed into the lounge, signed his name and his flight number and headed for the free coffee, Samantha, Georgia and Andrew did a simultaneous triple-take. But that was a meagre reaction from the group compared to the sight following close on his heels – Duncan and Clarissa Darrell.

Samantha, looking at Rankin, sat stock still. He, looking at her, took off his hat and grinned. Until a look of horror spread across her babyfaced features. Damn, he thought, this isn't working, and replaced his hat. But then he realized that he wasn't the object of her pained expression – she was looking at some couple behind him. What's going on here, he wondered, as he took in Georgia's presence as well. I wasn't bargaining for a group outing.

Georgia, when she first saw Rankin, smiled. The guy's got style, she thought, not to mention persistence. She looked over at Samantha, sitting beside her, and saw the horror too. 'Come on, Sam –' she started to say, but glancing back at John to give him encouragement, *she* caught sight of Duncan and Clarissa. Oh my God, she said, *sotto voce* and quickly turned to Eugenie, on her other side.

Eugenie hadn't met Rankin at the Fourth of July party and stared unabashedly at the blond, handsome character who was in the midst of doffing his white hat. Then she saw Clarissa. What's *she* doing here? flashed into her mind, and then Duncan's face exploded on her like a grenade, and she could feel Georgia grabbing her hand. All she could do was sit, transfixed by the sight of them, and ask herself why. Why, why, why? Why was he here? Why was she here? Why was he winking at her so manically? What flight were they on? They couldn't possibly – no, they couldn't possibly. She grabbed the sides of her chair.

'Eugenie, sweetheart – I'm sure they're on a different flight. Please try to relax. I don't have any emergency medical training.' Georgia, as she whispered this to Eugenie, began to feel faint herself, and quickly put her head down between her knees. 'Jesus,' she whispered, breathing deeply and feeling the colour come back to her face, 'we're not even on the plane yet and we're preparing for a crash landing.'

Andrew sat forward when he saw Rankin and pulled his eyelids down over his eyes with his fingertips. This was the final, the last straw. He was sitting on a sofa, at a right angle to Georgia, Eugenie and Samantha. He didn't even want to see Samantha's reaction as this man wearing a fucking panama hat walked in. Standing up and walking over to the hospitality bar, he saw his reflection in the mirrored tiles, saw the white panama hat on his own head. Turning around to avoid his image, he noticed Duncan Darrell and his wife, Georgia had pointed them out to him at the party.

'You are now entering the Twilight Zone,' he said to himself. A place where every man in love with a girl named Samantha Lewis wears a white hat, a place where strange people harbouring strange desires take strange trips with their even stranger wives. He did an about face and fixed himself a Bloody Mary.

Aha, thought Richard Holland – who, despite talking on the telephone, was in a position to see Duncan and Clarissa Darrell's entrance. The whole sick crew. I should have some fun with this. He finished his conversation abruptly, and walked over to them.

'Mrs Darrell!' He kissed her three times. 'I pray to every known deity that you're flying to St Lucia this morning. If not, I'll change my ticket. I couldn't bear it, really I couldn't. Tell me you're on our flight.'

'I am!' Clarissa knew for certain that she had never been so happy in her life. Images of hot tubs were romping through her brain.

'Aren't you the sly dog?' Rick addressesd Duncan, shaking his hand. 'Taking this gorgeous creature to the Caribbean in the summer. And here we are too. I can't help but wonder how such a lucky coincidence occurred.'

'I'm on a fact-finding tour.' Duncan knew two things for certain. That he hated this man with a passion and that he would rather be dead than be here right now.

'I'm sure there are a lot of facts to be found on this trip. And I hope the sun helps that nervous tic in your right eye. See you soon, you two. I can't tell you how pleased I am we're all in this together.'

173

Arms outstretched, Rick walked over to Georgia, Eugenie and Samantha.

'Beautiful, stricken people, guess what? The Darrells are on our flight.' He knelt down and put his hands on Eugenie's knees. 'Don't worry, little one, I'll help you through the pain, the suffering, the torment. I'll be your macho godfather. We're going to have a happy ending here.'

Samantha wished she had a macho godfather to help her through this. Why couldn't John Rankin just leave her alone? She stood up and walked over to him.

'Is this a coincidence, John?' Samantha looked up at him and had a strange desire to knock him flat.

'No. I'm here to take you away from all this.'

'I was *already* getting away from all this.'

'But I didn't think you should get away from *me*. You see, Ms Lewis, I know you found my – what should I call it? – my little version of *Who's Who*. And I don't think you understood.'

'It would be difficult not to understand. That list was pretty straightforward, John.'

'Yes, but don't you see, it's really a catalogue of the emptiness of my life, the meaninglessness of my encounters. Until you.'

You just earned five stars for bullshitting, Mr Rankin, thought Samantha, staring evenly into his blue eyes.

'That's really sweet. Tell me, do you picture us walking hand in hand over the sandy beaches together?'

'Yes, Samantha, of course I do.'

'Well, I don't. I'm going to get myself a drink now.'

Rankin watched as Samantha walked away from him. She was wearing white cotton trousers and a blue and white striped jersey with a grey collar and cuffs. Her straight, shoulder-length blonde hair swung as she moved. There had been something familiar about that last exchange, but he couldn't place it. She'd been unnecessarily rude, but then he'd expected that at first. He knew it would take a while to get back in her good graces, but he was at least in a position to do so now. The plane trip would be perfect – if he could manoeuvre himself into the seat beside her, he'd have her as a captive one-woman audience for ten hours. He turned his attention to Georgia, who was sitting in the corner of the lounge with a very beautiful dark-haired girl. The dark-haired girl had a man kneeling at her feet. Women, he thought. They've got us by the short and curlies.

'Look, Duncan, there's Eugenie Woodrow and Georgia Green. Let's go up and say hello.'

'They're talking to your friend Rick, Clarissa. They probably don't want to be interrupted.' Why hadn't Eugenie mentioned all these other people were coming on the trip? 'Besides, I need a drink.'

'Oh, good, I'll join you. I think a glass of champagne would be just perfect. I'm in a celebratory mood. I had no idea this was going to be such fun. I think I'll get drunk as a skunk.'

'Clarissa!'

'Oh Duncan, don't be such an old fart.'

'Clarissa!'

But Clarissa was already on her way to the bar. Duncan stood momentarily rooted to the spot. Should he go up to Eugenie now and explain? She was still talking to that brat of a man. I give up, he decided, and followed his wife. I'll just let events wash over me until we get on the plane. Then I'll find a way to explain to Eugenie. It will all be all right in the end. It has to be.

The receptionist in the First Class lounge announced the departure of their flight at that moment. Clarissa, Duncan and Samantha, standing beside each other at the bar, finished their respective glasses of champagne. Andrew, who had wandered over to where the newspapers were on display, finished his Bloody Mary. Rick, Georgia and Eugenie got up, collecting their hand luggage. They were all on the move, and all of them were hatching individual game plans for the Superbowl which lay ahead.

The eight trooped down the passageway and onto the plane, taking their assigned seats in the First Class cabin. Georgia beside Andrew, Eugenie beside Samantha, Duncan beside Clarissa, Rick and Rankin sitting solo. Nobody spoke as the steward and stewardess helped them sort their baggage and jackets, and settle comfortably in their seats.

For a moment it appeared that they were the only ones in First Class, but Georgia, nudging Andrew, pointed to a young man at the very front of the plane.

'What's he doing here?'

'What do you mean?'

'I mean he looks like a teenager – how did he get enough money to go First Class?'

'How would I know? Maybe he robbed a bank. Maybe his father is president of Barclays. What does it matter?'

'I don't know – he looks suspicious.'

'He's probably thinking the same about us. What do you want to do? Go up and see if he speaks in an Irish or Iranian accent. *He's* not our problem. The illustrious MP and his wife may be a problem. Mr Suave with the blow-dried blond hair may be a problem. What's *he* doing here, anyway?'

'John Rankin? He's a gynaecologist in love with Samantha. I guess he's pursuing her – isn't that romantic?'

Andrew grunted.

'And is the MP pursuing Eugenie with his wife in tow? That's romance for you.'

'I know – do you believe it? I have a hunch he didn't think wifey-baby was coming with him. Poor Eugenie.'

'Poor pilot.'

'Why poor pilot?'

'Because the combined weight of stupidity in this compartment alone will probably bring this machine down.'

The steward handed out free headsets as the stewardess distributed pre-flight drinks.

'I'm going to need this,' Eugenie said to Samantha, taking a glass of champagne from the tray.

'So am I.'

'Samantha, will you do me a favour?'

'Of course.'

'Can we talk about Charles Darwin or Donald Trump or Bruce Springsteen on this flight? The theory of evolution or the theory of money or the theory of pop music – anyone but Duncan Darrell and anything but sex?'

'Absolutely. And I have to ask you a favour. If John Rankin comes up to me, please help me ignore him – don't, please, offer him your seat or anything.'

'John Rankin? Is *he* here too? God, they should be selling tickets for this sideshow. Which one is he? Don't tell me he's that dishy –'

'Yes. But if you start raving about him, I'll kill you. I couldn't take it.'

'I promise I won't. I'm sorry. But he is …'

'Eugenie, stop.'

'Right. Of course. We've got a deal. So tell me, Samantha, what do you admire most about Bruce Springsteen?'

'His body.'

'Quite.' Eugenie signalled for more champagne. 'You know in his concerts when he gets a girl up on stage to dance with him? I would sell my soul to be her. It's something to do with his muscles, his unbelievably, cute bottom.'

'Eugenie.'

'What?'

'Maybe we should talk about Charles Darwin now.'

'Maybe we should.'

The doors of the plane were swung shut and locked as the engine started up and they began to taxi onto the runway. No one in First Class spoke while the safety procedures were explained. They all stared dumbly at the stewardess as she donned the lifejacket, pulled cords, and then told them about oxygen masks.

The jet took its position at the top of the runway, then built up speed, lumbering along until its nose began to point skywards and its wheels lifted from the tarmac. Within minutes it had broken through the light cloud cover and the safety-belts and no-smoking signs blinked off with a ping.

'Thank God for big favours,' said Eugenie, lighting up, Georgia immediately rose and went to perch on the armrest of Eugenie's seat.

'Well, girls. Looks like we're in for an interesting vacation. Should we take bets on who murders whom first?'

'George – Sam and I have made a pact. We're not going to discuss this unbelievable cock-up.'

'What else *is* there to discuss?'

'The theory of evolution,' Samantha replied.

'Spoilsports. All right then, I'll find greener pastures. I'll go collar Mrs Darrell and find out what the scoop is – what they're doing here together. Don't tell me you don't want to know. I'll come back with a report. And Sam, the altitude might be just the thing for Doc Juan over there. While you're talking about the theory of evolution, spare a thought for the Big Bang.' Halfway up from the armrest, Georgia stopped and sat down again. 'Would you take a gander at the guv up front?'

Samantha and Eugenie strained their necks and saw this figure of a boy standing with his eyes closed, his back resting against the front wall of the cabin, a Sony

Walkman in one hand, the other hand making strumming motions on an imaginary guitar.

'Does he think he's flying Virgin?'

'He's probably a famous rock star, George. Go sign him up for a book.'

'Uh-uh. He looks like a weirdo to me. Besides, I've got bigger fish to fry. Clarissa Darrell, here I come. I'm going to have a great time working this plane.'

'Sometimes I wonder whether Georgia is a true friend or just a sensation-monger,' Eugenie mumbled as Georgia made her way back to Clarissa and Duncan, sitting two rows behind.

'I think she just tries to see the humour in everything.'

'You know Sam, *I* haven't been a true friend to you. At first I just wanted to use you for my book. I still feel guilty about that. Even since we've become friends, since that night at my house when we all ended up in bed together, I've been studying you, watching how you've come out of your shell, figuring out how to make you my heroine. I'm just a fake – a fake writer and a fake friend.'

'Don't be silly. I don't mind at all if you use me for the book. I'd probably be disappointed now if you didn't. You and Georgia *have* helped to bring me out of my shell. You've both made me feel gutsier – if there is such a word. I'm not sure how to explain this, but I never really felt like a fully grown woman before.'

'What *did* you feel like?'

'A bystander. A curiously inept bystander.'

'That may be better than feeling like I do – an inept woman.'

'Eugenie Woodrow, you're hot shit. Don't let anybody make you feel otherwise. You know, I finally read *Let Yourself Go* and I loved it. You're a good writer; if the next book isn't as good, who cares? There aren't many people in this world who could've written the first one. You should be proud of yourself. And don't let any man drain your self-confidence.'

Eugenie leant over and kissed Samantha on the cheek.

'Thanks for the pep talk. I'll do you a big favour someday.'

'So …' Georgia stood hovering over the Darrells. 'This was a last-minute decision of yours, Clarissa? Duncan must have been thrilled.'

Duncan was close to committing a physically violent act. He wanted to go on a rampage – slap Georgia, kick Rick, stab Clarissa, ravage Eugenie. Do anything but sit there listening to people making fun of him. But all his political training stood him in good stead. He would absorb all the shit and find a way to use his aggressive feelings to his advantage, if that was humanly possible.

'He was surprised,' Clarissa replied. 'And I must say, he did try to stop me. But I was determined. And I'm so glad I was. Can I call you Georgia?'

'Absolutely.'

'Georgia, I have a confession to make. A little secret I haven't told a soul – not even Duncan.'

Duncan sat up, alert. She knows, she knows, she knows, he thought. This was her way to torture me. She knows.

'I read Eugenie's book the other day and I thought it was marvellous. I wish I could write something like that.'

Duncan's head dropped into his hands. Georgia and Clarissa turned toward him. Clarissa surreptitiously pointed to his bald patch and winked at Georgia. Georgia found herself winking back. What was going on here?

'Poor Duncan's such a highbrow – I knew my secret would shatter him. You must reintroduce him to

Eugenie. Maybe she can convince him that books like that aren't written by moral reprobates.'

His head popping back up, Duncan glared at his wife.

'I am *here* you know. I do *exist*. You *can* stop referring to me as if I were a patient and you were a nurse.'

'Well, I'll leave you two to your literary arguments. It was nice seeing you again, Clarissa.'

Georgia rushed back to Eugenie and Samantha.

'First news bulletin hot off the presses. *He* didn't know until the last minute that *she* was coming. Then he tried to stop her but couldn't. *She* loves *Let Yourself Go*, a fact which seems to have knocked *him* for six. Whew! It's getting hot in here.' Unsnapping the first two buttons of her country-and-western style shirt, Georgia proceeded to pull it out of her jeans and let the tail hang loose. 'I don't think we need to be formal for this occasion. *Now* I think its time to pay a visit to the doctor.'

Like a guided missile, Georgia shot off to the other side of the plane. The steward who had come to take their orders for lunch blocked Eugenie and Samantha's view of their friend as she plopped herself down in the empty seat beside Rankin.

'What would you like from the menu, ladies?'

'Can you get me a new life?' asked Eugenie.

'Make that two,' Samantha smiled at him.


'How many points do you think you scored by showing up for this trip?'

'I'm not sure if I scored any. I think you'll have to ask Sam.'

'Are you desperately in love with her?'

'Bone-crushingly.'

'And what are your intentions?'

Rankin grinned.

'OK, OK – don't answer. I've always wanted to ask

181

someone that question, though. If I were you, I'd make my first big move during the film, when the lights are down.'

'I appreciate the advice.'

'God knows why I'm rooting for you. No offence, but I think you'll probably be reincarnated as a rat. Still, you might convince Samantha to stay in England for a while and I'd like that. She's a special person.'

'And she has a special person for a friend.'

'Save that kind of shit for the stewardess, doc. Fake sincerity doesn't become you.'

Georgia leapt up and went to her seat while Rankin sat back slightly stunned. He *had* been sincere. These American women were so full of distrust. Make one comment they don't like and they pounce on you as if you had suggested rape. He wasn't sure he liked the idea of Georgia monitoring his progress. If he could convince Samantha, once they had landed, to branch off from the group and go on a side trip with him, he would feel much more relaxed and in control.

During lunch everyone stayed in his or her assigned seat, scoffing the free food and drink. No one was in a position to notice that the boy in the front managed to pocket one of the silver steak knives before his tray was removed.

The film started rolling immediately after the lunch was finished and all the passengers switched off their lights, pulled down the window shades and settled down to watch Crocodile Dundee II.

Within minutes of the opening shots, Duncan leant over to Clarissa. 'I think I'll take your advice and go talk to Miss Woodrow about her book. Perhaps I'll be able to understand what seems to be your new attitude a little better.' Lame, thought Duncan as he said this, a lame excuse, but I can't do any better. I'm too tired.

'Fine,' Clarissa replied, her eyes fixed on the screen

in front. That man Hogan's good-looking, she decided. As Duncan got up, Clarissa dived for her makeup bag stored under the seat in front. She pulled it under the blanket she'd spread over her, and reached in to find the electric toothbrush. Everyone will be listening to the film, she thought, they won't hear a sound. Stealthily she pulled her pants and pantyhose down over her hips, repositioned the blanket to hide her intentions, and reclined her seat. Then she lay back and proceeded to enjoy herself.

Duncan knelt down in the aisle beside Eugenie's seat and removed her headphones.

'We have to talk.'

'You may have to talk. I don't,' hissed Eugenie.

'This was not my fault, Eugenie. She decided to come last night and I couldn't talk her out of it. I'd wanted so much to surprise you. Like the old days.'

'You certainly surprised me.'

'Please. Just let me talk to you. I'm sure we can work something out. There are two seats free in the next aisle. You owe it to me. You owe it to what we had together. What we still have. You owe it to us.'

Samantha was trying not to pay attention to this conversation, but even though she had her headphones on and couldn't hear much, she could see Eugenie's body gradually soften in position and uncurl. So it was no surprise to her when Eugenie crept out of her seat and moved one row ahead with Duncan. She wondered whether Clarissa could see this, and couldn't resist rising from her chair, twisting round to peer over the top of her headrest and look two rows behind her. Clarissa was lying back, her eyes closed, with a strange expression on her face. It didn't appear to Samantha as if it were pain or jealousy. If anything, Clarissa looked almost religious.

Samantha sat back down, puzzled, to find John Rankin in the seat beside her.

'I brought you a glass of champagne.'

'Thank you, John.'

'Ms Lewis, can we please start afresh, wipe out the past and pretend we're two strangers who happened to be sitting together on an aeroplane?'

'Are you, by any chance, from Yugoslavia?'

She's playing the game, thought Rankin. I just have to take it from here.

'No. I was born in Katmandu, actually. Raised by the missionaries. My parents owned a pig farm, but were both gored to death by a wild boar. It's a tragic story.'

'John, I have to be honest with you. I think you're very handsome and funny and I admire your work. But you're not my type. I'm afraid you've wasted your money on this trip.' Samantha, stared straight ahead, as she delivered this knockout blow.

'You're not being honest with me at all. I *am* your type. It's that bloody list. Why can't you forget it? It's trivial, unimportant. For God's sake, Sam ...' Rankin grabbed her and began to kiss her aggressively. Samantha felt strangely numb. Is it possible, she asked herself as their tongues pushed, shoved and jostled for space in each other's mouths, that I don't fancy him? The whole world seems to think he's a latter day Valentino. What's wrong with me? Am I asexual?

Rankin's left hand began to travel towards Samantha's white trousers, but was stopped by the armrest separating the chairs. When he tried to lift it up in order to have unlimited access to Samantha's body, he found it was solidly built in.

'Samantha,' he whispered, breaking off his kiss and nuzzling her ear, 'I'm finding this difficult. Let's go to the loo. It will be the first time I've ever done it on a plane.'

'Does that put me at the top of a new list?' Samantha asked herself. Then she realized, with a shock, that she didn't care about him any more; him or his lists. He could make them till the cows came home, he could put her on them – it didn't matter. They had had one nice lunch and evening together – that was all there was to it. She didn't want any more, she didn't even want revenge on a Don Juan by treating him the way he treated all women. He was *not* her type. His looks and manner had affected her for a while, but she didn't want to be involved. In the end, she knew that she'd never be able to relax with him; they would always be fencing, there would always be power games. And she didn't care enough to play those games.

Samantha considered what would happen if she turned him down. He would believe it was another ploy, no doubt, and redouble his efforts. He was not the type of man to chase her all the way to the Caribbean and accept total rejection. She remembered a big legal case that had all of New York talking for a month: a man had sued a woman because she had gone out to dinner with him fifty times or so and never gone to bed with him. He had claimed that by accepting his invitations and letting him pay for all those dinners, she was tacitly agreeing to have sex. She had, in effect, signed a contract and welched on it. The implications were fascinating and endless. How many dinners could a woman accept without going to bed at the end? Two? Ten? Forty-nine?

Samantha hadn't asked Rankin to chase, her, true. But she felt responsible and guilty. Guilty that she didn't care about him any more. All that money and effort he had spent. Up until a minute ago, she *had* been involved with him. She *had* gotten a kick out of leaving him high and dry. Perhaps he had sensed that, perhaps she had willed him to chase her. Still, she was hardly morally obliged to have sex with him in the airplane toilet. That was carrying guilt and responsibility too far.

Rankin was hovering impatiently, waiting for her

'yes'. Samantha grabbed a cigarette from beside her and heard Rankin's annoyed sigh as she bent forward to light it. She struck a match and saw what she should have seen at the beginning of the trip, but had somehow missed as she talked with Eugenie. The airline in-flight magazine.

'Sam – careful, you're about to get burnt!' Rankin warned, and blew out the match she'd been dumbly holding. Samantha wasn't listening. She lit another match and confirmed what she didn't want to know. That *was* her on the cover – the girl David had been in bed with, the girl he'd gone off with. The long-legged, big-busted, blonde-haired beauty of a model, staring out at her in a flesh-coloured swim suit. David, no, doubt, had taken the photograph.

This time she blew out the match, and then threw away the cigarette. Sure, she thought, fine. No problem. I'll go to the loo with John. Do it in an airplane. Why not? Who says that women have to be emotionally involved with a man to have good sex? I bet Body Beautiful wasn't emotionally involved with David when they started up their affair. Maybe that's been my problem all along – thinking I should actually care about the man I sleep with. I'm back to the beginning – having sex with John Rankin for my own purposes. Only this time I'll go through with the act.

Knocking back her glass of champagne, she turned to Rankin.

'Let's do it,' she said. 'It's now or never.'

Rankin stood up and they walked back to where the 'toilet unoccupied' sign was lit. Samantha thought she saw Rick Holland sitting beside Clarissa as they made their way in the dark, but decided she must be hallucinating.

As John Rankin and Samantha Lewis were cramming themselves into the same toilet, Rick Holland was reaching over to rub Clarissa Darrell's left breast. Clarissa, toothbrush in hand under the blanket, hadn't noticed Rick's body quietly sliding into Duncan's seat. When she felt the hand, though, she knew it was Rick's. She didn't move. Instead, she opened her eyes slightly, staring at Crocodile Dundee. The toothbrush bristles were buzzing away. Rick's hand was doing dexterous moves, exciting already-excited nipples to a fever pitch, and all was right in Clarissa's private heaven.

Duncan Darrell was busy undoing the buttons of Eugenie's blouse.

'Duncan – what about Clarissa?'

'I don't care about Clarissa.'

'You don't care if she sees us? You have to choose now, Duncan. I'm not going to go through this routine again. I made you decide once before – this time it's final.'

All Duncan's pent-up anger and frustration had been concentrated in an overwhelming sexual urge. He *had* to have Eugenie and have her he would – right there on the First Class seat.

'You. I choose you!' He took her face in his hands and guided it down to his lap, forcing Eugenie into a contortionist's position – her feet still on the floor, her ribcage stretched over the dividing armrest, her neck straining to the side while she unzipped his trousers with her teeth.

Samantha, meanwhile, trousers and underpants shed, was straddling John Rankin, who was sitting on the toilet seat. Her arm kept bumping into the tissue dispenser as he bounced her up and down on top of him. And she was suddenly scared to death of clear air turbulence. What would happen if they dropped thousands of feet – would she be impaled on Rankin for life? She felt frightened and tipsy – but also, and more importantly, sexually bored. As she made the appropriate moans to accompany his, she realized that she'd been sexually bored by David too. She *was* asexual, she *was* frigid. The whole exercise was so pedantic, whether she cared about the man or not. In out, in out, shake it all about. Do the hokey-cokey and you turn around and that's what it's all about. She never had liked that song.

'Aaagghh!' she suddenly yelled.

'Oooh, Sam oooh' he moaned again, and came. 'Sam,' he hugged her close, 'was that great for you too? It sounded like a terrific orgasm. You see, I *am* your type.'

'God,' Samantha thought, thankful that it was over and that she could escape the claustrophobia. 'Don't gynaecoloigsts know about these things? I didn't have an orgasm. I hit my funnybone. It hurts like crazy.'


'Turn on the lights or I'll kill him!'

For a second the people who had taken their headsets off thought Crocodile Dundee was speaking to them from the screen. His knife was at a man's balls in a urinal.

But the lights were already on in the urinal.

And then the lights went on in the plane.

There at the front stood the boy, one arm around the steward's waist, the other holding the steak knife to his throat.

Duncan Darrell had just ejaculated into Eugenie Woodrow's aching mouth. She sat up and swallowed. Duncan leapt to his feet. Why hadn't he taken an SAS course on terrorism? What should he do? He did up his fly. Get the facts, size up the situation, he reckoned. How many of them are there? What are the odds? Instantly he scanned the First Class compartment.

The most obvious fact was that his wife wouldn't take her hand off Rick Holland's cock.

'Sweetheart,' whispered Rick, 'I think we're being

hijacked. And I *know* your husband's looking at us right now. I think we'd better call it a day.'

'Tell the captain this plane's under my control now,' the boy shouted to the stewardess, who had stopped halfway up the lefthand aisle, a drink in her hand. 'If you don't follow orders, I'll kill this steward.'

Samantha and Rankin, stumbling out of the toilet, saw the lights, saw the boy holding the steward. Neither of them moved.

'Oh my God,' said Samantha.

'Jesus wept,' said Rankin.

'Shit,' said Andrew.

'Fucking hell,' said Georgia, as she fainted and slumped over the armrest. halfway into the aisle, directly in front of the stewardess.

'I'll go tell the captain right away. But I think this woman needs medical attention. Is there a doctor in this compartment?' she asked.

'Yes,' Rankin spoke up, then looked at the hijacker. 'Am I allowed to examine her? I won't make any sudden moves.'

'What?' the boy yelled.

'Am I allowed to examine her?'

'What?'

'He's got his Walkman on,' Andrew shouted back at Rankin. 'He can't hear a thing. Come over here. Just don't make any sudden moves.'

'I wouldn't dream of it.' Rankin went forward slowly from his position outside the toilet, at the same time as the stewardess walked back down the cabin and up the stairs of the Jumbo leading to the cockpit.

A few seconds elapsed before Georgia came to. Her face was as pale as white chocolate, her whole body was slumped like a collapsed puppet.

'I knew I was bad in a crisis, but this is ridiculous,' she said to Rankin, who was taking her pulse. He then began to prod her stomach.

Andrew took her hand.

'Welcome to the human race, scumbag. We're all cowards. If you hadn't fainted, I was just about to. I may now.'

'Not for the same reason, Mr Green,' Rankin announced in his professional tone, whole he continued to prod. Georgia sat up straight.

'Why are you pushing my – hell, why didn't I think of that? I must have lost track – I mean I never count the days anyway.' She grabbed Rankin's shoulder with her free hand. He nodded.

'Will someone tell me what's going on?' Andrew asked.

'Andrew – we're going to have a baby.'

Andrew looked at Rankin. He nodded again.

'What?' shouted the boy.

Duncan Darrell didn't care about the hijacker. He didn't care about Eugenie. All he could think of was his wife with another man. *His* wife. His bloody wife holding another man's cock in her hand.

'What the bloody hell d'you think you're doing?' He was standing over Rick and Clarissa, his eyes popping. 'You have no right to touch my wife. She has no right to touch you. What I saw was disgusting.'

'You over there – sit down!' the hijacker yelled.

'Duncan, please, calm down. You can rant and rage any other time, but right now that boy up there may be about to kill someone. This isn't the time for a jealous fit.'

'I am not jealous. It's a matter of principle. It's just not done, not while I'm on the same plane for christsakes!'

'Sit down, you' the boy shouted. 'Now!'

Standing up quickly, Rick shoved Duncan down beside Clarissa.

'You two lovebirds work on your little tiff, I'm going

to sit this one out with Eugenie.' He dropped on all fours and crawled three rows up.

'Darling, do you mind if I join you?'

'Rick!' Eugenie was crying. 'He doesn't care about me. He still loves her. He just left me there like a sack of old potatoes. He *lied* to me.'

'*I* care about you, sweetheart, and I know all these emotional scenes are of cosmic importance, but honeycakes, we're being *hijacked*. And that kid looks like someone familiar.'

'Do you know him?'

'Not personally. But he looks familiar. And he has an American accent, which is reassuring. I don't know, maybe he went to the same how-to-be-a-mass-murderer seminar I did last year.'

'Rick!'

'No kidding. Charles Manson is the guest lecturer next term. He's going to tell us how to get those piercing, haunted, possessed-by-the-devil eyes. Did you ever notice Jackie Onassis has that look too? Oh dear, that steward's beginning to cry now, and *his* lover hasn't even lied to him.'

The steward's tears started to plummet unchecked down his face, over his chin, hurdling his Adam's apple like liquid ski jumpers.

'Doctor, tell him,' he sobbed.

'Tell him?' Rankin had resumed his seat, one up from Georgia's, on the aisle and he had motioned for Samantha to come beside him into the window seat. 'He still has his Sony Walkman on. How can I tell him anything?'

'Get him to take it off. I have something important to tell him. He'll let me go when he hears it.'

'I'll try.' Rankin stood up and pointed to the boy, then mimed taking off a set of headphones.

'Why?' the boy yelled back.

Rankin looked at the steward.

'Because I may have AIDS. And if he cuts me, he may get infected from my blood.'

'Look –' Rankin lowered his voice. 'I'm taking a chance here. I don't think he can read lips and I don't think he can hear over whatever he's got on that tape. Is that really true?'

'Yes. One of my partners just told me. I'm about to get a test.'

'I don't believe this.' Georgia turned to Andrew and threw her hands in the air. 'Some teenage nutso with headphones is hijacking the plane, the guy who just served me my lunch has AIDS, and I'm pregnant. This is *not* fair. Our baby's probably a basket case already. They're supposed to be able to sense what's going on, even from the womb.'

Rankin stood thoughtfully for a moment. Then, staring at the hijacker, mouthed, 'He has AIDS,' as clearly as possible.

'What?' the boy yelled.

'He has AIDS!' Rankin's mouth was the opposite of a ventriloquist's – stretched to its limits.

'What?'

'Oh, Jesus, I give up,' Rankin muttered.

'Let me try.' Samantha rose from her chair and edged past Rankin, into the aisle. She was facing the boy, who stared at her with suspicion. Then she held up one finger.

'One word,' the boy said immediately, and Samantha nodded vigorously. She pulled her earlobe.

'Sounds like,' he said. Samantha nodded again.

The hijacker watched with interest as Samantha pretended to tie an apron around her, then made vacuuming motions, sweeping an imaginary Hoover along the aeroplane carpet. Georgia, suddenly catching on, stood up and joined her, pretending to dust the armrests.

'I've got it,' shouted the boy. 'Cleaners!'

The two women shook their heads from side to side and started their charade again.

'Maids! MAIDS!'

Samantha and Georgia jumped up and down, pointing their fingers to their noses, then tugging their earlobes.

'This is the most surreal event I've ever witnessed,' Rick said to Eugenie.

'Sounds like maids.' The boy was pleased with himself. 'I'll start from the beginning. A. Aids.'

The two women jumped up and down again, pointing to their noses and then to the steward.

'AIDS?' the boy repeated, 'AIDS?' He ripped the Walkman off his head. 'Are you telling me this faggot has AIDS?'

'Exactly,' said Rankin. 'And if you cut him and he bleeds, he'll bleed on you and you're in big trouble.'

'Shit!' The boy let go of the steward, dropped the knife and backed off. At which point the captain entered the cabin.

'What's going on here?'

'I'm hijacking this aeroplane,' replied the boy. 'I didn't really need that knife. I just thought I should be dramatic. Actually, I can blow us all up with my running shoes.'

'Mm-hmm.' The captain nodded. He appeared calm. Uniforms do help, thought Samantha, watching his impassive face, and the fact that he has that slow Southern accent.

'And how do you propose to do that?'

'My shoelaces. I've hidden explosives in my shoelaces. If I touch the tip of my right shoelace to my left shoelace, they will detonate.'

'I see. Can I ask you now what you want from us?'

'I want my song to be played on every pop radio station in England and America. I want the people to get a chance to recognize my talent. When they hear it, they'll know I'm a genius. I don't care if I have to go to jail for it. At least then I'll be taken seriously.'

'Darling.' Rick stood up. 'A suffering artist. Of course your song should be played. I'm sure the captain here can see to that. If he can't, I will. I happen to know personally a shitload of famous disc jockeys just waiting for the next George Michael. What's your name?'

'Larry. Larry Moody.'

'What a name! That's just fabulous. And how old are you?'

'Seventeen.'

'Someone get this child prodigy a glass of champagne.'

'Good idea,' said Georgia, going back into the galley and quickly returning with a full glass. She approached him carefully.

Larry took the glass from Georgia's outstretched hand, then hesitated before putting it to his lips.

'I'm serious, you know. I'll blow this plane sky high if I don't get what I ask.'

'Of course you will. You *should*. We all deserve to die if we don't give art a chance.'

'Rick!' Eugenie was pulling at his jacket sleeve. 'I think you're overdoing it a little.'

'Sweetheart,' Rick whispered back, 'this guy no more has explosives in his shoelaces than I have a chance for an Oscar this year. He has to be placated, soothed.'

Samantha, standing beside Georgia in the aisle, took a step forward.

'Larry, could we hear your song?'

The boy's face reflected sublime teenage exuberance.

'Sure. I have it here on tape, but I guess it would be better if I sang it to you – you'd get more of a feeling for it then.'

'Absolutely. Good idea. Sam. Let's have a concert. Champagne for everybody.' Georgia turned to Andrew. 'I think the baby's starting to have fun here. Come back to the galley and help me dish out the drinks. Frankly, I don't want that steward doing it.' She turned back to Larry. 'Now don't start the show without us, and don't do anything silly with your shoes. We'll be right back.'

Andrew stood up. I'm going to be a father, he thought. Why did I think I'd never be a father? And why do I feel so intensely proud of myself? He followed Georgia and, as they reached the galley, hugged her.

'You're a star,' he said.

'I know,' she said. 'So are you.'

Andrew opened a bottle of champagne and began to pour.

'Do you think he's serious about the shoelaces?' she asked.

'No. But I'm not sure I want to test it.'

The crew-cut, uniformed figure of the captain came back to join them.

'I've told him I'm helping you out. He's so immersed in the thought of singing, he's not concerned about anybody's movements. Not that it matters. To tell you the truth, I don't believe I even have to report this right now. We're going to continue on our normal flight path. He's just a mixed-up boy needing attention. I'll radio ahead for an appropriate authority to meet us and deal with him.'

'What about the shoelaces?'

'The clever blonde lady up front has solved that problem. Apparently, she's the only one who's noticed he's not even wearing shoelaces. He's got those velcro running shoes on. She just whispered that to me a few seconds ago. The guy's a nutter, but he's not going to blow up my plane. You can do whatever you want. I'm going back to the controls.'

The captain stopped, a few steps up the spiral

staircase. 'You all might decide he's better entertainment than Crocodile Dundee.' He continued on his way to the cockpit.

'Sam – how brilliant of her. I can't believe none of us bothered to look at his shoes.'

At the mention of Samantha's name, Andrew experienced a sharp twinge. With a feeling of poignancy, he decided to shed his last vestige of hope. It had been a painful and exhilarating dream and now it was ending. He knew Samantha well enough to realize that even if she could be persuaded to forget about Georgia being her friend, she could never overlook the fact that Georgia was pregnant. Nor, for that matter, could he. Georgia was going to be the mother of his child. That placed her in an entirely new and foreign category.

'I'll take the left side of the plane,' said Georgia, 'and you take the right. If we're good enough at this job, maybe we can apply for it. I have a feeling that steward won't be around for long.'

Andrew laughed at his wife. Why had he criticized her so much lately for being funny? Nobody should criticize the mother of his child.

Making the rounds with the drinks as Larry waited at the front, biding time until the show began, Georgia and Andrew told their fellow passengers in whispers about Samantha's discovery.

'Thank God!' said Clarissa. Duncan was silent. And he was going to remain silent until he got Clarissa alone in a hotel room. Then he would haul her over the coals with no mercy. If she thought she could get away with cheating on him, she was wrong. He would see to that. How long had this affair with Rick been going on? Since that Fourth of July party? The idea that she could lie to him, that all the time they'd spent together since then had been based on a lie made Duncan indifferent about this supposed hijacker, about everything except

Clarissa's deceit. He wanted exact times, locations, every single detail. Duncan was experiencing the humiliation of betrayal. The fact that he had been doing the same to her was, in his mind, irrelevant.

'Are you ready now?' Larry was starting to chafe at the bit. 'Remember, I don't have my guitar with me, so it won't sound the same.'

'How bad do you think this is going to be?' Rankin whispered to Samantha, now sitting back down beside him.

'Very.'

'OK, here we go.' Larry cleared his throat. 'One, two, three ... "Feelings. Nothing more than feelings ..." '

'Barry Fucking Manilow,' Georgia mouthed to Andrew.

'Oh dear,' Eugenie whispered to Rick.

'A shmuck is born,' he whispered back.

'Feelings. Oh, oh, oh, feelings ...' Larry continued. His eyes were closed, he was swaying with the words. The plane was quiet as he finally finished, his voice quivering appropriately, his hands outstretched.

Clarissa Darrell stood up and clapped. She was crying, 'Beautiful, what a beautiful song. I think you're marvellous. I think you're absolutely right. That should be a number one hit. It's better than anything I've heard in a long time.'

'Are you going to give *him* a hand job too?' Duncan hissed at her. He grabbed her wrist and pulled her back down.

'Oh, do shut up Duncan,' she sighed.

By this time Georgia, Andrew, Rick, Eugenie, Rankin and Samantha had all risen as well and were giving Larry a standing ovation.

'You actually wrote that song?' Rick asked as the applause died down.

Larry nodded.

'I don't believe it.'

'Watch it,' Eugenie nudged Rick. 'Don't burst his balloon. He could still go crazy on us and open the door or something, you know.'

Rick gave her a you-should-know-me-better-by-now glance and turned back to Larry.

'I don't believe how talented you are. Any more where that came from?'

'Lots.'

'Oh my God, Rick's landed us with a Barry Manilow concert,' Georgia said under her breath. 'More champagne!' she said out loud. 'Hats off to Larry! Someone give him a drink.'

The stewardess appeared back from the upstairs of the Jumbo where she had led the still-sobbing steward, and brought out a tray with glasses of champagne. Larry took one and drained it. He was beginning to bubble.

'This next song is very special to me,' he announced, 'It's a little boastful, maybe. But given a chance, I think these lyrics will come true.'

'Uh oh,' said Eugenie 'I think I know what's coming.'

'One, two, three … I write the songs that make the whole world sing. I write the songs …'

'I knew it. I don't think I can take this for another four hours,' Eugenie groaned.

'Lie back and enjoy it, sweetheart. Have another drink.'


Flight 102 was the first hijacked plane in history to arrive at its destination ahead of schedule. Every First Class passenger with the exception of Duncan Darrell was drunk. Larry Moody, high as a kite, was singing 'Mandy' as the wheels touched down. Economy and

Club Class passengers, unaware of the drama which had occured during the flight, were stunned as they exited the plane to hear those in the First Class compartment doing an *en masse* rendition of 'Feelings'.

Larry Moody was shocked to see his audience begin to gather their belongings after the last chorus of 'Feelings'.

'What's happening?' he asked 'What about my demands? What about the air time for my songs? I don't understand. Why is everyone leaving? My shoelaces. Don't forget my shoelaces!'

'*You* forgot your shoelaces, Larry,' Andrew replied. 'Fun's over. I suspect you'll find some people here to greet you, though. People very interested in you and your demands.'

'Oh, well, that's cool then, isn't it?'

'That's just fine, Larry.' Rick moved over and clasped him around the shoulder. 'And don't you worry, I'll talk to all my friends about you. I'm curious, though. How did you get the money to fly First Class?'

'My uncle Barry. He's meeting me here.'

'I'm not even going to ask the obvious question,' Rick said. 'I don't want to know. Come on, people, let's get out and feel the warmth of the tropical sun.'

Duncan Darrell stopped Rick Holland as he loped down the aisle to the plane's exit door.

'I want a word with you.'

'You can't have one.' Rick pushed past him and caught up with Eugenie at the bottom of the steps.

'Your boyfriend's a relic, sweetheart. I suggest you consign him to the museum of your mind.'

'I already have.'

'That's a girl. Remember now, I'm always available for sex and sympathy. I'll give you approximately twenty-four hours to recuperate, then we can get down and get dirty.'

'What about Clarissa?'

'Mrs Darrell and I just did a little mid-air refuelling. What you and I can do on land is another matter.'

# Chapter Ten

John Rankin and Samantha were already in the airport terminal, waiting for their bags to arrive.

'Where are you staying Sam? That's the one bit of information I didn't have.'

'At the Coral Beach.'

'Fine. I'll check myself in there as well. Then we can have a rum punch or two on the balcony as the sun sets. I don't think they'll have any curry here.'

'John, I need some time. I'd like to be alone tonight, if you don't mind.'

Blast her, thought Rankin. Still playing hard to get.

'How about breakfast?'

'That sounds good.'

'Fine. Breakfast it is. Then we can play a game of tennis if they have a court.'

'Right.' Samantha wasn't even listening to Rankin. She was intent on getting away from him, from everyone. She wanted to be alone so badly that she raced as quickly as possible through customs and made a beeline for a taxi, not even wondering whether it would be more polite to share one with Eugenie or Georgia and Andrew.

Arriving at the Coral Beach she checked in, went directly to her room, ordered a banana daiquiri from room service and sat on her balcony sipping it, watching the waves break on the beach. For close to an hour she looked out on the ocean, musing about her life; about David, Rankin, Georgia, Eugenie; about sex, about friendship, about work. She had no answers to the various questions she posed herself, but for once she didn't worry. She felt relaxed, she felt as if nothing was quite so important as she'd once believed. Her life so far was like an accident which had occured on the other side of the road. She had slowed down to look at it, she had wondered what had caused it, but now she had travelled beyond it. She had a clear road ahead.

At some point during a school science course, she'd read about the Law of Entropy: everything in nature tends toward chaos. When chaos had broken in on her own emotions, she'd been unable to put it in perspective, she had let it swamp her. What she had to do now was to recognize the potential for chaos and live with it on her own terms. Even if she wasn't sure exactly how to do that.

Samantha was still pondering the meaning of life when she heard a knock on her door and opened it to find Eugenie.

'We're in luck,' said Eugenie. She had changed from her travelling clothes into a cool yellow sundress and sandals. Even in that, Samantha thought, she looked smart enough to go to Ascot. 'I took a quick walk on the beach and a very friendly native offered me a few joints. After that harrowing trip, I thought we could both indulge in a smoke.'

'That sounds good.' Samantha had smoked pot a few times before and liked it. 'Are you OK? What happened with Duncan? I was so engrossed in the Larry saga that I couldn't quite figure out what was going on in your side of the plane.' She and Eugenie walked out to the balcony and sat down. Eugenie lit the joint, inhaled deeply and passed it to Samantha.

'My erstwhile lover had a shit fit when he saw his wife engaged in sexual activities with Rick.'

'You're kidding!' Samantha took a hit and passed it back.

'No. I guess he really loves her. I would have thought he'd be relieved. But his feather's went up and I suspect the fur is flying in their room right now. Anyway, I give up. I'm not going to hang around with some man who's so jealous of his wife he leaves his supposed loved one abandoned in the middle of a hijack.'

'You're right. It's not worth it.'

'I know it's not. But it still hurts. It's my pride or something stupid like that. I kept thinking that if I could say the right thing, do the right thing, we'd go back to how it was at the beginning, the days of wine and roses. It's hard to believe that someone can forget the way they felt about you when you remember so vividly.'

She tossed her head back and her long silver earrings swung. Samantha wondered whether she would ever get used to Eugenie's particular form of beauty – it was not, as most great beauty is, distant or cold, it was a warm, welcoming beauty. She had a way of looking at you when she spoke that made you feel you were an integral part of her life, that she preferred you to anyone else. She was capable of doing this to a room full of people, enchanting them one by one without it seeming like a cynical use of power – an ability, Samantha thought, which was magical. She had observed it at the beginning of the *Let Yourself Go* party when Eugenie was dealing with the media. Before Duncan had arrived.

Perhaps that was why Eugenie had said all women want to be preferred – Eugenie could make other people feel that way, but no one, except Duncan, and then only for a short time, had made *her* feel it.

They passed the joint back and forth, smoking without speaking for awhile.

'The champagne's wearing off. Can we get drinks up here? Or do you want me to leave you in peace?'

'No,' replied Samantha, 'I'm in the mood to get peacefully stoned and tipsy. I'll go order some more daiquiris.'

After she'd phoned room service, Samantha rejoined Eugenie and they started on the second joint.

'What's up with Doc?' asked Eugenie.

'Not much. I'm a little surprised at myself, I guess. I mean, we had sex in the toilet of the airplane – well, on it to be precise, but I wasn't really interested. Do you know what I mean?'

'I think so.'

'Do you think I'm asexual or something? I'm beginning to wonder. Everyone says how attractive he is and I think so too, but it was all so mundane. I'm not really emotionally interested in him any more, but I don't understand why I can't be sexually interested in him. Do you understand that?'

'Yes.'

The drinks arrived and Samantha tipped the waiter. She was a little confused about time and motion – how long had they been talking? Had she just gotten up or had she been standing in her room holding the drinks for ages? And why did the balcony seem so far away? She sat down on the bed and tried to get her bearings.

'Sam?' Eugenie suddenly appeared before her, took a drink from her hand and joined her on the bed. 'We should be outside doing the limbo on the beach.'

'I know.' Samantha laughed. 'But my trousers are too tight.'

'Take them off, then.'

'Right. Of course. I'll take them off then.' She did. 'Boy it's easier doing that here than in an airplane loo, I'll tell you. You know,' she went on. She had forgotten what she'd just said. 'You know, I used to be a good gymnast. Well, not a gymnast exactly. Not Olga

Korbut. But I was really good at cartwheels and handstands.'

'Handstands?'

They both thought this hysterically funny.

'Look. I'll do one now. I'll do a handstand. Watch me. I'm definitely going to do a handstand.'

In her underpants and striped jersey, Samantha moved slowly to the end of the room and stood against the wall, facing the bed.

'Here goes.' She took a few short running steps, launched herself into the air, paused upright on her hands for a few seconds and fell over backwards onto the bed, her jersey flying up over her shoulders.

'Samantha, you are full of surprises.' Eugenie leant over to kiss her on the cheek. Samantha's eyes were closed. She had a triumphant grin as she felt her friend's lips touch her skin.

The upwards curve of her mouth turned into a straight, puzzled line when Eugenie's hand touched her, when it moved, cupping her left breast and then gently rubbed her nipple. But Samantha didn't open her eyes. Nor did she move. Eugenie's unseen hand moved, it moved down Samantha's stomach, tickling it lightly, before it reached her clitoris, where it stopped momentarily. Samantha could have halted its progress then, but she didn't. She lay still, holding her breath. As Eugenie's hand went into action, her fingers rubbing in a circular motion, Samantha exhaled very slowly and as that breath left her, so did any compunctions. Her thoughts had transferred from her mind to her body, she felt an entirely physical being.

Eugenie, who had been watching Samantha's face, swiftly readjusted her position, continuing to rub all the while, and then started to lick Samantha's erect nipple with snakelike movements of her tongue.

Samantha could feel herself on a ledge, a delightful but tormenting ledge. She wanted to jump off, but she

205

couldn't. She thought she would stay there forever, on the brink. She would never reach the other side. Eugenie's tongue slowed down as her hand sped up. Samantha felt, for a moment, as if her breast was a saucer of milk and Eugenie was a puppy lapping at it and the sensation pushed her a further step out onto the ledge where she hovered. Her lips began to move and her legs drew up. She silently willed Eugenie to rub harder. Eugenie did. Until with a spasm, a shudder, a jolt, she jumped, she fell, she landed.

Samantha opened her eyes.

Eugenie sat up.

Then she stood up and walked out to the balcony. Samantha lay still for a few minutes. Finally she rose from the bed, pulled on her trousers and went out to the balcony as well. Eugenie was standing, smoking a cigarette, her eyes focused on the horizon. She heard Samantha, but didn't turn to look at her.

'Samantha, I'm not –'

'I know.'

'I don't know why that happened. I shouldn't have done that. I've never –'

'I *know*. Look, I was there too Eugenie. It doesn't mean we're lesbians.'

'It bloody well better not.' Eugenie looked over at Samantha, then looked away. 'Are we still friends?'

'I hope so.'

'So do I. Shall we pretend it never happened? Do you think that's the best way?'

'I don't know.' Samantha picked up a cigarette from the table. 'Probably.'

They both stood smoking.

'You know I had an orgasm,' Samantha said quietly.

'I know.'

Eugenie finished puffing and flicked her cigarette over the balcony.

'It's simply a matter of knowing what's what, I

suppose. Plus the dope and the drink. It doesn't mean anything.'

There was a long and awkward silence. Samantha, watching a figure walk along the beach beneath, suddenly smiled.

'Look at it this way. Georgia was wrong. We didn't have to kiss each other.'

'Georgia ... oh, my god, Georgia. She would just die. Georgia would just keel over and die if she knew!' Eugenie began to laugh and Samantha joined her. But their laughter shared a nervous edge and Eugenie stopped abruptly.

'Sam, I think I should go now.'

'OK.'

'I think we're right. I think we should pretend this didn't happen.'

'OK.'

'We'll both be back to normal tomorrow morning.'

'Right.'

Eugenie turned and headed for the door.

'Eugenie,' said Samantha, 'wait a second. I think you're more upset about this than I am. It was a one-off under unusual circumstances. Can't we both look at it that way without being so self-conscious with each other?'

Eugenie, her hand on the doorknob, stood and looked directly at Samantha.

'You're perfectly right, Sam. I've been silly. But I'll be fine tomorrow, I promise.' Halfway out the door, she heard Samantha say her name again and stopped.

'I just wanted to say one more thing. Thanks.'

Eugenie paused.

'I was about to say "My pleasure",' she said, then laughed her natural, deep laugh and was gone.

# Chapter Eleven

Closing the door after Eugenie, Samantha stood and surveyed the room. Her sheets were rumpled, glasses of half-finished daiquiris stood on the floor, the balcony door was open, letting the tropical air mingle with and gradually dissipate the smell of marijuana. She wandered out to the balcony and sat down, crossing her legs underneath her. She supposed that she ought to be thinking about her experience with Eugenie, but she couldn't concentrate. The sounds of a steel band began to reach her and she thought of going to find them, but decided that she preferred to remain where she was, not thinking, not moving, just sitting and smoking and listening.

'I think they're on their fourth rendition of "Oh, Island in the Sun".'

Samantha looked over to the voice. There was a man, on the balcony next to hers, sitting with his feet up on the railing. He looked vaguely familiar. She laughed and wondered how long she'd been sitting there, how long he had been sitting there.

'What's your name?'

'Walter.'

'I'm Samantha.' She stood up and moved closer to him. They shook hands, over the balcony.

'We had quite a time up there today.' His Southern accent was slightly muted, and Samantha noticed that his jaw was unusually firm and motionless, even when he spoke.

'It took me a little while to recognize you without the uniform,' she said. He was wearing jeans and a blue checked shirt with the sleeves rolled up.

'Yes. People expect pilots to wear uniforms, like they expect priests to wear collars. I hope you're not disappointed.'

'No. I'm not.'

'I've been watching you for a while. You look happy.'

'I think I am.'

'Good. Now would you mind standing back?'

Samantha retreated a few paces. Walter climbed on top of the railing and in one quick, unconsidered leap, landed in front of her.

'Romeo,' she said.

'Why not? Besides, sometimes I have to prove I can fly without all that jet engine paraphenalia.'

'Romeo *and* Superman?'

'A brilliant and lethal combination.'

Samantha sat back down on her chair and Walter took the chair beside her, turned it around, straddled it, took a pack of cigarettes out of his shirt pocket, shook one out, lit it and tossed the packet onto the table.

'Do you want to talk?' asked Samantha.

'Not particularly.'

She studied him unabashedly – his tight jawline, sharp eyes, crew-cut hair, compact body. He is, she thought with a growing certainty, exactly what I'd like to be if I were a man. And then she looked away. What a strange thought to have, what a strange knowledge to have. I can't remember ever being in a mood like this – as if time had stopped, as if I were outside time altogether. I couldn't bear it if either of us moved.

They didn't. Until it started to drizzle – a sudden and preternaturally quiet fall of rain. Walter stretched his hand out from underneath their balcony covering, reaching for the rain. He let his hand absorb the water for a moment, then pulled it back in and wiped his forehead with it.

Samantha, seeing this gesture, immediately felt that she couldn't bear it if he didn't touch her. She wanted to be the rain. She leant over and kissed his forehead then sat back again.

He leant over, gathered her hair in his hands, and kissed the back of her neck.

Every single thing Samantha had read about or dreamt of began to happen. She had tingles shooting through her, her whole body ached for him to be inside her. Why hasn't anybody ever done that to me? Is it him or my neck? But she didn't have the time or inclination to wonder for long because he was kissing her lips. He had a harder and more thoughtful kiss than she had ever experienced, a kiss that didn't need wandering hands or touching bodies, a kiss that seemed to exist in and of itself.

When it ended, Samantha opened her eyes, stood up, took his hand. Together they walked inside the bedroom, where Walter undressed as Samantha watched his outline, half-hidden in the dark. She undressed as well and lay naked on the top of the sheets.

What Walter then did, Samantha realized gradually, with excitement and wonder and awe, was to tell her a story. Sex was his natural way of communicating. And he had a lot to say. In what is usually described as foreplay, he set the scene, he introduced the characters, he hinted at what was to come. His physical movements were like sentences with commas, exclamation marks, and full stops. Full stops which often led on to new paragraphs. And in a short time, she was joining in – she was turning the pages with him. She was doing things she hadn't even

210

thought of before; her imagination was keeping pace with his; they were exploring each other with abandon and with mutual delight, like children opening hoped-for presents under the Christmas tree.

When he entered her, Samantha felt immensely proud of herself. They were on to a new chapter and she was co-authoring the book. They found they could afford to tease each other – they could, reaching a height of excitement, stop and go back to the beginning. Lie back and kiss and fondle and explore until they were ready to start again. Samantha had learned that afternoon about orgasms; now she was learning about multiple orgasms, about different kinds of orgasms, about orgasms which made her legs and arms buzz. Was this what David had been talking about when he said there were things she didn't know? Samantha had time, during a short lull, to consider that question. No, she decided. David was talking about specifics, specific tricks like the ones Georgia and Eugenie had told her about, probably. If David had known about making love like this, her ignorance couldn't have stopped him. There were, obviously, a lot of things David didn't know he didn't know. She felt sorry for him, briefly, then she forgot all about him.

When Walter and she finally finished, when he came, with a Southern rebel yell, they looked at each other and laughed. Samantha found it very hard to stop laughing. She sat up and punched the air, laughing.

'What's happening to me? I want to go run on the beach or something. I've never had so much energy.' She began to jump around in bed on all fours.

'Come here, Samantha.' Walter pulled her back down to him, 'There are better ways to expend energy.'

# Chapter Twelve

John Rankin woke up early, jet-lagged. He pulled on his white bathrobe and shambled out to his balcony, passing his hand through his hair and yawning. He looked out on a couple swimming in the ocean beneath him.

They're up early, he thought. They must have had a good night. Samantha and I should be doing that now. We will be doing that tomorrow morning.

Rankin stretched, still watching them. Probably a honeymoon couple, he decided. Frisking away in the surf, splashing each other, hugging. The perfect advertisement for a holiday.

The man and woman emerged from the water, onto the beach and John Rankin stepped forward to check out the girl's body. Good pair of tits, flat stomach, thin, reasonably long legs. Not bad at all. He wouldn't kick her out of …

Rankin almost fell over the railings. He closed his eyes and opened them again slowly. He stomped his bare foot on the floor. It hurt. Every part of his body hurt. He collapsed on the chair, holding his foot and swearing. He had been made such a fool, such a bloody ridiculous fool. He began to pound the table with his fist. Until that started to hurt too.

And I thought you were an innocent little lamb, he said, a sweet young thing with all your silly bets and questions and games. Bugger it. What a laugh. You're just as bad as I am. Just as bad.

Then John Rankin tipped his chair onto its back legs, shook his head and grinned ruefully.

Georgia strode to the beach after breakfast, wearing her bikini and a baseball cap, dragging a deck chair behind her and a bag slung over her shoulder. She staked out her spot, covered her fair-skinned legs with a towel, scrabbled in her bag for the necessary sun block and sunglasses, then settled down to relax. 'How're we doing down there?' she asked her stomach, giving it a quick pat. 'Enjoy it while you can – you've only got a nine-month lease, kiddo, then you're out into the cruel, cruel world.'

'Don't disillusion it so soon.' Eugenie had appeared from behind her in a one-piece dark swimsuit, and was stretching a towel out on the sand. 'Why didn't you tell me you were pregnant?' She applied some suntan oil to her body and lay down beside Georgia's deck chair.

'I didn't know. We hadn't fucked that much lately – so I was dumb. I wasn't thinking about it.'

'That *is* dumb. But congratulations. I'm really happy for you. And very jealous, of course. My biological time clock just keeps ticking. Do you think it will sound an alarm when it's about to run out altogether?'

'What? At the sound of the beep, your child-bearing days are over. Quick, go find any available sperm.'

'Mmmm. Something like that might be useful.'

'You have plenty of time. Besides, I want you to wait a few years. Then if I have a boy and you have a girl, think what havoc they'll cause together. We'll have to lock them in their rooms for decades.'

'Georgia, I better get going on this next book and make you some more money soon. I can only imagine the psychiatrists' bills you'll have to shell out for that poor kid in there.'

Georgia patted her stomach again.

'This baby is not going to be neurotic. This baby is

going to be perfect. Intelligent, sane, funny and able to serve me breakfast in bed at the age of four.'

'We'll see,' said Eugenie. 'How's Andrew taking the news?'

'He's thrilled, actually. He was so sweet to me last night, I even dared asked him about the Other Woman.'

'What did he say?'

'He said that nothing had happened, that he had been attracted to someone else, but that nothing had actually happened. You can't imagine how relieved I was – I know it's a technical point, but it helps. He also said that he'd grown tired of our constant banter and wished we could just relax and be nice to each other sometimes. Take each other seriously. Whereupon I told him that I thought I *had* to keep up the banter or else he'd get bored. And that I wasn't sure I could take anybody seriously, but I'd try my hardest.

'If I understood him right, he thinks I'm too tough, too cynical. What appealed to him about this other woman was her vulnerability. I've been thinking about that one. I figure he wants me to be vulnerable as long as I don't cry, or ask him for any help. I'm not sure how I'm supposed to do that, but I know I'll have to try. I love the creep, that's my problem.'

'Did you ask him who the mysterious other woman was?'

'No. Not because I don't want to know. I do. But I also know that this isn't the time to badger him. I've gotten so many points for being pregnant, I don't want to throw them all away by being a jealous shrew. Especially if I'm jealous of someone he hasn't screwed. Even *I* know when to stop sometimes. I'm sure I won't be able to resist nailing him to the wall about it later – maybe when I'm in labour. That ought to distract me from the pain.'

'Hi, guys!' Samantha threw a towel down on the

other side of Georgia and sat down on the middle of it in Eugenie's borrowed shorts and a white T-shirt. Her hair was wet and slicked back off her forehead. 'Have you set the world straight yet?'

'Samantha Lewis. What have you been up to? I'm the one that's supposed to look glowing, but you look positively – ah, I see it. I *know* what you've been up to.' Georgia took off her sunglasses and sat up straight in her deckchair. 'Tell all.'

Eugenie turned on her stomach and buried her face into her towel.

'I'm in love,' Samantha said and smiled. 'It's as simple as that.'

'Did you hear that Eugenie? Rick said there'd be happy endings. What are you doing down there? Sit up and listen. The doc has won the day at last. This is hot stuff.'

Reluctantly Eugenie sat up, pulling her cigarettes out of her bag and staring at the sea. Sam can't be, Eugenie thought, she can't be talking about me. This is horrible.

'Nope,' Samantha shook her head, 'Not the doc, I'm afraid.'

'Whoa. Well, whoever it is is a fast worker.'

'Mmm hmm,' Samantha was grinning. Eugenie was puffing madly on her cigarette.

'So who is he?'

Eugenie's shoulders hunched up.

'Walter Peyton. Our Captain yesterday.'

'What?' Both women exclaimed. Eugenie snapped her head around so quickly she looked as if she'd been shot in the neck.

'Yup.' Samantha began to sing. 'Some enchanted evening, you may meet a pilot …'

'You may meet a pilot across a hijacked Jumbo,' Georgia continued, and she and Samantha laughed.

'A pilot! I love it. Good at the control panel, no doubt. An expert at take-offs. Smooth landings.'

Samantha just sat there, smiling lazily.

'Well, well, well. Where is our hero now?'

'Sleeping. He has to fly out this afternoon.'

'Shit. So we don't get to check him out properly? When are you going to see him again?'

'Next week, in New York.'

'God, Sam. This is wonderful. Just perfect. You won't have to see him too much, so you won't get bored. You can worry about him crashing all the time which will give your life a real edge. And stewardesses these days are way over the hill, no threat at all. As for the stewards, the less said about them the better.'

'Sam? When did you meet him?' asked Eugenie.

'Yesterday evening. A little while after you left.' Samantha answered, smiling at Eugenie. Eugenie sank back on her elbows.

'I see,' she said. 'Poor John Rankin.'

'He'll get over it,' said Georgia.

'Look. I think he already has.' Samantha pointed to a couple walking past them – John Rankin, shirtless, in white flannels, was strolling arm in arm with a diminutive brunette. He glanced over at the three women and waved nonchalantly to Samantha. She waved back, then realized that the brunette was, in fact, the stewardess. The brunette started to walk faster and Samantha began to chuckle. 'Thataboy, John, add another name to the list. You know, I actually like that man. He's one of a kind.'

'Aren't your feelings hurt? I mean, he came here to chase you. He can't know about the pilot. And he's already off with someone else.'

'I suppose my ego should be damaged, but it isn't. We were never meant to be together. It was all a game, just a one-off ...' Samantha stopped and looked down at her toes. Eugenie put her cigarette out in the sand, then buried it.

'A summer romance, but the weather was lousy,

right? Now you can have a proper one.' Georgia replaced her sunglasses and lay back against the chair. 'Much as I love my gynaecologist, I have to admit I had niggling doubts. Can someone who works down the mines all day be really enthusiastic about going back down at night?'

'Will you shut up for a second, Georgia? I'm beginning to understand Andrew's problem with your smart remarks. Sam –?' Eugenie stood up and walked around Georgia's chair, putting her towel down next to Samantha's. 'Do you think this is such a good idea? Aren't you being a little hasty with this new man? What if he disappoints you? I mean, he appears out of nowhere and you're blissfully happy – as if Prince Charming had just arrived. Isn't it a little dangerous to believe in fairy tales?'

'Jesus, Eugenie, why don't you go soak that towel in the sea and *literally* put the wet blanket over her. Just because Duncan's been such an asshole doesn't mean you have to ruin Sam's fun.'

'I'm concerned. I care about her.'

'And I don't?'

Samantha was sitting in the middle, as these exchanges flew over her head. She felt like the rope in a tug-of-war game.

'I'm not saying you don't care, I'm just saying that maybe, just maybe, a man is not the answer to all problems. I don't want her to get hurt.'

'Oh, I *see*.' Georgia sat up again. 'She should be happy within herself, is that it? Centred and balanced and in harmony with life – then, if a wonderful man does come along, she's guaranteed not to get hurt? Come off it. You can be the most balanced person in the world and still go loopy if a romance hits the skids. *Skid Romance* – that would be a good name for a book.

'Anyway, what's wrong with fairy tales? Fairy tales are great. Eve gets dumped on in the Bible for biting

217

the apple, but look at Snow White – she does the same thing in a fairy tale and winds up with a Prince.

'Every woman is looking for the tall, dark stranger or short mousy-haired pilot to fly her away. Shit – if it were up to you, you'd put gypsies out of business.

'And it's not like you to be sensible, Eugenie. Besides, I'm worried. If you start writing like you're talking, all those fantasy-prone women out there will stop reading your books. Lighten up.'

'Maybe you're right.' Eugenie was looking at Samantha.

'Of course I'm right, aren't I Sam? Look at you, you still have that shit-eating grin on your face. God, that's worth at least a couple of months of misery if it doesn't work out with Chuck Yeager.'

'I think she's right, Eugenie. I couldn't stop the way I feel right now, even if I tried, and I don't want to. Maybe it isn't love, maybe it's just sex – I don't care. It feels like love. If it doesn't work out with Walter, it doesn't mean it was a mistake to try.' Samantha turned to Georgia. 'I'll just come back to London and stand on your doorstep in my dumpy black dress looking forlorn and miserable, I guess.'

'Great!' Georgia slapped Samantha on the shoulder. 'And then we'll set you up with a lifeguard. I heard the other day that the new craze is to make it while you're going down the Richmond water slide. I need to know if that's physically possible.

'Meanwhile, Miss Woodrow, I'm going to stop being your literary agent and start my new career as your love agent. My first inspired move is to set you up with Rick. Tonight. Go dancing with him. You'll be a born-again romantic, I promise. OK?'

'I don't know,' said Eugenie.

'Come on, Eugenie,' said Samantha. 'Go for it. He's so funny. He'll make you laugh. You need that now.'

'That's true.'

'That's settled, then. That's you taken care of. I'm going to be busy comforting Sam on the absence of the Incredible Hunk. Sam, sweetheart, there was a cute little waiter at breakfast this morning. I don't think Walter would mind infidelity this early on in the relationship, do you?'

Clarissa Darrell stood in her new, one-size-too-small bikini, studied the beach scene and spotted the three women to her left. They were, she thought, having fun. Sitting gossiping. Not stuck with some maniac husband seething with jealousy and anger. Not stuck with Duncan. Duncan who had kept her up until 3 a.m., berating her, quizzing her, refusing to believe she hadn't had an affair with Rick – aside from that little dalliance on the plane which, of course, she couldn't deny. It wasn't as if Rick had actually done anything, and in the end, Clarissa knew, she had defended herself brilliantly. After all, hadn't Duncan gone on and on about Ronnie Ferguson's right to go to massage parlours if he so chose? Ferguson wasn't hurting anyone, Duncan had argued at the time, he hadn't actually gone to bed with those women. He had simply paid for some fairly innocent enjoyment.

Clarissa reminded him of this, and made the point that she hadn't had to pay for hers.

Duncan had exploded at that. 'We're not talking about women going to massage parlours, although for all I know at this point you could be doing that too. But Ferguson's wife wasn't *there*,' he'd yelled. 'Aren't you forgetting? I was *there*!'

Keeping her cool, Clarissa decided it was time to bring out the big guns and silence him.

'Duncan, darling,' she had said in the tone she generally reserved for servants, 'I may not have been there in the room when you had your affair, but you weren't what I would call discreet. As far as I'm

219

concerned, the slate is now clean between us, although, frankly, I'd say that is very generous of me. Now I'd suggest you get some sleep. As you've reminded me so often, you have a lot of work to do here. You have a hectic week ahead.'

Duncan's face had the expression of a woman who sits down on a toilet only to find the man before her had forgotten to put the lid down.

Clarissa wanted more than anything to join those three women, but she was a trifle hesitant. They were younger, working women. What could she say, how could she become a part of that group? She wrapped a towel around her waist to hide the cellulite on her thighs and approached them, bracing herself for rejection.

'Excuse me,' she said, standing opposite Georgia. 'I wanted to get my hair done in those braids. Do you know where I can do it, or do you think it's a frightful mistake at my age?'

'Clarissa!' Georgia was momentarily lost for anything to say. Eugenie stood up then immediately sat back down again.

'*I* know,' said Samantha, smiling up at Clarissa. 'There's a woman who'll do it for you on the beach. I saw her earlier this morning. I was just thinking I'd like to have my hair done like that as well.'

'Of course you're not too old.' Georgia had recovered herself. 'Sit down with us.' Clarissa did.

'I think I'll do it too,' Georgia continued. 'I mean everyone who does it wants to look like Bo Derek, but I think I'll look more like a red-haired version of Bob Marley.'

'Perhaps' – Clarissa's voice was like an excited teenager's at a sleepover party – 'we could all do it together?' She was staring at Eugenie.

Eugenie looked at Samantha and Georgia and saw

220

what they wanted to say. Give it up, Eugenie. The man is a shit. He doesn't love you. Your arch-enemy Clarissa here will most probably be nicer to you than he was. He doesn't love you.

Eugenie pretended to have problems lighting a cigarette as she avoided Clarissa's glance. Her sense of order had upended itself. The day before she had found herself in bed with another woman. Now she was supposed to make friends with her ex-lover's wife. What was happening?

Her mind was doing quick video flashbacks of times in bed with Duncan, then it stopped on the last. She could hear him admitting he hadn't read her book. *He had not read her book.* She would have read a book of his even if it were a Jip the Cat kindergarten primer.

With what felt like a thumb and forefinger clicking, her heart snapped to attention. He *doesn't* love me. For the first time, she truly believed it. Then she inhaled, and the nicotine and tar going down her throat passed by a rebellious wave of feeling travelling upwards from her gut to her brain. And I'm not so sure I love him either.

'Why not?' she said. 'If we look like fools, at least there'll be four of us.'

Clarissa winked at her. It was a nicer wink than Duncan's.

'So ...'

Clarissa was sitting on a stool beneath the shade of some palm trees as the black woman behind her fashioned her hair into tight single-braided strands.

'I told him that he hadn't been exactly discreet about his affair either, and *that* put paid to all his nonsense.'

Eugenie, Georgia and Samantha were sitting on stools as well, forming a circle. The braid-maker had called in three friends to help, and all four women were being transformed at the same time. Eugenie bit her lip and began to blush. Sam and Georgia stared at each other, then at Clarissa.

'Can you imagine getting involved with that little tart Sarah Frawley? I suppose you don't know her.'

'*I* do,' said Georgia.

'So do I,' added Samantha.

'Clarissa?' Eugenie crossed her legs. Her left foot was bobbing. 'Duncan and Sarah Frawley? Did he ... When did he have this affair?'

'Oh, about five years ago.'

'I see.' Eugenie's foot relaxed. At least it was before me, she thought. That's some consolation.

'I suppose I should have left him then. But it's different when you have children.'

'Tell me about childbirth, will you?' said Georgia. 'I want to know all the gruesome bits. Like is it more painful than anal sex?'

All four black hairdressers behind the stools glanced at each other and rolled their eyes.

'I don't know,' Clarissa sighed. Then her face brightened. She was the centre of attention. None of the others had experienced labour.

'I had an epidural anyway, which I must say was heaven. You're numb from the waist down, but you're totally conscious of what's going on.'

'That's for me,' said Georgia. 'None of this underwater bullshit with Mozart playing in the background. Twisted Sister, maybe.'

'And at the end my gynaecologist did the most amazing thing. The epidural had worn off enough so that I could bear down and push, and as the baby – Rupert – started to come out, I felt like a champagne bottle being uncorked. It was an incredible experience. Then my gynaecologist said, "Give me your right hand," and I thought, "Why does he want me to shake hands with him now? He hasn't even finished." But he put my hand into Rupert's tiny little hand and said,

"Pull," and I did. I pulled this beautiful little creature out into the world. It's the most heavenly experience on earth. And nobody, nobody can ever take that away from you.'

The three women were riveted by Clarissa. Nobody spoke. The black women looked at each other and nodded, smiling.

'But you know what's a bit odd? I know that the husband is supposed to be important in all this. These days he's helping you breathe and taking those videos and things, but I have to tell you, at that point, I couldn't have given a toss about Duncan. He was there, but he was, well, irrelevant. It was me and the baby and the gynaecologist. *He* was the man I wanted to be near me, he was the one I was sharing it with. When the epidural wore off and it began to hurt, I wanted to be brave for him. Strange, isn't it? I could have kissed him afterwards. I could have ...'

'Seduced him in the delivery room?' asked Samantha, laughing.

Georgia began to laugh. Eugenie began to laugh. The three friends laughed so hard they fell off their stools and doubled up on the sand. Clarissa didn't know what was funny exactly, but the laughter was so infectious that she joined in. The hairdressers began to laugh. A couple strolling by the palm trees saw eight women convulsed with laughter, and they began to laugh too.

All Futura Books are available at your bookshop or
newsagent, or can be ordered from the following address:
Futura Books, Cash Sales Department,
P.O. Box 11, Falmouth, Cornwall TR10 9EN.

Please send cheque or postal order (no currency), and
allow 60p for postage and packing for the first book
plus 25p for the second book and 15p for each additional
book ordered up to a maximum charge of £1.90 in U.K.

B.F.P.O. customers please allow 60p for
the first book, 25p for the second book plus 15p per
copy for the next 7 books, thereafter 9p per book

Overseas customers, including Eire, please allow £1.25
for postage and packing for the first book, 75p for the
second book and 28p for each subsequent title ordered.